Praise for Catheri‌ ‌ee

Wife by ‌

"A fun and sizzling rom‌ ‌c trade verbal spars like fist punches, and the ‌ ‌oyal wedding!"

—‌g Hot Book Reviews, 5 Stars

"A good holiday, fireside or bedtime story."

—Manic Reviews, 4½ Stars

"A great story that I hope is the start of a new series."

—The Romance Studio, 4½ Hearts

Married by Monday

"If I hadn't already added Ms. Catherine Bybee to my list of favorite authors, after reading this book I would have been compelled to. This is a book *nobody* should miss, because the magic it contains is awesome."

—Booked Up Reviews, 5 Stars

"Ms. Bybee writes authentic situations and expresses the good and the bad in such an equal way . . . Keeps the reader on the edge of her seat."

—Reading Between the Wines, 5 Stars

"*Married by Monday* was a refreshing read and one I couldn't possibly put down."

—The Romance Studio, 4½ Hearts

Fiancé by Friday

"Bybee knows exactly how to keep readers happy . . . A thrilling pursuit and enough passion to stuff in your back pocket to last for the next few lifetimes . . . The hero and heroine come to life with each flip of the page and will linger long after readers cross the finish line."
—*RT Book Reviews*, 4½ Stars, Top Pick (Hot)

"A tale full of danger and sexual tension . . . the intriguing characters add emotional depth, ensuring readers will race to the perfectly fitting finish."
—*Publishers Weekly*

"Suspense, survival, and chemistry mix in this scintillating read."
—*Booklist*

"Hot romance, a mystery assassin, British royalty, and an alpha Marine . . . this story has it all!"
—Harlequin Junkie

Single by Saturday

"Captures readers' hearts and keeps them glued to the pages until the fascinating finish . . . romance lovers will feel the sparks fly . . . almost instantaneously."
—*RT Book Reviews*, 4½ Stars, Top Pick

"[A] wonderfully exciting plot, lots of desire, and some sassy attitude thrown in for good measure!"
—Harlequin Junkie

Taken by Tuesday

"[Bybee] knows exactly how to get bookworms sucked into the perfect storyline; then she casts her spell upon them so they don't escape until they reach the 'Holy Cow!' ending."

—*RT Book Reviews*, 4½ Stars, Top Pick

Seduced by Sunday

"You simply can't miss [this novel]. It contains everything a romance reader loves—clever dialogue, three-dimensional characters, and just the right amount of steam to go with that heartwarming love story."

—Brenda Novak, *New York Times* bestselling author

"Bybee hits the mark . . . providing readers with a smart, sophisticated romance between a spirited heroine and a prim hero . . . Passionate and intelligent characters [are] at the heart of this entertaining read."

—*Publishers Weekly*

Treasured by Thursday

"The Weekday Brides never disappoint and this final installment is by far Bybee's best work to date."

—*RT Book Reviews*, 4½ Stars, Top Pick

"An exquisitely written and complex story brimming with pride, passion, and pulse-pounding danger . . . Readers will gladly make time to savor this winning finale to a wonderful series."

—*Publishers Weekly*, Starred Review

"Bybee concludes her popular Weekday Brides series in a gratifying way with a passionate, troubled couple who may find a happy future if they can just survive and then learn to trust each other. A compelling and entertaining mix of sexy, complicated romance and menacing suspense."

—*Kirkus Reviews*

Not Quite Dating

"It's refreshing to read about a man who isn't afraid to fall in love . . . [Jack and Jessie] fit together as a couple and as a family."

—*RT Book Reviews*, 3 Stars (Hot)

"*Not Quite Dating* offers a sweet and satisfying Cinderella fantasy that will keep you smiling long after you've finished reading."

—Kathy Altman, *USA Today*, "Happy Ever After"

"The perfect rags to riches romance . . . The dialogue is inventive and witty, the characters are well drawn out. The storyline is superb and really shines . . . I highly recommend this stand out romance! Catherine Bybee is an automatic buy for me."

—Harlequin Junkie, 4½ Hearts

Not Quite Enough

"Bybee's gift for creating unforgettable romances cannot be ignored. The third book in the Not Quite series will sweep readers away to a paradise, and they will be intrigued by the thrilling story that accompanies their literary vacation."

—*RT Book Reviews*, 4½ Stars, Top Pick

Not Quite Forever

"Full of classic Bybee humor, steamy romance, and enough plot twists and turns to keep readers entertained all the way to the very last page."
—Tracy Brogan, bestselling author of the Bell Harbor series

"Magnetic . . . The love scenes are sizzling and the multi-dimensional characters make this a page-turner. Readers will look for earlier installments and eagerly anticipate new ones."

—*Publishers Weekly*

Not Quite Perfect

"This novel flows extremely well and readers will find themselves consuming the witty dialogue and strong imagery in one sitting."
—*RT Book Reviews*

"Don't let the title fool you. *Not Quite Perfect* was actually the perfect story to sweep you away and take you on a pleasant adventure. So sit back, relax, maybe pour a glass of wine, and let Catherine Bybee entertain you with Glen and Mary's playful East Coast–West Coast romance. You won't regret it for a moment."

—Harlequin Junkie, 4½ Stars

Doing It Over

"The romance between fiercely independent Melanie and charming Wyatt heats up even as outsiders threaten to derail their newfound happiness. This novel will hook readers with its warm, inviting characters and the promise for similar future installments."

—*Publishers Weekly*

"This brand-new trilogy, Most Likely To, based on yearbook superlatives, kicks off with a novel that will encourage you to root for the incredibly likable Melanie. Her friends are hilarious and readers will swoon over Wyatt, who is charming and strong. Even Melanie's daughter, Hope, is a hoot! This romance is jam-packed with animated characters, and Bybee displays her creative writing talent wonderfully."

—*RT Book Reviews*, 4 Stars

"With a dialogue full of energy and depth, and a twisting storyline that captured my attention, I would say that *Doing It Over* was a great way to start off a new series. (And look at that gorgeous book cover!) I can't wait to visit River Bend again and see who else gets to find their HEA."

—Harlequin Junkie, 4½ Stars

Staying For Good

"Bybee's skillfully crafted second Most Likely To contemporary (after *Doing It Over*) brings together former sweethearts who have not forgotten each other in the 11 years since high school. A cast of multidimensional characters brings the story to life and promises enticing future installments."

—*Publishers Weekly*

"Romance fans will be sure to cheer on former high school sweethearts Zoe and Luke right away in *Staying For Good*. Just wait until you see what passion, laughter, reconciliations, and mischief (can you say Vegas?) awaits readers this time around. Highly recommended."

—Harlequin Junkie, 4½ Stars

Making It Right

"Intense suspense heightens the scorching romance at the heart of Bybee's outstanding third Most Likely To contemporary (after *Staying For Good*). Sizzling sensual scenes are coupled with scary suspense in this winning novel."

—*Publishers Weekly*, Starred Review

Fool Me Once

"A marvelous portrait of friendship among women who have been bonded by fire."

—*Library Journal*, Best of the Year 2017

"Bybee still delivers a story that her die-hard readers will enjoy."

—*Publishers Weekly*

HALF
Empty

Also by Catherine Bybee

Contemporary Romance

Weekday Brides Series

Wife by Wednesday
Married by Monday
Fiancé by Friday
Single by Saturday
Taken by Tuesday
Seduced by Sunday
Treasured by Thursday

Not Quite Series

Not Quite Dating
Not Quite Mine
Not Quite Enough
Not Quite Forever
Not Quite Perfect

Most Likely To Series

Doing It Over
Staying For Good
Making It Right

First Wives Series

Fool Me Once
Half Empty

Paranormal Romance

MacCoinnich Time Travels

Binding Vows
Silent Vows
Redeeming Vows
Highland Shifter
Highland Protector

The Ritter Werewolves Series

Before the Moon Rises
Embracing the Wolf

Novellas

Soul Mate
Possessive

Erotica

Kilt Worthy
Kilt-A-Licious

CATHERINE BYBEE

HALF
Empty

BOOK TWO IN THE FIRST WIVES SERIES

Montlake
Romance

Text copyright © 2018 Catherine Bybee
All rights reserved.

Published by Montlake Romance, Seattle

www.apub.com

Amazon, the Amazon logo, and Montlake Romance are trademarks of Amazon.com, Inc., or its affiliates.

ISBN-13: 9781503903555
ISBN-10: 1503903559

Cover design by Letitia Hasser

Cover photography credit by Belief Agency, LLC

Printed in the United States of America

For Ellen
My unexpected new friend
Thank you for helping me find my new home

Chapter One

Trina Petrov sat on the edge of one of the many canals in Venezia, Italy, drinking an Aperol spritz and listening to the conversations going on around her while not taking part in a single one. Eavesdropping had become part of the solo traveling experience, and the best part was when those around her didn't think she understood a single word they said. With three languages fluently under her personal belt, and a fourth quickly becoming a part of her skill set, Trina had returned to this particular café because the locals had told her that the tourists didn't frequent it. Admittedly, she was a tourist, but was on the quest to immerse herself in the Italian language in an effort to learn. When she sat in the larger cafés, she overheard many people speaking English, and if she wanted to eavesdrop on that language, she might as well go home.

Venezia wasn't a location picked by accident. Venice, as much of the world called it, was a city of love. Complete with romantic gondola rides and lovers cuddling on a single seat while the gondoliers swept the small watercraft through the many canals of the famous sinking city. With couples dominating the landscape, Trina hadn't found herself the target of unwanted male attention. It helped that she often played with the four-carat diamond wedding ring she usually wore when traveling.

Two Italian men, somewhere in their seventies, were sitting in the same place they had the day before, doing the exact same thing. With a bottle of wine on the table and a chess game sitting between them, they took painstaking time calculating each move while together they solved the world's problems. The lower the volume of fluid the bottle held, the more convinced they became that they had all the answers to the troubles of today.

Trina kept her head ducked into an e-reader, pretending to have lost herself in a story.

"*Bella*, you're here again." Luciano, the owner of the small restaurant, spoke to her in English. His accent was pure Italian.

"I haven't perfected your language," she responded in Italian.

"It sounds good to me," he said.

A group of giggling teenage girls sat huddled around an adjacent table making not-so-shy advances toward Luciano's son, who waited tables. He had a Justin Bieber vibe about him, even though he was a tad bit older than The Bieb. But age didn't stop this group of backpacking teens from flirting, giggling, and sending poor Marco handwritten notes.

Good sport that he was, Marco smiled, winked . . . and flirted, which probably earned him plenty of phone numbers.

"Shameless," Luciano said under his breath in Italian.

"They're just having fun."

"He's practically engaged."

Trina took a second look. "Those girls are too young for him anyway. He's just making sure they have something to grin about tonight when they give each other . . ." Trina struggled with the word for *facials* in Italian before finally giving up. "Doing each other's makeup."

Luciano, hair slightly gray around the parts that hadn't paled altogether, placed a hand on his head before smiling into his thoughts. "I suppose."

Trina looked between father and son. "I would bet money you were exactly like your son when you were his age."

Luciano's mirth turned to a light shade of wicked, and Trina knew she was right.

"See . . ."

Luciano didn't try to deny her claim. "The boy takes after his father."

"If he is half the cook you are, he will make the future Mrs. very happy."

Luciano's smile waned. "Adriana is perfect for my Marco."

They both held silent as Marco smiled and walked by.

"So why the frown?" Trina knew the word *frown* wasn't right, but it was the closest one she knew in Italian to voice the look of stress on Luciano's face.

Trina's lack of the right word didn't stop her meaning from getting through. She made a mental note to look up the word *distressed* when she was back at her hotel.

"She has more than we do. It worries my Marco."

Trina felt her heart hurt. "Money isn't everything." No one knew that more than she did.

"He loves her. Would do anything for her."

"Then what's stopping him?"

Luciano turned his attention away from where his son had disappeared into the back of the café. "He wants to give her the world. I told him that he could be her world if he just asked for her hand."

Trina liked that.

"He is young and thinks fortune is easily gained."

Trina squeezed her eyes shut.

"The youth of today . . ." Luciano said the words as if Trina and he shared a similar birth decade. They were a good twenty years off.

"But enough about my family . . . where is yours?"

Trina blinked her eyes open. "My parents live in California."

Luciano's smile fell completely. His gaze moved to the ring on her left hand.

The answer to his unasked question fell from her lips. "I'm widowed."

His face went white, quite the feat for a man with an Italian complexion. He pulled up a chair beside her and sat. "I'm so sorry," he said in English.

She tried to smile. "It's okay."

He wasn't convinced.

"I am. It's been nearly a year." She knew how lame that sounded the second it left her lips.

Less than a year from *I do* to *goodbye*, she thought but didn't say. The complication of her short marriage wasn't something she wanted to discuss. The world didn't need to know the truth, and she didn't feel the need to spread gossip.

"I'm at a lack for words . . . in English or Italian," Luciano said.

Marco walked by in that moment and glanced at the two of them. Trina watched him walk away and sighed. "We can only plan for the moment. Tomorrow isn't promised. You're old enough to know that."

He placed a hand over hers. "You're too young to say that with such conviction."

Trina smiled. "Then I'm ahead of the game, right?"

Luciano tapped his chest and dipped his chin.

A few minutes later he left her side. Trina tossed enough euros on the table to pay for her drink and walked away.

Just the thought of her real life—the one she lived when she was pretending to be someone she wasn't—made her want to flee.

She'd be back to see Luciano again, she knew that as she left the café. But for now, she needed to search out busy, touristy crowded streets where she could disappear.

Half a dozen switchbacks of tiny alleys framed by bridges and buildings that looked exactly like the others yet unique in their own way, and Trina found herself in Saint Mark's Square.

The sun was starting to set, and the massive plaza had already started to fill with water. With a city destined to sink into the ocean sometime in the next hundred years, the Venetians were used to the sight, while tourists tossed off their shoes and made light of the water rising from the drains normally used to rid the square of seawater.

But for today, the city wasn't sinking. It was simply enduring another day of lovers strolling the city and small vignettes of six-piece orchestras playing everything from classical music to modern pop while tourists drank their wine.

Trina paused in the moment.

She slipped off her sandals and walked through the ankle deep water in the center of the square.

A stranger in a wedding dress held the train of her gown and smiled into a camera.

Trina walked around until she stood at the space between the church and the sea.

I'm hiding, she thought while the world moved by. Here she was, a single woman walking the streets of a touristy Italian city where not one soul knew who—or what—she was. The anonymity of it all drove her here.

Learning the language had been an excuse.

Still, she walked through the crowd, purposely forgetting.

Here she was just *Trina.*

She accepted the occasional appreciative glance from the opposite sex, smiled, and moved along. Never once did she stop to try and see if that glance could turn into something else.

She wasn't interested.

As the streets thinned out and the last of the scammers attempted to pawn their final trinkets to unknowing visitors, Trina made her way back to her nondescript hotel.

She pushed through the swinging doors of the hotel and made her way up the two flights of stairs to her corner room with a double window view of one of the canals below.

Locking the door, she tossed the key, which was still a key and not a card, onto the secretary. Moving to the windows, she opened them wide and pushed back the shutters.

The occasional pedestrian walked over the bridge closest to her room, their words muddled in her ears.

She flopped on the bed and glanced at the grandiose glass chandelier above. It was something Trina would expect to see in a hotel in Vegas.

She closed her eyes and ignored the loneliness that knocked on the back of her skull.

Everything was fine.

☙

A loud voice had Trina shooting out of bed.

She blinked a few times, orienting herself to the room.

"I'm working here!"

"Make way!"

The voices came from outside her window. Trina glanced at the clock in the room and winced. Six thirty was too early for shouting.

While the men outside her window kept yelling at each other in Italian, she gave up and moved to see what they were arguing about.

The canal below had two side-by-side delivery boats that were manned by half a dozen men unloading supplies. Sacks of flour, cases of paper goods, everything a restaurant would need to stay in business. The man doing half the yelling was a gondolier, standing at the back of his gondola, waving a hand in the air.

"The tourists are still in bed." This from one of the men trying to unload his boat. "You can wait."

The problem was the lack of room between the two delivery boats for the gondola to pass.

"For God's sake, move so the man can get through and the rest of Venezia can sleep!" Trina yelled from her window.

Seven pairs of eyes looked up at her.

Trina lifted both hands in the air as if emphasizing her point.

Three men started yelling at the same time, a mix of arguments of being in the right-of-way.

Trina leaned out farther and added her complaint to the chaos. "A bunch of grown men acting like children," she growled.

Another window from across the canal opened and a woman twice Trina's age let out such a rapid stream of Italian she only caught every fourth word. While Trina hadn't been able to put it all together, it was obvious the men unloading their goods did.

A few minutes later, one of the larger boats had moved enough to allow the gondolier to pass through.

"My apologies, beautiful lady," the gondolier said with a dramatic bow in Trina's direction.

Tall, dark, and Italian. The man's smile had Trina grinning back.

∽

"You're ignoring me!" Avery Grant paced around her high-rise condominium in downtown Los Angeles with her cell phone pasted to her ear. The connection to Trina, halfway around the world, was surprisingly clear.

"I'm not ignoring you."

"Three text messages and two phone calls. If that isn't the definition of *ignoring*, then I don't know what is."

"I've had bad Wi-Fi."

"Lame-ass excuse, lady. How long are you planning on being in Venice anyway?"

Avery stood looking across the city skyline as the sun dipped across the buildings. Sunset was always worth watching from this high off the ground.

"How . . . how did you know where I was?"

7

"Oh, please. I have you on Friend Finder, remember? So you know where I am when I'm out on a date."

"Oh, yeah . . . I forgot."

Avery rolled her eyes and walked away from the window, giving Trina her full attention. "Lotta good that app is going to do for me if you never look at it."

"Sorry. I'm . . . I'm in a weird place right now."

"I know you are. But you need to find your way out of it. The First Wives meeting is this weekend, and it's your turn to host. Or have you forgotten?"

"I, ah . . . didn't forget."

Avery sucked in a deep breath, knowing damn well Trina not only forgot, she hadn't planned anything either.

"Uh-huh . . . right. Tell you what. You just get back to the ranch and I will plan everything."

"I have six days."

"None of us wanna see you sleep off jet lag. So start working your way west, woman!"

"I'll be okay."

"Don't make me come there and get you. Cuz I will!"

Trina laughed, which made Avery smile. "I know you will. Just give me a few more days."

"Okay, but if you flake, not only will I come and retrieve you, Lori, Shannon, and Sam's team will be right there with me."

"I heard you, Avery. I'm hanging up now."

"Why? Do you have a hot date?" For a brief second Avery wondered if her joke was an actual possibility.

"No. Of course not."

"Well, that's a damn shame. You're in Italy. The men there are gorgeous."

"They are."

Lotta good that did for her friend, the woman who hadn't so much as smiled at a man in the year Avery had known her. "Try and kiss one for me."

"I'll do that."

Never gonna happen.

"I'm stalking you until I see you blip online in Texas."

"I'm hanging up now, Avery."

Hearing the fight in Trina's voice was better than the sorrow.

"Love you."

"Love you, too."

Avery disconnected the call and immediately called Lori.

When her neighbor, lawyer, and fellow First Wives Club member answered the phone, Avery drove right to the point. "I got ahold of Trina."

"Is she okay?"

"I think we need to do an intervention."

Chapter Two

The deep baritone of a man singing woke her the next day. The clock said seven. The sun streaming through the window suggested another hot day lay ahead.

Trina pushed out of bed when the voice didn't stop or move farther away.

Unlike the day before, the canal had only one occupant.

Mr. Tall, Dark, and Italian looked up from his gondola to her room while he sang.

Words of love and inspiration lifted to her ears. He made grand gestures with his hands as he finished the song.

She clapped and smiled when he took a sweeping bow.

"A free ride for you, beautiful lady. For aiding me in my plight yesterday."

"That isn't necessary," she replied in Italian.

"You're American."

"I am."

"Americans love our gondolas."

She leaned against the window. "Another day."

Her words gave him the hope he needed. "What is your name?"

"Trina."

He placed a hand on his chest. "I am Dante. I will see you tomorrow."

She opened her mouth to argue, but he pushed away from the dock and started to sing.

❧

Trina's day buzzed by, faster than the previous three weeks. Because she hadn't given herself an end date to the trip, she realized how little of the island she'd seen. Trina felt the sudden need to start touring.

A short boat trip brought her to the neighboring island of Murano, famous for its handcrafted glass. While mosquitoes nipped at her ankles, she took a reprieve from the sun by stepping into several stores. She'd never been much of a shopper, but with a pocket as deep as the one her late husband and his mother had left her, Trina took advantage of the merchants' offers to ship goods to the States. She knew, as she was shelling out three thousand euros apiece for the four vases that had caught her eye, that the gifts were going to be an *I'm sorry I missed our quarterly meeting*. Still, the sculptures were phenomenal and would help her friends forget her flaking on them.

She was already practicing what to say when they gave her hell.

"As soon as Avery reminded me of the meeting, I went on a quest to see all of Venice. I bought these gifts in my rush to see everything."

Avery wouldn't buy it.

Lori, a divorce attorney by day, would know damn well she was lying but wouldn't call her out.

Then there was Shannon. She was harder to read. She'd probably just thank Trina, pat her on the back, and then let her know if she ever wanted to talk, she'd be there.

Avery was going to take some work. Considering Trina and Avery were the closest out of all of them, Trina would do her best to sweeten the pot.

Maybe tomorrow morning she'd take the gondola ride with Tall, Dark, and Italian. She'd snap a selfie of the two of them and tell Avery she was distracted by Dante. Just the thought of Trina smiling at the opposite sex would help Avery get over her absence.

With a plan in motion, Trina finished the paperwork on the expensive glass and strolled the rest of the island without a worry in the world.

⁓

Dante was much better looking up close. "No singing today?" Trina asked when she exited her hotel at seven o'clock sharp. If she asked enough questions, she'd forget that she was on a kinda date. Or maybe she was reading into the situation.

He jumped off his gondola and approached her as if they already knew one another. First a kiss on the right cheek, and then another on the left. Trina stepped back to regain her personal space.

"If it is song you want, then song you shall have." Before she could laugh and tell him she was kidding, he let out a note that shook the walls of the buildings around them.

Trina put a hand on his arm. "Kidding. I was kidding," she said in English. "Shh, you'll wake everyone."

"You're right. I want to keep your beauty to myself."

He had a sly smile and a playful wink. "Come . . ." He extended his hand to help her into the small boat. "Have you been on a gondola before?"

"No."

He shook his head, the white-brimmed hat casting shadows on his face. "Such a shame."

"You really didn't have to do this," she told him.

"It is my pleasure. I'll show you many hidden gems in my city."

She settled into the seat facing forward. Dante stood in the back and used a single paddle to power and steer the handmade vessel. "I've been here for almost three weeks. I think I've walked every street."

"But you haven't sailed every canal."

She glanced over her shoulder. "True." Before she forgot, Trina slid her cell phone from her back pocket and pretended to take a picture of the scenery in front of her. Instead, she snapped a selfie, capturing Dante behind her. *That* would hold Avery over.

The city had yet to wake, and the temperature had cooled down quite a bit from the day before. "This is the best time of day," he told her.

It was easier talking without looking at him. "How long have you been doing this?"

"Five years."

"You enjoy it?"

"What's not to love? I see beautiful women like yourself. Spend my days on the water and sing for a few extra euros."

A simple life. "You make it sound romantic."

"It's Venezia. Even the buildings drip of romance."

Trina looked up at the vertical brick and stucco walls in varying colors and stages of decay. "Is it really sinking?" she asked him.

"Sadly. But our government has vowed to keep the city afloat."

One good earthquake off the coast and that government effort wouldn't mean a thing.

"Let's hope their efforts aren't in vain."

Dante put his foot to the side of a building and steered them down a smaller canal.

"Your Italian is impressive. Have you lived in Italy?"

"No. I've visited a few times."

"Then you have family who taught you as a child."

She leaned back. "I've only studied Italian for six months."

He stopped rowing briefly. "Again, I'm impressed."

His shameless flirting brought a lightness to the inside of her chest. She didn't take him seriously. Not completely, in any event. The flirtation had to be limited in light of the fact that she needed to make an effort to leave Venice in a few days. Even if she had to switch planes in Paris, and perhaps end up delayed there for a few days, or a week. She had half a chance of convincing the First Wives that she was sincere in her struggle to get home, even though she'd be channeling Pinocchio while she smiled.

"What are you thinking of, *Bella*?"

"That my trip here is coming to an end."

He grunted, and she looked over her shoulder.

His bottom lip was pushed out in a childish pout.

Trina rolled her eyes.

"We just met, surely you can stay a little longer," Dante pleaded.

She shrugged, looked forward again. "We'll see."

"These words I can work with." And with that, Dante started to sing.

Halfway through his song, the wind kicked up, and the sky above them started to darken.

"It appears that we must cut this short," he said as he pushed the gondola toward the nearest dock. Luckily for him, the docks were on every corner.

A boom of thunder brought her attention to the change in Dante's smile.

He secured the gondola to the dock with a single rope and used his weight to hold the rocking vessel steady while helping her onto dry land.

Lightning flashed, and the thunder rolled quickly behind.

Dante scrambled over his boat to cover the seats with a fitted tarp. He was halfway through when the rain started to pelt down.

Trina wanted to help but knew she'd just be in the way.

Instead, she stood in the warm Venezia thunderstorm and proceeded to get soaked. There was something cathartic about purposely standing in the rain and letting the water run down her hair. Standing there with someone, even a someone she didn't really know, was better than being there alone.

The second Dante finished covering the gondola, he jumped to her side, grasped her shoulders, and rushed them down a small alley that opened into a plaza. As in most of the squares in Venezia, there was a church with a large overhang to protect them from the rain.

Not that it mattered—they were both dripping in the shadow of the building.

Thunder ripped through again and the rain flew at them sideways.

They both moved as close as they could to the door, and still the rain managed to reach their feet.

Looking down at her soaked shirt and cotton shorts, Trina started to laugh.

Soon Dante joined her.

"This is nuts," she said in English.

"It can last for hours or minutes," he told her.

She poked her head out from under the eaves and looked at the gray sky.

"I think we're somewhere in between." When she looked at Dante again, he was standing closer. He reached out and pushed a wet strand of hair from her face.

Kiss one for me. Avery's voice buzzed like an annoying fly in her head.

"You are so very beautiful."

"And you're a player."

"Guilty," he said as he stepped closer.

Just one kiss. It wouldn't kill ya!

"Shut up, Avery," Trina whispered in English.

Dante licked his lips. "Talking yourself out of my attention, or into my affections?"

She shivered, knowing before he leaned in that she would not have to lie to her best friend.

He moved slowly, giving her time to back away.

Trina didn't.

And when Dante kissed her, she forced her eyes to close and her head to tilt back.

It was nice . . . okay, maybe a bit more than just nice. It had been so long since she'd kissed anyone, she thought maybe she'd forgotten how.

Dante, on the other hand, knew exactly how to kiss.

When his hand reached around her waist, and he pulled her into his arms, Trina panicked.

"*Bella.* You're so lovely," he said again, his lips set close to her ear. "We could make beautiful love."

Yeah, that wasn't gonna happen.

She put a hand on his chest. "I don't think . . ."

"No one needs to know. Just you, and me. I won't tell your husband and you won't tell my wife."

Trina froze, her gaze moving to the hand she had on his chest.

Fedor's ring stared her in the eye.

She pushed. "I'm not." *Oh, God.* "But you are? You're *married?*"

Dante didn't stop smiling. "Don't deny. It's okay. I don't care."

Trina ducked out from under his arm and into the pouring rain.

Only then did Dante's grin fall.

"I'm not married, asshole!" she said in English. And because it sounded even harsher in Russian, she tossed that language at him, too.

"My condolences to your wife," she yelled before running to the closest exit from the square.

He didn't chase. Then again, he wouldn't have to, since he knew where her hotel was.

For twenty minutes, she zigzagged through the never-ending maze of streets until she found a familiar path.

She wiped her lips with the back of her hand and cussed all the way back to the hotel.

Chapter Three

She lugged her overstuffed suitcase down two flights of stairs since the small hotel didn't have an elevator.

"Mrs. Petrov . . . you're leaving us?"

"I am. I'm going to need a water taxi to the airport."

"You're booked through the end of the week."

She eyed the door. "Change of plans," she said in English before switching to Italian.

The older man typed a few things into his computer before pulling up an invoice for her to sign. When she did, she once again caught Fedor's ring out of the corner of her eye.

This is ridiculous.

"Shall I call for a taxi now?"

Her gaze fell on her suitcase, then the ring.

She held up a hand. "Hold off. I need to do something first."

"Oh . . ."

"Watch my suitcase. I'll be back."

She didn't run, but it was one of the fastest determined walks she'd done since her days as a flight attendant when she was late for work.

Luciano's was only an hour into their day, and only one table was occupied.

"You're early today," Luciano greeted her, a kiss to each cheek.

"I'm not staying."

Luciano looked disappointed.

"I'm actually on my way home."

"You're leaving Venezia?"

"I am."

He kissed her cheek again. "It saddens my heart, even though I knew your time here wouldn't last forever."

"Thank you, Luciano. You've been one of the best parts about my visit."

"Will you return?"

"I'm sure I will. This will be one of the first places I find when I do." Trina looked over his shoulder. "Is Marco here?"

"Of course."

Luciano yelled out his son's name, and the younger man stepped out from the back of the restaurant, placing a long apron around his waist.

"Ms. Trina is leaving us," Luciano announced.

"I wanted to say goodbye."

"We will miss you," Marco said.

Trina hugged Luciano first, and then turned to his son.

After she hugged the younger man, she pulled away and captured his hands in hers. "Follow the dream, Marco . . . and the money will come. If you love her, don't let her go."

He smiled.

She patted his hands, knew he felt that she'd slipped something in his, and squeezed.

"Ciao," she said to both of them as she left the restaurant nearly as quickly as she'd run in.

Behind her, they called her name.

Trina started to run.

An hour later, as she sat in the airport lounge, she looked at her naked hand and released a long-suffering breath.

◦❥

I'm at the airport. Trina texted Avery instead of calling.

It had taken two hours, but she'd managed to grab a standby seat en route to Paris. As Trina had planned, a storm was descending upon that part of France, and the chances of planes being grounded were actually quite high.

Having been a flight attendant for most of her young adult life, she knew which regions to avoid to minimize nasty weather and delays. Now she used that knowledge to do the exact opposite. London was known to have fog all times of the year, but summer storms were a much more likely issue in the southern regions.

If the rain over France didn't delay her, she'd find her way to Florida, where a tropical depression would. No matter how you spun the wheel, she'd end up arriving in Texas after the weekend she was supposed to see her friends. She didn't want to face them.

More importantly, she wanted to trudge through the anniversary of Fedor's death by herself.

Their marriage had been on paper, something the First Wives would remind her of. But for some reason, Trina had grown to care for her late husband more since his passing than she had during their marriage. She'd stepped into his world as a hired bride. She was supposed to end their marriage after a year and a half and leave with five million dollars.

Only Fedor had eliminated the need for a divorce with the use of a gun.

His suicide had been in the papers for weeks.

Then, when his mother died of incurable cancer, the reason he'd wanted to marry in the first place, the papers had blown up.

Alice left her entire fortune to Trina, along with one-third say in the oil company she co-owned with her sisters, Diane and Andrea.

When all was said and done, Trina became one of the wealthiest women in the world, with well over $350 million in assets.

The fact that she was sitting between an overweight man and a teenage kid who smelled as if he'd been living in a hostel during his backpacking experience in Europe was quite ironic.

Avery would no doubt call her out on not chartering a private plane to reach her destination on time and in style.

Private jets were smaller and didn't risk bad weather conditions like the larger commercial airlines did. Maybe she should consider chartering after all, she mused.

I tried, I did . . . but the only thing available was a small Lear, and they refused to fly.

Yup . . . the line would work and wouldn't be a lie.

She'd even lose ten or twenty thousand on the booking just to stay away a few more days.

Trina spent two nights in Paris before the storm blew past and she inched her way toward Florida.

There again, she booked a hotel and glanced at flights without trying hard to find something to get her to her Texas ranch.

Her phone lit up as soon as she landed in Miami.

"Where the hell are you?" Avery was ticked.

"Miami. In baggage claim." Trina watched the conveyer belt that unloaded luggage down two chutes at a painfully slow rate.

"Are you connecting in Miami?"

Trina was more than a little irritated that the call wasn't losing its connection. "I tried booking, but there weren't any flights. I'm going to find a private charter."

"You know, if you'd actually planned on coming home for our club meeting, you wouldn't be scrambling."

She switched the phone to her other ear after catching sight of her bag sliding down the chute.

"I was on an open-ended vacation. I'm allowed to forget. Are you in Texas?"

"I am. Lori and Shannon will be here late tomorrow night."

"Great. I should be right on their heels."

Avery was silent.

"Are you still there?" Trina reached for her bag, holding the phone to her ear with her shoulder.

Once she managed to grasp the handle of her suitcase, her purse slid off her shoulder, and her phone took a nosedive to the cement floor.

"Shoot." She fumbled while tossing her bag over the side of the metal conveyor belt, nearly taking out the woman on her left. Trina bent down to retrieve her phone and cussed.

The image of a call in progress was distorted by the cracks that now spiderwebbed all over her screen. Trina put it back to her ear right as Avery called her a name.

"I dropped my phone."

The woman Trina had nearly taken out now pushed around Trina to grab her luggage. Trina shuffled to the side, once again attempting to multitask.

"What are you doing?"

"I told you I'm in baggage claim."

"You sound like a hot mess."

"I am a hot mess. And now my phone is toast."

"Okay, okay . . . call me when you have a plane booked so I can pick you up from the airport."

With an irritated grunt, Trina turned the phone off completely and shoved it in her purse.

The humidity of Miami slapped her once she breached the doors. She scanned men in dark suits holding signs with last names, looking for hers.

Petrov stood out like a beacon.

"I'm Trina," she told the driver she'd ordered with her service.

He was short, dark . . . and spoke with a thick Cuban accent. "Mrs. Petrov."

"Trina's fine, thank you." *No more Mrs. Anything, thank you very much.*

With a nod, he took the handle of her rolling bag and led their way out of the airport.

⤳

"What do you mean my room isn't available?" Trina stood at the check-in counter and stared at the registration clerk.

"There was a mix-up. Our guest that is staying on the penthouse floor has the suites for tonight."

"One guest has the whole floor?"

"I'm afraid so."

"Must have a big family." Which ultimately meant noise.

"We do have a junior suite available a few floors down."

Trina glanced around the crowded lobby. She normally didn't book a massive suite for just herself, but she thought the quiet of an executive floor would give her what she needed to work off some of the jet lag that was already setting in. Since money wasn't an object . . . why not?

"If that's all you have."

The clerk smiled and went through the motions of processing her credit card and activating a key.

"We are truly sorry for the inconvenience. We'll be giving you the junior suite for a regular room price for your trouble."

"It's not an issue."

Once settled in her room, Trina kicked off her shoes, washed the miles off her skin with a shower, and fell face-first on the bed. Thirty minutes into what was meant to be a four-hour nap in an effort to get back to a normal sleeping pattern, an infant in the next room howled.

And jet lag officially started kicking her butt.

~~✤~~

Wade Thomas kicked his boots up on the coffee table while his personal assistant, Ike, put on Wade's hat. It wasn't really Wade's, but it was one exactly like it, which they used when they split up at the end of a tour.

"A few more hours at that gym of yours and you'll really be able to be my double."

Ike turned to the mirror and lowered the brim of the Stetson to hide his eyes. "No amount of bulk can hide the fact you're prettier than me."

Wade chuckled. "You mean you're uglier."

"Women like rugged."

"You keep telling yourself that."

Ike turned back around and stood taller. "Well?"

"Looks about right to me. Jeb, what do you think?" Wade asked his personal bodyguard, standing at the door.

"I won't let anyone close enough to tell the difference."

Folding his hands behind his head, Wade made himself comfortable. "Enjoy the flight home, boys."

"You have the charter booked for tomorrow night. You sure you don't want me to have the hotel car take you to the airport?"

"Plain yellow taxi is less conspicuous."

Ike didn't look convinced.

"Hey, it worked last time." And the time before that, and the time before that. Wade's idea of having his assistant dress like him, and having the posse escort Ike out the front doors of hotels so that Wade could catch some peace, had been a welcome change. Eventually his mob of fans would catch on. But in a metropolitan city like Miami, he was less likely to be discovered.

Both men looked him up and down, as if they were forgetting something.

"Go." Wade made a shooing motion with his hands.

Once he had the penthouse to himself, he studied the street below from his perch. It took a bit of time, but eventually a stretch limousine pulled away from the covered turnaround, while several cars followed it in a rush.

His cell phone rang.

"Looks like we've drawn their attention."

Wade felt a fifty-pound weight lift from his shoulders. "Text me when you're on the plane."

"Will do."

Alone at last. Seemed he wanted that more and more in the past couple of years, and it wasn't easy to get. He'd turned in his privacy for fame. Something he knew came with the bill, but he had yet to get used to it.

Now he was headed for some much-needed time off. He had the occasional gig here and there, but his official tour was over, and would be until he had another album out. That would take well over a year.

Wade kicked off his boots and stretched out on the king-size bed. He didn't bother closing doors or turning off phones. He'd hibernate in the room until he received the all clear from Ike.

Until then . . . sleep.

Chapter Four

Trina jumped out of bed as if the hounds of hell were pulling her into the blazing depths of molten heat.

It was solid dark, with only the ambient light from the digital clock casting a dim light in the room.

The time flashed eleven thirty.

"Oh, no."

She flopped on the bed, knowing she'd overslept her limit and was now going to drag through jet lag for days.

The crying in the next room had kept her from sleeping when she wanted to, until she simply crashed. Obviously the baby was up, since the whining was permeating the walls once again. You would think a hotel that cost as much as this one did would have soundproof walls.

She rolled out of bed and padded into the bathroom. One look in the mirror and she cringed. What she really wanted was a shower, but that would prepare her circadian clock to be up for a full day instead of a few hours and probably mess her up for a week. Trina settled on a washcloth to her face and a brush through her hair.

Once finished in the bathroom, she found the room service menu right as the baby let out the loudest scream to date. Instead of fighting the inevitable, Trina threw on a pair of jeans and a tank top, grabbed her purse, and headed down to the hotel bar.

The dim lighting of the glass-and-mirror decor made it easy for her eyes to adjust as she slid behind a stool and picked up the bar menu.

The bartender, a man somewhere in his midforties, slid a cocktail napkin in front of her and smiled. "Good evening."

"Hello," she greeted him.

"What can I get you?"

"Cabernet."

He nodded. "The kitchen closes in ten minutes."

Her stomach growled. When was the last time she'd eaten?

"I'll take the sliders."

He started to turn away.

"And fries."

He took a step.

"And wings."

He looked her up and down. "Hollow leg?"

She dropped the menu. "Jet lag."

He hesitated. "Anything else?"

"I should probably have a vegetable."

"Side salad it is."

That sounded perfect. "With ranch."

He waved and walked away.

While she waited for dinner, Trina sipped her wine and thumbed through the many messages left on her phone from Avery.

Not that she could read them very clearly, since her screen was cracked all to hell. It was surprising the thing still worked.

Her salad arrived at the same time a tall man slid into a seat two bar stools away. She vaguely heard him order a beer before she dug into her first course.

Her stomach happily accepted the food and she hummed with approval.

"Well, hello," the man to her left said in her direction.

With a full mouth, Trina glanced up, fork in hand, and met his blue eyes. He had sandy blond hair, a face meant to make women melt, and a sly, mischievous smile.

Trina slowly started to chew.

She'd seen that grin before.

From a certain *married* Italian.

Another forkful of lettuce and dressing made it to her mouth. "Not interested," she said around her fork. Maybe if she floored the man with bad manners, he'd look the other way.

His laugh sat low in his chest.

When she looked again, he smiled with dimples that reached the corners of his eyes.

"That's a first." There was a southern drawl to his words.

She kept chewing as the bartender handed him his beer. Trina took note of his clothing. A T-shirt was hidden beneath a light jacket, blue jeans . . . and boots. If she had to guess, she'd say he left his hat in his room.

"He's a fool," the stranger said without a prompt.

Trina wiped her mouth with her napkin. "Excuse me?"

"The man who put the chill in your tone. He's a fool."

His observation collided with a compliment. "Most men are," she decided to say.

He winced. "Ouch."

She'd been raised better than that. "Sorry," she said, hoping he wouldn't continue his path. "Bad timing."

He seemed satisfied with her apology. "I understand." He turned in his seat, leaned against the bar.

Before he could say anything more, the bartender brought her a parade of food. Once it was all sitting in front of her, it filled the empty space between her and her unwanted admirer.

"Now this I have to see," he said.

"Me too," the bartender added.

She popped a fry into her mouth and looked to find both men staring.

"Enjoy." The barkeep walked away.

"I'll take an order of those burgers our friend here is eating," the stranger announced.

"Sorry, the kitchen just closed."

"Seriously?"

"Yeah. Midnight."

Mr. Country, minus the pearl-snapped shirt, groaned.

"The room service menu has some premade sandwich wraps."

"That sounds about as appetizing as a long walk in cold rain."

Trina bit into her tiny burger and closed her eyes as the hot meal hit all the right spots.

When she opened them again, Mr. Country eyed her food almost as intently as he had watched her.

She blinked, looked at the two remaining sliders, the plate piled high with chicken wings, and a basket of french fries. "Fine," she muttered as she slid the plate of sliders toward the stranger.

"You sure?" His eager smile reminded her of a six-year-old holding back excitement at the candy counter.

"If you don't want it . . ."

He slid out of his seat and to the one right next to hers faster than she could blink.

He glanced over his shoulder and pulled his beer closer. "What's your name, little lady?"

"Let me guess, Texas?" She'd been there long enough to hear the twang and tell some of the subtle differences in the dialect.

He lowered his voice. "Just outside of Austin."

"I recently moved to Houston."

"Is that right?" He picked up the tiny burger with his big hands. He glanced at her, then the burger, and laughed.

She took a second bite out of hers as he put the whole thing in his mouth in one swallow. It was amusing to watch him try to chew. It didn't take long before he was washing it down with his beer.

"Did you taste it?"

"Mmmm."

Shaking her head, she followed her bite with a fry.

Her companion's stomach growled, and instead of waiting for his eyes to ogle her food, she pushed the plates between them.

He didn't ask, he just helped himself.

"I'm Trina," she offered.

"I'm in your debt, Trina. Seems I slept through dinner."

"You and me both."

"I'll count it as a blessing, since I've met you."

Trina lifted a hand as if saying *No, thank you* before digging into the chicken wings. "I'll share my food, but I'm still not interested." Attracted, but not willing to go there. The last thing she wanted to ask was if his wife knew he was burning the midnight oil in Miami.

"Shame, that."

She chased the spicy wings with her wine. "What brings you to Miami, Mr. . . . ?" She left his name open, hoping he'd fill in the blank.

He was staring again.

"What?"

"You really don't know who I am, do you?"

Trina stopped chewing long enough to look closer.

She shrugged. "No."

He laughed under his breath, glanced behind him. "My name is Wade," he whispered.

She lowered her voice. "Why are you whispering?"

He leaned closer. "Wade Thomas," he said even lower.

She blinked again. "Am I supposed to know that name?"

Wade squared his shoulders and sat taller. "Well, I'll be . . ."

The bartender approached. "Can I get you another wine?"

"Please, and I'll take another. Put all this on my tab," Wade said.

"No, no . . . that isn't necessary."

"I insist."

She looked at the bartender. "He can buy my second glass of wine, but the rest is on my room."

When Wade didn't argue a second time, the bartender left to refill their drinks.

"That's a second first," Wade said.

"A second first?"

"First you flat-out turn me down. Now you refuse to let me buy the meal I'm eating." He paused. "Oh, and you really have no idea who I am . . . I guess that makes it a third first."

Trina finished off her wine. "Am I supposed to be following your train of thought?"

He laughed in a way that made her smile with the infectiousness of it.

"What brings you to Miami?" she asked.

Wade laughed harder. Too much more of that and she'd start to believe he had a screw or two loose.

"Did I say something funny?"

He shook his head. "No, no . . . Uh, work. What about you?"

"Working my way home from a vacation."

He helped himself to a wing. "Oh? Where did you go?"

"Italy. Venice."

"How was that?"

"Hot and filling."

"You didn't like it?"

"Oh, no . . . I loved it. I'd still be there if it wasn't for my friends."

Wade questioned her with his eyes.

"It's our weekend to get together, and I was trying to avoid it. I love my friends, but I just needed some time alone. You know?"

He nodded as he chewed. "Do I ever."

"I booked my flight to Miami hoping this tropical depression would ground flights."

"Did it work?"

The bartender dropped off their round of drinks.

"I'm not sure. I planned on checking flights after I eat. Which I wanted to do hours ago, but the baby in the next room kept me up until I couldn't keep my eyes open even if a bomb were going off."

"That doesn't sound good."

"Yeah, I booked a quiet room on the top floor, but someone took the whole penthouse floor as their own."

Wade stopped smiling.

"What?" she asked.

He looked away. "Nothing . . . So, what do you plan to do now?"

"Find a flight tomorrow . . . or maybe sleep in until it's too late."

"You really don't want to see your friends."

She thought about how their conversation would revolve around Fedor's death the previous year, and how she should be seeking some testosterone in her life. Avery would remind her that she was too young to be alone, Lori would analyze her as if she were a psychologist instead of an attorney, and Shannon would passively agree to everything the others said until she found Trina alone. Then she'd talk sense and make Trina look a little too hard inside herself. Something she didn't want to do. Not now, in any event.

She shook out of her thoughts to blue eyes peering close.

"Do you realize how much emotion you show on your face?" Wade asked, jaw slack.

Trina lifted her chin. "Guess I'll have to work on that."

They closed the bar and took their last round to the hotel lobby.

Wade had to admit he was a bit more than tipsy, and Trina wasn't exactly sober. She'd tucked her feet under her on the lobby sofa as she described Venice in a way that made him want to visit.

"There isn't one car?" he asked.

"No place for them. You only get around on foot or boat. Which is probably best to help counter the pasta you consume while you're there."

"So why did you pick Venice?"

Her eyes drifted away, something Wade had noticed happened a lot when she was lost in thought. A hint of sorrow quickly came and went, almost as if she caught herself. The smile she flashed felt forced. "I wanted isolation so I could study."

"Study?"

She rattled off something that went completely over his head.

Her dark brown eyes glistened with her smile. "I'm learning Italian."

Wade blew out a breath. "Oh, thank God. I thought maybe that last beer was one too many."

"I like languages."

"As in many?"

"A few."

He was happy to speak English. "I'm impressed."

"Don't be. Most Europeans are fluent in a minimum of two languages."

"Are you from Europe?"

"No. Born and raised in Southern California. My grandparents on my mother's side are from Mexico. Spanish was always spoken in our home."

"So you speak Spanish as well?" He squirmed in his chair.

"Yup."

"Now I'm feelin' a bit inferior."

"Language is my hidden talent," she said.

"So how did you end up in Texas?"

Her gaze met his before she wrinkled her nose and gave a quick shake of her head. "It's a long story."

"Which is your way of saying *Don't pry*."

She stretched out her arms. "It's my way of saying that we've had a pleasant conversation, and bringing up my recent move will change all that. I'd just as soon keep this light."

Wade wasn't expecting her reply. "Now you've piqued my interest."

"Another time," she said.

He offered a smile that usually had women crawling all over him. "Am I going to have that chance?"

"Chance for what?"

"Another conversation."

Her eyes bored into him as if he wasn't the sharpest tool in the shed. "I told you, I'm not interested."

He lifted one eyebrow, flashed a dimple. "What if I told you I was rich?"

She burst out in laughter.

His smile fell.

"Sorry . . ." She appeared to pull in her mirth. "You're gonna have to do better than money."

"Good lord, woman."

"Sorry."

He scratched his head. "I'm famous."

She bit her lip. "That explains the arrogance."

Wade placed a hand on his wounded chest. "I am not."

Trina tossed her head back, and her deep laugh filled the empty lobby. "My name is Wade Thomas, you don't know who I am?" Her mimicry of him was off by several octaves.

Her laughter tickled his gut.

"I can teach you the two-step."

She pinched her lips together, trying to contain herself.

"That was Wade." They approached the steps of the jet. "Listen, I have to go. We have a tiny stop in Nassau, something about picking up a straggler. But I can't be picky, it isn't my charter."

"I knew there was a catch."

"Not a catch, just a quick stop. Only a few miles away from Miami. Didn't want you to be shocked when you saw my radar headed east."

"I swear, Trina . . . if you don't get here, I'm going to track you down."

"I'm on my way. Don't worry."

At the foot of the steps, a flight attendant greeted them. "Hello, Mr. Thomas."

"Good afternoon . . ." Wade spoke with the attendant while Trina ended her call.

"I'll be there, Avery. I admit I wasn't in the mood to face the anniversary . . ." She glanced over her shoulder, saw Wade duck inside the plane. "But I'm better now."

"I'm worried about you." Avery put her anger aside for a minute.

"I know. I'm sorry for that. It's been a strange week."

"Trina?" Wade called her from the plane. "We need to get in the air before the storm hits."

"Right . . ."

"Storm?" she heard Avery ask.

"Just a small one. But I gotta go. I'll text when we leave Nassau."

"Text on the plane, I wanna know who the *we* is."

"My phone isn't acting right since I dropped it." Which wasn't a lie. "Trina!"

"Gotta go. Wade is waving at me."

"Wade who?"

"Thomas. Love you." Trina hung up.

She climbed the few steps and grinned.

"Did she buy it?"

"Yup."

He moved aside so she could walk in. It wasn't the largest private jet she'd been on, but it wasn't the smallest either. The interior was made of white leather and sleek lines and would comfortably seat six people. It wasn't large enough for a bedroom, but all the seats reclined enough for a person to sleep.

"Can I take your purse, Miss . . . ?"

The flight attendant—tall, thin, and twentyish—flashed a perfectly manicured smile.

Trina couldn't help but feel a certain companionship with the woman. She dropped her phone inside and handed her the bag. "Trina is fine. What's your name?"

"Nita."

"Thank you, Nita."

Nita took her purse and stowed it before closing the door and securing the lock.

Wade encouraged Trina to sit across from him. "The pilot told me we needed to get in the air as quickly as possible. He anticipates the need to stay in Nassau for a minimum of six hours."

Trina smiled. "I'm sure we can push that off until tomorrow."

Nita walked by them again, and this time she brought two glasses of sparkling wine. Trina didn't feel the need after the late night before but took the glass anyway. Within minutes they were taxiing onto the runway.

"So you really didn't google me when you went back to your room last night?" Wade asked.

"I did not." They'd started this conversation in the car over. "It was late. I was tired. Besides, I'd rather you tell me what you want me to know than read about you online."

Wade sat back in his seat and played with the stem of his glass. "You have more restraint than I do. I would have googled you if you'd shared your last name."

Her last name would have pinged more pages than his, or so she thought.

"Are you married?"

She snapped her gaze back to his. "No. No, I wouldn't be here . . ."

He leaned forward and glanced at her left hand. "I see a tan line."

"When did you notice that? Last night when you were trying to convince me to date you?"

"When we got in the car. I looked for a ring last night."

She thought of her sleazy Italian. "A ring would have stopped you?"

Wade sipped his wine. "I am many things, but I don't sniff around another man's woman."

The plane started to pick up speed. "No one says things like that anymore."

"I'm Texas, born and raised, and I've always talked like that." The smirk told her he was proud of it.

Trina took a deep breath and spat out the truth as the plane lifted off the ground. "My late husband shot himself one year ago this weekend."

Her confession wiped the grin off Wade's face. Before he could comment, she continued. "I was in Italy because I didn't want to see that look of pity hovering in every corner of my life. Which is why I'm not in a hurry to get home and see my friends."

"Whoa."

"So I would appreciate it if you could just absorb the fact and move past it."

"I think that might take me more than a few minutes."

She looked out the window at the rain, which was starting to run down the side of the plane. If she told him they were married less than a year before she buried Fedor, it would only prompt more questions. The answers wouldn't be something she wanted to give. She sat alone in her thoughts for a few minutes before changing the subject. "What would I have found out if I had stayed awake and looked you up on the Internet?"

The pity in his eyes slowly faded. "I'm a singer."

She'd guessed maybe an actor when he'd told her he was famous. Since she hadn't been to the movies in over two years, he could have been the latest and greatest without her knowing.

"A country singer," he added. "I just finished my tour in Miami."

"That's why I've never heard of you. I don't listen to a lot of country music."

"I'll see what I can do to change that." He'd turned on his charming smile.

The plane hit a pocket of air and dipped left, then right.

Wade glanced at the ceiling.

"Just a little turbulence."

"You fly a lot?" he asked.

"I was a flight attendant, before . . ." She dropped the end of her sentence.

That look of pity started to cross his face again.

"None of that. Please, Wade. I'm not worthy of your pity on the subject. I wouldn't have mentioned my late husband if I could have gotten around it."

Wade closed his eyes and shook his head. "I'm glad you told me. It's all adding up now."

"What's adding up?"

"The not wanting to go home. Your desire to dis me last night and never see me again."

She couldn't help but smile. "We are on a jet together, so my conviction to stay away obviously wasn't that strong."

"Yes, but you're sitting over there instead of in my lap, which is where I'd rather you be."

That had her laughing. "You're so blatant."

"I'm honest. It's a curse, though my mama would say differently."

The plane dipped again, forcing Trina to hold her glass up to avoid spilling the wine. The intercom system inside the plane made a noise, and the voice of a man she assumed was the captain started to talk.

"We're hitting some rough weather, Mr. Thomas. I'd suggest you and your guest stay seated with your seat belts fastened until I can get us away from this storm."

Wade sat a little taller and looked out the window. "Don't have to tell me twice."

Trina took a drink of her wine to keep it from spilling. "They wouldn't have taken off if it wasn't safe. It's just gonna be bumpy."

Trina peered at the flight attendant, who was sitting several feet away, the phone to the cockpit to her ear.

"This doesn't bother you?"

"Not at all. In fact, I was working in the private sector as a flight attendant before my marriage. I'd planned on creating a company for private flight attendants."

"That didn't work out?" Wade asked.

"I didn't pursue it. I might, eventually. I've had other priorities this year."

"I can imagine."

"Enough about me. What's your story?" The way he was watching the rain against the window told her Wade was nervous. In her experience, the best way to quell that was to get him talking.

"I started singing in the shower as soon as I realized a hairbrush could double as a microphone."

The image of a young boy covered in soap, holding a round brush, popped into her head.

"When I was about eight, me and my buddy started a two-man band. He used an old paint bucket as a drum, and I had a hand-me-down guitar I learned how to play on my own."

The plane dipped again. This time Wade's glass fell to the floor and started rolling around, spilling wine everywhere.

Trina looked at the flight attendant, who reached for her seat belt to cinch it tighter.

"Whoa."

"It's okay—"

"Sorry for the turbulence, Mr. Thomas. This is the captain speaking. It looks like we're being encouraged to land on Grand Bahama instead of Nassau. There are lightning strikes on the smaller island, and turning back to Miami would have us chasing this storm. We're very sorry for the inconvenience. As soon as the weather clears, we will get you to your destination."

"That's not good," Wade said, looking behind him toward Nita. "Is everything okay up there?" He pointed toward the cockpit door.

"Just lightning, like the pilot said."

Wade turned his wild eyes on Trina.

"Hey, it's fine."

"Easy for you to say. Musicians always die in small plane crashes."

Trina couldn't help but take the blame for being on the plane with a storm approaching. Not that she felt they were at risk of falling out of the sky, but Wade obviously considered it a high probability.

"Do you need me to come over there and sit next to you?" she asked, trying to tease him.

His eyes locked on hers. "Don't you dare take that seat belt off."

The plane started to descend and bank to the left. Trina tried to see the ground but only saw clouds.

"Does your friend still play the drums with you?"

"What?"

"The drums. You said you had a friend who played when you were a kid."

Wade shook his head. "No. He ah . . ."

Trina noticed his hands fisting on the armrest. His knuckles turned white.

"He what?" Trina kept her concern about the bad weather to herself. As flights went, this was one she could have done without. The small plane made it worse.

"Married his high school sweetheart, had a daughter within the first year."

"Married life and your job aren't compatible?"

"I'm not sure about that. Drew didn't have the same drive. Took the excuse of a wife and a kid to stop trying and went to work with his father." Wade looked out the window again and released a relieved sigh. "Land. I see land."

Trina leaned forward and rested a hand on his knee. "Hey . . ."

He turned her way and tried to smile.

He sucked at it.

"I'm sorry. This was a bad idea."

Wade covered her hand with his and squeezed. "It was my bad idea."

"You were just trying to get me to go out with you."

There was a pause and a tilt of his head that she'd seen him do before. "I think after this flight, the least you can do is say yes to a date."

Oh, yeah, he was definitely playing it hard. Not that she thought for a second his anxiety about the flight was a show. White knuckles and wild eyes were a dead giveaway.

"How about dinner at whatever hotel we muster up once we land?"

His thumb stroked her fingers.

On instinct, she pulled away, only to have him hold her tighter. "That was a given. I'm talking about when we get back to Texas. I still need to teach you the two-step."

The plane rocked back and forth as the runway approached. Wade squeezed her hand a little tighter.

"Who says I don't already know the two-step?"

"Do you?"

"It's two steps, how hard can it be?"

The first punch to the tarmac and Wade squeezed her hand hard enough to have her tense. Once the wheels made decent contact and the nose bounced before leveling out, Trina placed her free hand over his fist.

Wade glanced at his hand. "Oh, damn, sorry." He let her go the second he realized the grip he had.

Trina shook out her hand with a laugh. "I don't need my hand for the rest of the day anyway."

Tilting his head back and closing his eyes, Wade let his shoulders fall. "That was not fun."

"We landed. We're good."

"Little lady, I haven't worked this hard for a date since I was in Miss Kuhnar's third grade class."

She laughed. "Third grade? You started early."

"Patty refused to let me walk her home up until the last week of school."

Trina had a strong desire to learn more about Patty.

The airplane came to a stop, and Nita stood from her seat as quickly as she could.

"Sincere apologies, Mr. Thomas."

Relaxed now, Wade flirted with his eyes and put Nita at ease. "I'll use this in a song," he told her.

The younger woman seemed to like that idea. "I can't wait to hear it."

Wade winked.

⁓

"Do you know who Wade Thomas is?" Avery glanced up from her cell phone to find Lori's and Shannon's eyes.

"The name sounds familiar," Lori said.

Avery turned her phone around and showed the others the image on her screen. "He's a country western singer. A friggin' musician!"

Lori blinked. "Okay . . ."

"Trina is in a private plane with a cowboy rock star. This isn't good." Avery hated to think of her vulnerable friend being taken advantage of by some sweet-talking, *yes, ma'am* kinda man that had women throwing themselves at him in a different city every night.

Shannon and Lori didn't share her distress.

"Remember Miguel?"

They all exchanged glances in a memory of the man that had latched on to Trina during their weeklong cruise in the Mediterranean last year. The man had put drugs into Trina's drink, his intentions never truly revealed, since they had intercepted their friend before anything tragic happened.

"One case of bad judgment isn't a reason to assume Trina isn't capable of picking up a decent guy," Shannon said.

Lori was biting her lip with a frown.

"What?" Avery asked.

"I seem to remember something in Trina's file saying she had a track record of dating lousy men." Since Lori was the lawyer who wrote up the prenuptial agreements for all the First Wives, she would know. Alliance, the company that had arranged all of their fake marriages, procured painstaking background checks. Those reports included everything from criminal behavior to previous relationships, bad behavior on and off the record, financial issues good and bad, all the way down to the skeletons in the family closets.

"She's too trusting."

"There isn't a lot we can do about it until she comes home," Lori told her.

Avery pushed off the couch in the middle of Trina's Texas ranch estate. A home Trina had inherited from her late mother-in-law, a mansion way too big for a single woman, even if it had a staff of half a dozen people milling about at all times of the day. "Oh, yeah, there is. We can go to her. She isn't planning on coming home."

"She wouldn't ditch us," Shannon said.

Avery moved around the great room until she found a pen and paper. "That's exactly what she's doing. It's been a year since Fedor offed himself. The only people who know about her other life are here. Everyone out there only knows what she tells them. If you haven't noticed, Trina hasn't exactly fostered any new friendships since all this went down. According to Andrea, she has made several excuses about going into the office, except when they have board meetings." Trina had inherited a third of Everson Oil, including a place on the board. Shortly after coming into her inheritance, she'd embraced the company and her mother-in-law's sisters, Andrea and Diane. That was up until a month before, when she escaped to Europe. She'd pulled away then, and hadn't emotionally returned.

"Maybe she needs some time alone," Shannon said.

"Or she needs her friends to step up and make sure she's making good decisions. If she isn't, we're there to catch her when she's dealing with the memories of last year."

Lori glanced at Shannon. "She has a point."

"Damn right I have a point. If my fake husband had splattered his brains all over the wall in the den, I would have run off to find God in India or some such place."

Shannon winced. "Thanks for the visual."

"Sorry, I'm just worried. You guys are the best thing, other than the money, of course, that my marriage to Bernie has given me. I don't want Trina making a mistake that we can help her avoid. A cowboy singer handing her a bunch of country lines so she can bankroll his next indie project is not gonna happen so long as I have some say in the matter."

"Maybe this guy and her are completely platonic." Shannon was forever the optimist in the group.

Avery and Lori exchanged doubtful glances.

Avery turned her phone back onto the image of Wade Thomas. "Look at that ass and tell me you wouldn't take a handful?"

A slight pull to Shannon's lips in the form of a smile told Avery what she already knew.

Avery started to dial.

"Who are you calling?" Lori asked.

"Sam. She said if there was ever a need for her jet, to call. I think now is a good time."

Chapter Six

Umbrellas proved useless when rain splattered horizontally across your body.

Dripping wet and laughing at the plight of it all, Wade opened the door to the hotel lobby and let Trina step in before him. Behind them, their driver dealt with their luggage.

Trina held both hands out in front of her and pulled her wet shirt from her chest. "That is nuts."

Wade shook his head and rain splattered everywhere.

"Hey!" Trina laughed and stood back.

"What's the matter . . . ?" He did it again. "Afraid of getting wet?"

Trina stepped close and twisted her ponytail over his frame.

"Oh, it's *on*." He snaked a hand around her waist and shook his head until she squirmed away.

"Uncle!"

When they stopped laughing, half the lobby was staring at them like they were nuts.

Trina tried to keep a straight face. "His fault," she told anyone who listened.

Wade took the liberty of placing a hand on the small of her back as he pushed her through the lobby. "I'll get ya for calling me out."

"It was your fault," she whispered.

They both stepped to the registration desk at the same time.

"Good afternoon," the man behind the counter greeted them.

"Hello," Trina said.

"Hi," Wade said at the same time.

The clerk looked between the two of them. "We're here to check in," Wade told the man.

He turned to the computer. "What is the name on the reservation?"

"Oh, we don't have a reservation. Our plane had to land here unexpectedly—"

The man stopped typing and the smile on his face fell. "I'm sorry, but we're completely booked."

Yeah, Wade had heard that before. "I'm sure you can find something."

He shook his head. "Many of our guests were forced to stay an extra night because of the storm."

Trina leaned forward. "What about your penthouse suite, or whatever your top floor has to offer? Money isn't an issue."

Trina pulled her wallet out of her purse.

Not to be outdone, Wade removed his wallet. "Exactly."

The clerk typed on his computer again. "The only thing we have is the presidential suite—"

Wade put his credit card down before Trina could. "We'll take it."

Trina nudged his card away. "I'll pay."

Shaking his head, Wade picked up her card and pushed his forward. "Not this time, little lady. Use this, please."

The clerk ping-ponged his gaze between them.

"I'm the reason we're here. I pay for the room," Trina insisted, grabbing at her credit card.

Wade held it out of her reach.

"I haven't had a woman pay for my room since I was in diapers." He turned to the clerk. "On my card."

The clerk held up his card and hesitated. "You sure?"

49

"Yes."

"No."

Wade turned to Trina.

"I pay for half or I'm going to find another hotel," Trina insisted.

"Seriously?" What was up with this woman?

She placed her hands on her hips and cocked her head to the side. "Don't I look serious?"

"You look like something that fell into a pond."

Trina rolled her eyes, grabbed her card from his fingertips, and turned as if she was walking away.

"Fine! Half."

With a smug smile, she handed her card to the clerk without words.

"Presidential suite for one night—"

"Two," Wade interrupted the clerk. He glanced at Trina. "I'm not getting back on that plane until my liver settles to where God meant it to sit."

She sighed. "Fine."

஧

"You take the master," Trina suggested when the bellhop left them.

"Why? Are you going to argue about that, too?"

He had this pouty look that stretched from his eyes to his lower lip. Trina wondered if he used that look to get his way with all the women.

"I won't argue. But my guess is the bed in there is a king, and you're taller than me. It's the practical choice." She picked up her suitcase and started toward the master. "But if you insist." Blowing right past him, Trina passed into the larger bedroom and tossed her case on the footstool by the bed. "Oh, this is nice."

"Now you're just teasing," Wade said from the other room.

Trina laughed to herself.

"I'm going to shower and change," she told him.

Wade moaned.

She turned around and bit her lips.

"You're loving this," he said.

Trina shrugged. "Could be worse."

"I can't figure you out, lady."

"Good." With that, she stepped back from the door and closed it. Wade chuckled as he walked away.

Once she kicked off her shoes, she found her half-broken phone in her purse and attempted to access her messages.

The screen had cracked to the point that bright globes followed the shattered glass and distorted the information. She tapped her messages but nothing happened. Instead of fighting it, she tossed it back in her purse and told herself to call her house phone later that night.

It might be nice to live without the distraction of a cell phone for a couple of days.

Shedding her clothes as she went, she made her way into her private bathroom and smiled at the size of the space. How many times had she stayed in hotels on layovers all over the world? None of which had rooms like this.

But this was how she lived now.

Penthouse suites and bathrooms you could throw a party in if you chose to.

She still packed light, even when going to Italy for an extended period of time. She had bought a few things along the way and simply shipped them home instead of dealing with the luggage. A luxury she never would have used in the past.

Her reflection in the mirror looked back. Her long black hair had stopped dripping down her back somewhere between checking in and taking the elevator to the top floor. Through her beige shirt, she saw the outline of her bra. Hardly wet T-shirt contest worthy, but it was close. To give Wade credit, he hadn't noticed. Or if he did, he didn't stare.

He seemed like a nice guy—therefore, she wondered what was wrong with him. If there was one thing Trina knew about herself, it was that she trusted them all way too soon. She thought they all said what they meant and meant what they said. She couldn't read them before her fake marriage to Fedor, and she'd certainly failed with her husband in their brief time together.

Unable to stop her head from going there, she thought about the last time she saw Fedor alive. It was the night before he shot himself. Alice, his mother, had slipped into a coma, and he spent most of his time in the hospital, by her bedside.

Trina had found him in his den. In his hand were two metal balls that he often fiddled with when he was thinking. She wondered, briefly, what had happened to those balls. They were real silver. The only reason she knew that fact was she'd asked him shortly after she moved into his Hamptons home.

Trina closed her eyes and forced the image, and the memory, away.

It had been a year. Why was she thinking about it all again now?

She flipped off her thoughts and turned on the water in the shower.

                                              ☙

"We could always find a swimming pool until it's time for dinner," Wade propositioned Trina, who was watching the rain fall in heavy sheets outside the windows of their room.

"First, I just took a shower, and second, the pools here are outside."

"What about a hot tub?"

Trina glanced over her shoulder and sent him a look that women had perfected for centuries. It said, *Are you kidding, Give me a break,* and *Stop,* all at once. "You just want to see me in a bikini."

As hard as he tried, Wade couldn't stop his head from going there and his eyes from traveling down her one-hundred-percent-clothed body. "Yes, ma'am, there is that."

"Do women ever say no to you?"

He paused and tried to remember the last time he'd been rejected for a drink, a date . . . or anything that might follow. He'd been on tour for six months, and there were plenty of opportunities, and perhaps more than just a couple of women along the way.

He shifted on his feet, tried to bring up the months before the tour.

"Oh my God."

"What? I'm trying to think."

"You're a womanizer." She called him out.

Wade was pretty sure she meant that as an insult. "I make it a rule not to see women I work with. It's too complicated when things don't work out."

"How noble."

"So that leaves me with . . ." The image of a concert venue filled with flirty eyed women wearing everything from jean skirts and cowboy boots to bras they used as shirts with tight shorts. Every once in a while, some backstage guest or a wife of a producer would come on to him.

"Thousands of adoring fans?" Trina finished for him.

Wade kicked his feet up on the coffee table and leaned back. "I'm not gonna lie, there are plenty of them who offer, but I don't dip into that pond as often as you might think."

Trina turned to watch the rain again. "If I was interested, I'd ask more about the ones you cast off, but I'm not."

Yeah, he didn't buy that.

"Being on that stage gives a lot of women the feeling they know you."

"I can't imagine."

He pushed to his feet almost as quickly as he'd sat. "Well, we can sit in this room and banter for hours, or we can check out what this island does when it's on lockdown. I don't know about you, but I've had just about enough of the inside of a hotel room. As much as this one is nice."

A hotel room was a lot like living in a stale, staged home. It had everything you needed, but nothing that fit you perfectly.

"I need to find a store to fix my cell phone."

"Okay, then. We search for that and stop at whatever else draws our eye."

Trina agreed with a shrug and disappeared into her room.

Wade cursed his eyes for lingering on her ass.

His mouth watered. Lordy, what was it about her that made him want to strut like a cock in a henhouse? It didn't matter, he was strutting and doing everything possible to get this woman to agree to see him once their little adventure was over.

"Ready." She appeared at her door, purse in hand, light jacket over her shoulders. Her hair was down and flowing over her back. He wondered what it would look like with her in her birthday suit.

You're a womanizer.

Yup, he needed to change his thinking or the images in his head would be teleported into hers. Because if there was one thing he'd figured out about this woman so far, it was that she read him like an open book.

The concierge hooked them up with umbrellas and slickers that were nothing but glorified trash bags with a place for your arms and head. Trina pulled the plastic over herself without thinking twice.

"Aren't you going to put it on?" she asked him.

He held up the folded plastic. "I'll look ridiculous."

Trina looked around the lobby, noticed several people wearing the rain gear. "You and everyone else."

"I think I'll just stick with the umbrella."

She lowered her voice. "Look at it as camouflage. No one will recognize you if you're wearing this."

"I'll risk it, besides, no one noticed me when we ran through earlier."

"That's because everyone was preoccupied with being soaked. That or you're not as famous as you think you are."

Wade lifted an eyebrow as if to say she would eat her words.

"Suit yourself." She pulled the hood over her head and turned toward the door.

The second they were out in the rain, Wade thought twice about his decision to look good over being dry.

Two blocks down and one block over, they rushed into a storefront that sold and fixed cell phones.

It didn't take long for the clerk to tell Trina her phone was jacked and she should probably replace it. Unfortunately, they didn't have the iPhone she was using. "I can get one here in the morning. It's on the other side of the island."

"Are there any other stores that sell new phones?" Wade asked.

"Yeah." The clerk smiled. "Mine, the one on the other side of the island."

Trina looked at her damaged phone. "We'll come back tomorrow, then."

"Tell you what, leave it with me, and by the time you come and pick it up, I'll have all the information transferred over. I just need you to fill out a few things."

"You sure?" Trina asked.

"My sister will bring it tonight when she closes the shop."

Trina filled out a few forms and paid the man for her new phone and told him they'd be back.

"Now what?" Trina asked as they stood under the eaves of the shop and managed to keep some of the rain at bay.

Across the street was an open-air bar, one where the walls were sheets of plastic and the patrons were already well ahead of Wade and Trina. "Happy hour?" he asked.

"Might as well."

They ordered the house recommendation. Something rum infused that tasted a bit fruity for his liking. A three-piece reggae band was playing in the corner. Their music was loud enough to keep whispered conversations outside, but soft enough to talk somewhat normally inside.

"I assume this is nothing like what you sing?" Trina asked him.

"No, ma'am. But it's nice."

"*Ma'am* makes me feel old."

He'd heard that before. "It's not meant that way."

"I know. I've heard it a lot since I moved to Texas. Which fits, since I feel like I've aged ten years in the past year."

That last part was said without her looking up from her drink. Although he didn't want to bring up her past, he couldn't help but ask a few questions.

"Did your late husband move you to Texas?"

"No, no . . . we lived in New York."

"The city?" She didn't seem like a Manhattan kind of woman.

"The Hamptons." She smiled. "Sounds snooty, but it was rather nice."

He sipped his drink, decided he'd switch to something less sugary on the next round. "So how did Texas happen?"

He wasn't sure at first if she was going to answer. But then she squared her shoulders as if drawing up the courage to open up.

"Oil."

He blinked.

She squeezed her eyes closed. "I suppose now that you've heard my last name a few times, it's only a matter of time before you look me up."

"Petrov is unique and hard to miss when someone is checking your credit card information."

She shifted, took a drink. "There's this little oil company . . . Everson Oil."

Wade laughed. He couldn't help himself. "That's not little, sweetheart."

"Right. Well, I somehow ended up inheriting a third of the company."

It took a lot to shock Wade, but her words did the job. He looked her over again. She wasn't wearing anything terribly fancy. No flashy jewelry or anything else to give away her wealth. He blew out a long, slow whistle.

"I know. So, yeah. I moved to Texas. Most of the last year, I've been learning about the alternative fuel side of the company. Which is really interesting, if not a little ironic, considering fossil fuel is our bread and butter."

"Do you like the work?"

She laughed. "I don't think you can call it work. Most of the time I'm shadowing people on the management team for different divisions to learn what their functions are. It isn't like I have any real job, or boss. When I said I was going to Italy for an extended vacation, there wasn't one person who suggested I was needed."

"Oh."

"They're probably happy I'm not hovering over them."

"So it's not fulfilling."

"I think it could be. I'm on the board, and my vote actually counts, so I felt the need to learn as much as I can. I'll continue to when I get back."

He didn't see her at a desk. "Why bother, if you don't like it?"

She took another drink, sat back in her chair. "What else am I going to do all day? It isn't like I can go back to my old life. I'll never work as a flight attendant again, or any service job. I don't need to work for money . . . what does that leave?"

"Philanthropy."

"Right, and the ambassador of goodwill to the less fortunate. But I'm nobody. People just want the check, they don't want me cheering them on to fulfill their dreams. Besides, I'm too young for long days on the golf course or the opera house, where philanthropic individuals congregate and network."

He opened his mouth, only to have her cut him off.

"Not to mention the fact that because I'm young, the wives of the men who play in the same taxable income that I have automatically assume I'm gunning for their husbands."

"That can't be true."

Trina gave him that *you've got to be kidding* look again. "I have attended several events since moving to Texas. Fundraisers for kids, causes for cancer, Everson Oil holiday parties where whole pigs are roasting on an open fire for what seems like days. Every single one of them is bursting with men in their sixties and their wives, who look twenty years younger. Not one time was I left beside a married man to have a conversation about anything without someone dodging in and taking that person away. Even if I wanted to impart some of my wisdom learned while watching the staff at Everson, I've never had the chance."

She paused.

Wade opened his mouth.

Trina kept going. "On the occasion a single man, old or young, approached me . . . it was never to talk about the company, or the cause. It was only to see if it had been long enough since Fedor's death for me to consider dating."

Fedor? Her late husband's name was *Fedor?*

"You're a beautiful woman."

"With a brain," she said, pointing to her head.

He made a rolling motion with his finger. "Can we go back . . . Fedor? That's a very unusual name."

"His father is Russian. Alice Everson was his mother. American."

Something clicked in the back of his head. "This was in the news."

The waiter walked by and Trina flagged him down. "Can we have a menu?"

"Sure."

"Mother and son died close together," Wade remembered out loud.

"Yeah. It was not a fun time."

"I suppose escaping to Venice was a good plan for the anniversary of it all."

She tilted her drink in the air in his direction. "See, that's what I thought."

Her eyes lost focus again. There was so much going on inside her head, Wade could practically hear the wheels turning.

"Anyway . . . now I need to figure out what to do. That's proven harder than it would seem."

"Because you planned your life with someone who is no longer here."

Her eyes snapped to his, and he wondered if he got that wrong.

"Yeah, I guess." Trina looked away. "Tell me about you."

The change of the subject told him that more talk of her late husband was off the table.

"What do you want to know?"

Trina finally looked at him again, her eyes less guarded. "How has fame and fortune changed your life?"

The waiter stopped by, took their order, and left again.

"It's changed everything. Even my friends, I'm sorry to say."

"How is that?"

"Money changes how people look at you. You know that."

"I do."

The memory of Drew filled his thoughts. "Jealousy is often followed by his ugly uncle, Envy. When that happens, things change. Much as you want your friends to come along for the ride, they often don't."

"Chances are they weren't that good of friends, then."

"Maybe. Real friends are hard to find in my world. Some of the people I relate to the most are other singers, some as successful or more so. They get it."

"So celebrities hanging out with other celebrities happens because no one else understands?"

"You could say that. Have you ever had the paparazzi outside your hotel or home?"

She nodded. "Actually, yes."

That was not the answer he was expecting. "Really?"

"They called me the black widow."

Wade lost his humor. "They did not!"

"You're familiar with the media. You know how they are."

He'd been called many things, but none terribly hateful. "I'm sorry you had to deal with that, darlin'."

"It's okay. I have a group of really wonderful friends now."

"The ones you're avoiding."

Her eyes narrowed. "Aren't we supposed to be talking about you? Tell me about your mother."

His head fell back as he laughed. "Now you're a therapist."

She laughed along with him. "Or you can tell me about your last real girlfriend."

Hand on his heart, he said, "My mother is the best woman in the world."

Trina roared with laughter. "Boundaries are set. Okay . . ."

Chapter Seven

The sound of fists hitting the door met the pounding in Trina's brain. She cracked one eye open and protested the sunlight blaring through the hotel window.

Shots . . . they had ended the night drinking shots.

Trina never drank shots.

Her eyes drifted closed again.

". . . is she in here?"

What was Avery doing in her hotel room?

The door opening didn't wake her up, but the voices that followed did.

"What the hell, Trina?"

With a hand to her forehead, Trina faced the glare of the light to find the very women she was trying to avoid standing over her.

"What are you—?"

Behind Lori, Shannon, and Avery, Wade leaned against the door-frame. "We had a bit to drink last night." Wade wore a hotel-issue bathrobe and a smile.

Lori moved to the bed and Avery turned on Wade. "You had better not have—"

"Whoa, feisty lady. Hold your fire."

"Back down," Trina said, a little loud. She winced at the sound of her heartbeat behind her eyeballs. "Oh, God."

"I know that look." Wade's voice was closer than the buzz of women in the room.

An arm wrapped around her shoulders at the same time her stomach reminded her why she never drank shots.

In the space of five seconds, the covers on the bed were thrown off and she felt her body lifting and a flat chest pushing against her cheek.

She held back a burp that promised to be so much more until her knees felt the cold tile floor of the bathroom.

Then she lost it.

"I'm getting ice," someone behind her said.

Her body protested the evening before while someone held her hair back.

"It's okay, little lady. Give it all up. You'll feel better."

Wade. God, how embarrassing.

If her head wasn't pounding so much, she might actually encourage him to leave the bathroom.

But she was pretty sure he was the one keeping her from falling face-first into the toilet. She peeked out of the corner of her eye.

Yup, it was Wade.

She groaned.

"I advised you against that last round," he reminded her.

A smirk found its way on her lips.

From her other side, someone produced a cold washcloth.

"Thank you."

"No worries," Lori said.

Trina swiveled her head, slowly. Her stomach was finally empty. "What are you guys doing here?"

She started to stand to find Wade helping her up.

"If you won't come to us, we will come to you," Avery said.

Shannon walked into the bathroom with a bucket of ice, which sounded like a really good idea on the back of her neck.

"Do you want to go back to bed?" Wade asked.

Trina finally looked him straight in the eye. "I think I need to brush my teeth."

Avery pushed past him and dislodged his hand from Trina's arm. "We got this, Cowboy."

Wade put both hands in the air and stepped back. "I'll just take a shower and let you all work this out."

Lori regarded him without emotion and Shannon offered a polite smile.

"You do that," Avery snapped.

Trina smacked at Avery's hand. "Stop it." She turned to Wade. "Thank you."

He winked before zigzagging through the women and out of the room.

They fell in like hungry wolves on fresh meat.

"What is going on with him?" Avery asked.

"Are you okay?" asked Shannon.

"We needed to make sure you were all right," Lori added.

Trina took an ice cube and placed it directly behind her neck. "Outside of a hangover, I'm fine."

"You ditched us."

Trina looked at Avery. "I know. I just couldn't deal."

"That's what we thought," Shannon said. "But disappearing only results in others worrying."

"I'm sorry for that. I don't want anyone to worry."

"You could have just told us," Lori said.

"You would have come running either way." Trina was sure of that. When no one protested, she knew she was right.

Shannon moved to the shower and turned it on. "Let's get you cleaned up. Order something mild for breakfast."

That sounded good.

Avery started for the door.

"Don't give Wade a hard time. He hasn't so much as touched me."

Three sets of doubtful eyes met hers.

"Not that he hasn't suggested it. But he's been nothing but respectful, regardless of my late night indulgence."

"He better not have."

"Avery!" Trina gave a warning.

Her feisty blonde friend left the bathroom and the others followed.

Alone, Trina stepped to the mirror and dared a look.

Green was not her color.

～⑨

There had been many times in Wade's life when he had been in a hotel room surrounded by beautiful women, but never, not even once, could he recall a time when three women stared him down with such doubt against his moral character as this pack of females. It was as if three lovers all got to talking and figured out he was seeing each of them.

Wade was smarter than that. He never dated three women at the same time. When he was in between girlfriends, when he was free to date as many or as few women as he liked, he did so in different states. Making a situation like the one he was in right now next to impossible.

It seemed his quiet little weekend without a crowd had come to a close, and he was the cog in the wheel of an all-girl party.

With a smile, he greeted the women as he moved to the room service cart to pour a cup of coffee. "Ladies."

"So you're Wade Thomas," the woman with a chip on her shoulder the size of Texas said.

"I am. And you would be?"

"I'm Avery." She pointed to the tall, thin, dark haired, model look-ing woman. "That's Shannon."

"I'm Lori," said the slightly less hostile blonde. "Trina's lawyer."

Wade's eyebrow went up with that. *What an interesting introduction.* "Funny, I thought you were all just her friends."

"We are. Just making sure the introductions are thorough."

Lawyers. He had yet to find one he truly liked.

He took his first swig of coffee, happy to have the caffeine on board.

"How did you two meet?"

He could see the end of this conversation before it began. "In a bar in Miami, and before we begin twenty questions, let me sum this up. Yes, I hit on her. She is stunning and was oddly sad, and I had a desire to make her smile. But instead of taking me up on my offer, we drank and talked until the early morning hours. We ended up here, where there has been more talkin' and drinkin', but no foolin' around." He looked directly at Trina's attorney. "My mama taught me never to mess with a girl who has had too much to drink or I might end up needing someone in your profession." He sipped his coffee. "Anything else you wanna know, you're gonna have to ask your friend."

He took a piece of toast from the table and ate half in one bite.

Once he washed it down, he headed for the door. "Tell Miss Trina I'm going out to retrieve her broken phone. I'm sure I'm leaving her in capable hands."

Once he escaped the henhouse, he felt the weight of the women inside lift. It was good for his ego, he decided . . . to have so many women *not* falling at his feet. It had been a good long while since that had happened. If ever.

The sun outside was a bright contrast to the day and evening before. The storm had blown through and left fresh, albeit humid, air behind.

He hid his features with dark sunglasses as he walked down the still, quiet streets.

Some debris left over from the storm littered the sidewalks, and sand made tiny drifts along the buildings. He managed a glimpse of the sea as he ducked around until he found the phone store.

The clerk recognized him when he entered.

They greeted and shook hands. "Where is your friend?" he asked.

"We had a little bit too much fun last night at the place on the corner." He pointed in the general direction of the bar they'd closed the night before.

"Those tropical surprises have a kick."

"Sure do."

He produced the phone and turned it on. "I did a direct transfer overnight. It looks like everything is there, but if it isn't, just have Ms. Petrov download it from the cloud."

"I'll do that."

Wade placed the phone, and her old one, back into the bag. "What do I owe you?"

"She already paid."

Oh, yeah . . . he'd forgotten. "I guess that's all, then."

The clerk stopped him before leaving. "One more thing."

Wade smiled, expecting some kind of comment on his music or recognition.

"There was a hiccup during the download."

"Oh?"

"Some kind of tracking app kept kicking an error message."

"Okay."

"It was strange," he went on. "The icon wasn't something I'd ever seen before, and it kept flashing, but so fast it would have easily been missed."

Wade shrugged. "What kind of tracking app was it?"

"That's just it, I don't know. I saw it flash a map, and then the airport in Miami, then it brought up a map of London and flashed the name of London Heathrow."

"Probably just a glitch."

The clerk shrugged. "It also kept flashing text in a different language. Something Slavic, I think, which was what caught my attention."

Wade smiled. "I'm sure it's nothing."

"It seemed to be causing some havoc rebooting. I finally got it to work without an issue, but it wasn't easy. When I looked in her app menu, there wasn't anything there. Almost as if it was a virus running in the background. But since she said she dropped her phone in Miami, I assumed it wasn't there by accident. If the app clogs up the phone, you might tell Ms. Petrov to remove it and download it again."

Wade nodded. "I'll do that."

Instead of heading straight back to the hotel, Wade stopped at a small diner and ordered a big, greasy breakfast. For him, nothing combated a night of drinking better than a big meal. He doubted the women were done getting all the details out about how he and Trina had met, and he doubly doubted that Trina would want to watch him eat. Poor girl was bound to be ill all day after the night they'd had.

He smiled. Not because she'd gotten drunk, but because even though she didn't know him that well, she'd felt comfortable enough to do so in his presence. That sadness he'd told her friends that had lingered in Trina's eyes had slowly faded in just a couple of days. When she smiled, something bright pierced his breastbone and lit him up. Maybe it was the chase, the fact she didn't fall all over him. Or maybe it was just her.

He liked her and really wanted to see her again.

He'd have to make her posse of friends like him if he was going to get anywhere. Not to mention the reason he'd been chasing the sorrow from her eyes since they met. Who was the man she'd been married to?

Why the hell did he commit suicide and leave her to pick up the pieces? Trina's friends, he could manage . . . women had a hard time resisting his charm when he turned it on. But the man talking to angels? That might prove more difficult.

Trina's warnings about bad timing weren't going to stop him.

No way.

He took her phone from the bag and typed in his personal number. When he typed in his name, he did so with a little extra. Wade, You Owe Me A Dance, Thomas.

That should get her attention.

He put the phone away and finished his breakfast.

Before he left the restaurant, he called the pilot and asked how quickly they could fly home. He figured his welcome back at the hotel would be limited, and there was no reason to hang around to keep Trina smiling now that her friends had found her.

Of course, he would make sure she was okay with him ducking out before taking off. He felt he owed her that.

On his way back to the hotel, his phone buzzed in his back pocket.

"Where the hell are you?" The roughness of Jeb's voice had Wade smiling.

"Miss me?"

"Seriously. How am I supposed to sit still when I don't know where you are?"

"Calm down, Jeb. I'm in the Bahamas."

"What . . . why?"

"I met a woman."

Jed groaned. "A phone call would have helped."

"Good thing you called, then." Wade turned the corner and onto the street of the hotel.

"I assume there aren't any flash mobs around."

"It's an island. I'm safe. I'll probably be heading back today."

"That was quick. Did you at least get her name?"

Wade rolled his eyes. "Trina Petrov, and it isn't like that, so knock it off."

Jeb was unusually silent on the other end.

"You still there?"

His phone clicked twice before he heard a dial tone. "Guess not," he said to himself.

Chapter Eight

"You don't have to leave."

"If I value my head, I think I should just make my way back to Texas, where the women are a tiny bit nicer than the ones in this hotel room."

Trina glanced over her shoulder to find Avery and Lori staring.

Trina narrowed her eyes, and they both looked away.

"I'm sorry."

"Don't be," Wade told her. "I'm glad your friends are loyal enough to hate me on sight just out of principle."

"Misguided as that is."

Wade chuckled.

Heaviness sat in the back of Trina's throat.

Wade stood before her, suitcase at his side, cowboy hat on his head. Their goodbye felt oddly out of place.

She tried to smile. "Kinda glad you hit on me in Miami," she told him.

His killer smile and flirty eyes took over. "Still bummed you didn't take me up on my offer."

"Bad timing."

"I know that, darlin'."

She sighed.

"Well, I'll get back to my regularly scheduled life and leave you to your friends."

Trina rubbed her hands on her pants, not sure if she should shake his hand or hug him.

Apparently she was the only one unsure of what to do.

Wade wrapped his arms round her shoulders and pressed his frame against hers in a hug that fueled her soul. When he pulled away, he pressed his lips to her forehead, stood back, and picked up his suitcase.

"Oh, by the way. The clerk at the phone place said there was a tracking app that was messing things up, and that if you had any problems, you should delete it and reinstall."

"Tracking?"

"Like one of those friend apps you women use to keep track of each other."

"Oh, okay, thanks."

She walked him a few feet to the door.

He opened it. "I might have put in my number, in case you wanted to take me up on those dance lessons."

Trina saw herself accepting his offer. She placed a hand on his arm, caught his eye. "Thanks, Wade."

He winked before turning away.

His jeans sure did hug his hips well.

She started to close the door before she heard him say, "You can stop staring at my butt now."

Trina laughed. "Vain much?"

Wade just chuckled as he sauntered out of sight.

Avery clicked her tongue when Trina walked back into the room. "A country singing cowboy? Really?"

"He's a nice guy," Trina defended.

Lori lifted her phone and started to read. "'Wade Thomas, thirty-four years old, and one of the most celebrated country singers of this decade, and how he loves the ladies. It's said he has broken hearts all over the country and a few places in Europe, as well.'"

"Gossip magazines. We all know how accurate those are."

Lori twisted her phone around. "This was in the *Austin Press*."

"Still sounds like gossip," Shannon said.

"Thank you, Shannon. Glad to know someone is on my side."

"But most gossip holds some truth," she added.

Trina stuck her tongue out.

"He is very cute, though," Lori said with the first smile Trina had seen on her since they arrived.

Trina felt her face heat up. "I kinda like that Texas drawl."

"Oh. My. God!" Avery exclaimed. "He's a musician."

"I think you have to call him more than that." Lori held up her phone. "Sold out concerts, platinum records . . ."

Avery wanted nothing to do with it. "Every single musician I ever went out with was a total douchebag."

"And how many was that?" Trina asked.

"I couldn't even tell you. I did the whole groupie thing in college just to tick off the parents, then found myself attracted to a long stream of jerks. They all cheat. They all lie. They *hey baby* you until you're out of sight, and then they *hey baby* someone else. Trust me on this one, Trina, stay clear."

"Not to be a total bitch, but didn't you just describe yourself this last year?" Ever since Trina had met Avery, she hadn't seen her with the same guy twice.

"No, they all know I'm free and single. It's agreeable for all parties involved."

"Doesn't matter anyway. Wade was a weekend companion that didn't involve one kiss," Trina told them.

Lori turned her whole body in Shannon's direction and her back to Trina. "Funny, but it looked to me like Wade Thomas wanted to lick the cherry right off the top of Trina's ice cream sundae."

Shannon laughed and made eye contact with Trina. "He was salivating."

"Y'all are barking up the wrong tree. I'm not interested in Wade Thomas. Or any man right now."

The room went silent for several seconds.

"Y'all?" Avery said slowly.

"I'm living in Texas, cut me some slack."

"Okay, okay . . . let's get on to the subject that brought us here." Lori stood and crossed to the small kitchenette. "First Wives Club meeting is called to order. Which means wine."

Trina moaned. "I'll have water."

"Fine." She went through the motions of opening the bottle while talking. "Since we've been picking on Trina already, let's start with you, Shannon."

Their normal method of operation during these meetings was to talk about what they were doing, or not doing, in their dating lives. What worked and what didn't. They also spent a good amount of time discussing what they were doing with the money they'd made from their temporary marriages.

Shannon accepted the wine and relaxed on the sofa. "I signed a lease for a studio."

"That's fantastic news," Trina said. "Do you have any clients yet?"

Shannon had a semisuccessful career as a photographer that she wanted to expand postdivorce. But when she was no longer the first lady of California, she ended up closing her business, since the majority of people requesting her services were members of the press searching for a story. Or worse, the activists and lobbyists of the general population that thought she could plead their cause with her ex-husband.

"I do. An engagement party and two weddings."

"No more lurking jerks walking through the door?" Avery asked.

"Not yet. I'm sure I won't escape them forever. But I think the public finally realized I'm no longer Mrs. Paul Wentworth."

"What about you?" Lori asked. "Have you realized you're no longer married to him?"

Shannon shook her head. "Don't be ridiculous."

Avery tucked her feet under her in the chair she sat on. "So you're dating, then?"

Silence.

Yeah, Trina didn't see Shannon dating anyone when she had fallen hard for her temporary husband.

Unfortunately, the feeling hadn't been mutual.

"It's hard to meet men."

Avery laughed. "Dating apps, bars, clubs, walking on the beach, Uber drivers, waiters—"

"Uber drivers, really?" Trina asked.

Avery answered with a smile.

"Please, I can't pick someone up at a bar," Shannon said.

"You're right. You have to actually go into the bar before you can pick someone up," Lori told her.

"I go to bars."

"The no-host bar at a wedding reception doesn't count," Avery exclaimed.

Shannon didn't deny Avery's claim. "Well, dating apps are out."

"Yeah, those suck. Half the guys on there aren't real, anyway." Trina had tried those things before she married Fedor. It wasn't her pace.

"Good for hooking up, but that's about it," Avery said.

"Have you ever considered taking up bowling, or sailing . . . something like that? Something that has tons of testosterone around by default. Football games, anything?"

"Sports aren't my thing."

"It doesn't have to be *your* thing, it has to be *their* thing." Avery was like a dog with a bone.

Shannon passed glances around the room. "Maybe I'll try sailing. I love the ocean."

"Okay, then. That's a direction, at least."

Trina could almost hear Lori tapping a gavel on a desk with her statement.

"Anything new with you and Reed?" Avery turned her attention to Lori.

Lori slowly smiled, as if the mere mention of her boyfriend warmed a part of her soul. "He's a good man. He cooked stir-fry for us last Tuesday."

"Reed can cook?" Shannon asked.

"No. It was awful. Took three days for the soy sauce to leave the back of my throat."

Trina chuckled. "So what was good about it?"

"He wore an apron."

They all stared at her.

"And nothing else."

"Ahh, so, sex in the kitchen," Avery said.

"Any wedding bells yet?" Trina asked.

Seemed like every time they all got together, they asked if Reed had hinted at the next step.

"He is taking me out of town for our anniversary. I think maybe . . ."

"Let us know as soon as he pops the question."

Shannon lifted her glass. "I'll be your wedding photographer."

"I'll help plan the wedding. I love that stuff," Trina said.

"Hold up, guys. He hasn't asked me yet."

"It's only a matter of time. That man adores you." Avery unfolded from the couch to refill her glass. "So now that we have the obligatory 'Is Shannon dating' questions out of the way, and 'Where is Reed on the commitment meter' conversation behind us, I think maybe it's time to dig into what is eating at Trina that made her ditch us."

Three sets of eyes turned on her.

"Is this an intervention?"

Lori shook her head. "Give it up, Trina, what's going on in your head?"

After sucking in a long breath and blowing it out slowly, Trina tried to form her emotions into words. "I don't know what to do. I thought I could find a place at Everson Oil, and maybe I still can, but it feels like everyone there is placating me. My financial goals when I married Fedor are completely obsolete now. I have all the money in the world and nothing to do. I have no cause, no reason to get out of bed in the morning and face the day."

All the stares in the room turned to worry.

Trina went on. "I started having dreams about Fedor about a month ago."

Lori set her glass down. "What kind of dreams?"

"Memories. His body . . ." She closed her eyes and tried to erase the image that would forever live with her. The housekeeper had found him after he shot himself, and started screaming. By the time Trina made her way to his detached office at their home in the Hamptons, the entire household staff was there. She rushed into the room to see Fedor at his desk, lifeless, blood everywhere. She only had one look before two people pushed her out of the room and called the police. Once the coroner removed him, and the authorities cleared the room for her to go into, she didn't. They'd hired an outside company to clean the space, paint the walls, and replace the rug. Trina knew the work had been done, but she never went into the room again. Within a month of his death, Lori had pulled her, along with Avery and Shannon, onto a ship to cruise the Mediterranean to help her forget the tragedy. When she returned, she packed her personal belongings, sealed up the Hamptons house, and moved to Texas.

"Why now?" Avery asked quietly.

"I don't know. Maybe because it's been a year. I've been thinking of selling the house. Before I do that, I should probably go there and make sure anything personal of Fedor's is found and given to his aunts."

"You don't have to do that. You can hire—"

Trina interrupted Lori. "No. I need to do it. I need to face that home and the memories that are there in order to move on. Do you realize I was still wearing Fedor's ring until last week? Who does that? We weren't even married for love and forever."

"I noticed you put it back on when you moved to Texas," Avery said. "I didn't want to ask."

"It started out of respect at the company. I was there a lot, and the ring reminded people that I had been Fedor's wife. People expected me to be the mourning widow. Young widows wear their wedding rings."

"Makes sense," Shannon said.

"It's been a year, and the ring is gone, and with it the obligation of playing the sad widow." That was her plan, in any event.

"It sounds like you have a direction," Lori said.

"Maybe. I wouldn't mind a divine sign from above letting me know I'm not on a detour that's just going to lead me back to walking in circles."

"Like Wade Thomas?" Shannon asked.

Avery scoffed.

Lori leaned forward. "Have you received any letters from Alice yet?"

Trina shook her head. "The mystery letters from the grave have yet to show up."

"I wouldn't be surprised if they are triggered by the anniversary of her death," Lori said.

Alice had told Trina, in her will, that letters would be sent explaining Alice's reasons for her final wishes regarding the estate. An estate that should have been left to Fedor. Alice was already in a coma when Fedor killed himself, so it wasn't as if she knew that Fedor wouldn't be around to collect. The entire thing baffled Trina's mind. For the better part of the year, she'd managed to not think about Alice's motives. Only now, that was all Trina seemed to contemplate when she was left alone with her thoughts.

And she was alone with her thoughts a lot.

"When did she die?" Avery asked.

"Sixteen days after Fedor." Trina looked between each of the women in silence. "His death was a year ago tomorrow."

Silence met her words.

Then Avery added, "Sounds like a good reason to get drunk."

"Or date a cowboy." Shannon winked.

For a moment, Trina felt herself smile. Maybe learning the two-step was a good idea, so long as the dance was in the forward motion of moving along in her life.

What a protective lot they were. Usually he was a hit with the girl squad when he put his focus on one of them. Not Trina's friends. Good thing his ego was firmly in check or he would have been offended. But as one of his songs told the world, being humble in the face of fame is the only way to live. *Keep it real,* his mother always preached.

"Someone got quiet."

He squeezed her shoulder and let her go. "I'm hungry," he told her. Suggesting he had a woman on his mind would only prompt questions, and he had a few of his own tickling his head before he dealt with his mother's. Would Trina use the number he typed into her phone? When would he use the one he jacked from hers? Maybe if he gave her a day or two . . . enough time for him to look up a bit about his competition. A dead ex was hard to navigate, not that he'd done that before.

"Hungry?" his mother asked, her sharp eyes drilling into him.

"Yup. In need of some Texas-size Angus beef grilled by my own hands." He turned to make his way back to the house.

"There is something you're not telling me," she called out.

He smiled over his shoulder. "Yeah, there is. I'd like some apple pie with that steak. Any chance that can happen?"

She skipped a step to keep up with him. "How about cobbler?"

He draped his arm over her shoulders again and walked the rest of the way back.

❧

After the First Wives intervention, Trina skipped the flight to Texas and detoured to New York. Lori and Shannon both returned to Los Angeles, and Avery tagged along with Trina.

The Hamptons home she'd shared in her brief marriage to Fedor had been vacant for nearly one year. She stood at the steps, looking up into the dark windows and pulled shades. The gray, cloudy sky matched her mood.

"You know what this place is missing?" Avery asked.

"What?"

"Eerie Halloween music and fake fog."

Avery's reference to All Hallows Eve wasn't because there were over-grown weeds and dead trees, but the air that surrounded the house itself.

The outside was perfectly maintained, and inside, Trina knew she'd find the same. The company she'd hired to manage the home after she'd moved was in charge of weekly cleaning and maintenance, and Cindy, her old housekeeper, supervised. Something Trina had become very accustomed to dealing with after inheriting nearly half a dozen homes. This one she had no intentions of ever living in again, so she'd let the staff go with severance packages and letters of recommendation.

Trina looked over her shoulder and past the gates and wondered if any of the neighbors paid attention to who came and went. Probably not. The homes were spaced out enough to not see those who lived next door for weeks, if at all. One would think a home that would fetch over fifteen million dollars would have someone living inside, but many of the homes in this area were weekend and summer getaways. This one going unoccupied for a year probably wasn't even noticed.

"It's going to take me a few days to go through everything," Trina told Avery for the third time.

"Yeah, you've already said that. Like you, I don't have a job, so here I am. Ready to go through the Ghost of Christmas Past's shit."

Trina was glad for it. She didn't want to do this alone. Her mother had volunteered to help, but Trina wasn't about to encourage that. Her parents still had no idea her marriage to Fedor was a complete fallacy. The lie she'd told the world was only known by the First Wives, Fedor, and the employees of Alliance. That was the way it would forever stay.

"Let's do this." Avery took the first steps toward the door.

Inside was exactly as Trina remembered. Dark stained wood floors, high ceilings, white painted walls, and lots of windows where the shades and window treatments were closed. She caught the alarm and pressed in the code to disarm, and then stood in silence.

"We need to open this place up." Avery went to work even as she said the words. She marched through the foyer and into the main living room and pulled back the drapes. Even the gray light coming in from outside helped the mood of the house. She pushed open the window with a grunt. "Deal with the cold. It smells like a coffin in here."

Trina winced.

"Sorry."

Rooted in place, Trina just stared at the familiar space. "Wait until you go into Fedor's office in the back."

"Point me in a direction and I'll do it."

"Let's deal with the big house first." Trina shook out of her fog and headed back outside. "I'll get our suitcases."

It had started to drizzle in the few minutes they'd been inside. Instead of rushing, Trina took her time pulling her suitcase from the trunk of the rental car she and Avery had picked up at the airport. She looked toward the four-car garage and remembered the car she had inside. She wasn't even sure if the registration was paid on the thing. Fedor had bought it for her when she'd moved in and said he would take care of all of it, even after they were divorced. Now it sat in a garage with two more of Fedor's cars, collecting dust.

What a shame.

A waste of life Fedor had pissed away by squeezing the trigger.

The Hamptons home was never meant to be hers. Although he did promise a postdivorce compromise that would keep anyone from guessing their marriage was an arrangement. That compromise was never fully developed. Once again, cut short by Fedor's decision, and that of Alice's estate landing in Trina's lap.

With Fedor's death, the money he'd earned on his own had ended up back in the family money with Everson Oil. He'd known his mother wasn't going to live long, so he'd had his attorney write up a plan to give his estate to his aunts. If his attorney questioned why the money wasn't to be left to Trina, she'd never heard.

After Fedor's death, and Alice's, his aunts wanted to give Trina all of Fedor's assets.

She outright refused, and the funds went in the general pot of the oil company, which still ended up giving Trina a third of Fedor's estate. It was obvious she wasn't going to escape the money, so when Andrea and Diane asked that Trina deal with the Hamptons home, Trina agreed. Considering the aunts had only been in the place a couple of times, it only seemed right that Trina manage the sale.

A twig snapped behind her, making Trina swivel her head in that direction.

Nothing.

She glanced down to find a cat sitting and watching her expectantly.

"Who are you?" Trina asked, as if the cat would answer.

She knelt down and put out her hand, willing the animal to approach. Instead, the gray and white cat scurried in the opposite direction and disappeared behind the garage.

Another noise to her left had her thinking that maybe there was a colony of feral cats close by. But instead of seeing another feline friend, there was nothing.

She sighed and hoisted Avery's suitcase from the car, pulled the handles on both bags, and closed the trunk.

Trina screamed.

"What?" Avery jumped back.

Trina blinked, her heart in her chest. "Don't scare me like that."

"I thought you heard me coming."

She willed her pulse to slow down. "No. Geez."

"Here, let me help."

Trina let Avery drag her own overstuffed bag and quickly followed her inside.

Not that the interior of the house helped at all with the calming of her nerves.

"We need some music in here," she told Avery.

"Maybe a certain country singer?" Avery teased.

That made Trina smile. "Not a bad idea. I don't know if I've ever heard Wade's music."

"I doubt that's possible."

By the time Trina dropped her bag in her old room and placed Avery's in the closest guest room, Avery had already found the stereo and Bluetoothed her phone to it.

Sure enough, Wade's lighthearted southern drawl filled the house and made Trina smile.

"I know this song," she said, surprised.

"Told you." Avery held a pen and a notebook. "Let's start a list so I can go to the grocery store. I think it's going to take at least a week. This place is huge."

"Yeah."

"Are these originals?" Avery asked, looking at the art on the walls.

"I have no idea."

"If they are, there will be paperwork somewhere. We should find an art dealer. Unless you want any of them."

Trina looked at the wall as if seeing the art for the first time. "No, I don't . . ."

Avery spun around. "I forgot how big this place was."

"Me too."

"Show me around again."

Trina headed to the stairs to do just that.

Chapter Ten

They'd finished a bottle of wine, which seemed to be the theme of their friendship, and boiled some gourmet pasta, which they ate with a tossed green salad.

But when Avery couldn't keep her eyes open any longer, Trina was faced with sleeping in her old room. Not that there were memories of Fedor there. But beyond the adjoining door was his personal space, which she hadn't yet tackled.

With a laundry basket full of clean clothes, she pulled on a nightgown she hadn't seen in a year and went through the motions of getting ready for bed. Once she kicked her feet up, her eyes traveled to the door between the rooms.

She tapped her fingers, looked away, and then jumped from the bed.

She hesitated for only a second before swinging the door open.

There wasn't a bogeyman, or even a ghost, just an empty room with a perfectly made bed and clean floor. Like her bedroom, Fedor's was left the way he had kept it. The nightstand held a book, but the title wasn't one Trina had heard of. She padded barefoot to his dresser and lifted the cologne she recognized as his unique scent. Three of the wooden figures he himself had carved sat perfectly placed next to a lamp. He often carried a whittling knife and dabbled in the pastime when he wanted to relax. A picture of Fedor and his mother sat next to a picture of the two of them on their wedding day.

Trina lifted it up and remembered when she'd picked out the image to print. Very few of the pictures captured her in a relaxed state. Much as she had to be an actress for everyone watching, it wasn't a job she was good at. But this picture was caught with Fedor whispering in her ear. She still remembered his words. "Just think, everyone in this room is going to have sex tonight except you and me."

She had laughed and whispered back, "I knew your mom had something going with Steve."

Steve had been Alice's nurse. While there was no way Steve was doing anything with Alice, Trina had kept the joke going with Fedor and Alice whenever spirits were low. Even Steve played along from time to time.

The wedding picture in her hand had captured a genuine smile between the both of them. No one would have guessed after seeing the image that their entire wedding and marriage was a farce. They looked the part of a couple in love. Truth was, Trina loved and respected Fedor for everything he had done to make his mother happy in her last days. She meant everything to him, to the point of marrying Trina. Something Alice didn't think she'd see her son do before she died. It hadn't been a complete surprise that Fedor couldn't cope with her imminent death after a stroke left her oblivious of everything around her.

Still, Trina cussed her dead husband for his choice.

She'd lost a friend and gained a life she hadn't wanted with his suicide. Maybe he thought he was doing them all a favor. She'd never know. Fedor hadn't left a note or ever indicated his desire to die.

"You know something, Fedor?" she said to the empty room. "You never struck me as a coward. Mama's boy . . . but for the right reasons. But not a coward."

The room screamed its silence.

"Nothing to say?" she asked again. "I thought so."

Trina padded back into her room and closed the door behind her. With the ghost flushed simply by looking beyond the door, she welcomed the warmth of the bed and the quiet of the house.

Until her phone rang.

She didn't recognize the number, and the name for it was written as Wade, You Owe Me A Dance, Thomas.

"Hello?"

"Hey, little lady."

Trina's heart kicked and her lips spread into a huge grin. "Wade?"

"Is someone else calling you *little lady*?"

"What are you doing?" She chuckled.

"I'm checking up on you. Thought maybe something had happened, since you haven't called yet."

She tucked her bare feet beneath the covers and pulled her knees into her chest. "I didn't realize we had a phone date set up."

"It was implied."

"Well, bad on me, then."

He laughed. "Did you survive the inquisition of your friends?"

"Barely. Did you survive the flight home?"

"With lots of whiskey."

"Oh, you're traumatized."

"I survived by thinking of how calm you were on our flight out of hell and felt the need to man up."

"Glad I helped."

He paused. "Are you home yet?"

She looked around the room she once called home. "No. I'm in New York, actually."

"Oh?"

"I've put off dealing with the house here long enough."

"Sounds painful. How are you doing with that?"

She glanced at the closed door. "I'm okay. It's not the easiest thing I've ever done, but it isn't the hardest either."

"Do you need any help?"

Trina processed his question. "Uhm, ah . . . ," she stuttered. "Avery is here with me."

"The blonde pit bull?"

Now Trina was laughing. "I'll be sure and tell her you said that."

"Come on, darlin', I thought we were friends."

"She won't bite."

"I doubt that."

Yeah, Trina did, too. "She's protective and apparently my disappearing act brought out her mom gene."

"Does she have kids?"

"No . . . but my guess is when she does, her kids won't think about crossing her."

"That's a good thing."

She moved the phone to the other ear. "I have a confession to make."

"I'm all ears."

"I might have listened to your latest album today."

Wade paused, and when he started talking, she could tell his ego had been stroked. "Might have, or did?"

"Did. I even recognized a few of the songs."

Silence.

Trina bit her lip.

"And?"

She hummed a bit. "It was all right."

"All right?" he asked, deadpan.

Trina tried not to laugh. "Yeah, one of the songs was even pretty good."

"One?"

She giggled in silence.

"Well, uh . . . I'll see what I can do about impressing you with my next album."

She snorted and gave in to her laughter. "You are so easy."

"You're pulling my chain," he said.

"*So* easy."

"You're the most unusual woman I've ever met."

"I'm not sure if that is a good thing or a bad thing."

"Me either," he confessed.

"I like your music, Wade."

There was relief in his voice. "Well, thank you, little lady."

"Don't expect me to ask for your autograph the next time I see you."

It was Wade's turn to hum. "So I *am* going to see you again."

"*If,*" she retracted. "*If* I see you again."

"Oh, no, no, no. You said *next time*. I'm holding you to it."

Her heart warmed. "You're an insufferable flirt."

"And you're flirting back."

"I'm teasing. Not flirting."

Wade made a ticking noise on the phone. "Fine line drawn between those two things. If you're flirting, your cheeks would be rosy and warm."

Trina placed the back of her hand to her cheek.

Oh, shit.

"They're warm, aren't they, Miss Trina?"

"No," she lied.

"Why do I doubt your ability to tell me the truth right now?"

"Because you're not a naturally trusting person?"

"I trust that I have wiggled under your skin enough to make your cheeks warm when you're talking to me."

She ignored her hot face.

He started to laugh.

"You're really full of yourself, Wade Thomas."

"Maybe," he said. "But I have a confession to make myself."

"Oh?" This she wanted to hear.

"Yeah, my cheeks are warm right now, too."

~

"Are we done in here?" Avery stood in the center of Fedor's bedroom, hands on her hips, and looked down on all the boxes they'd managed to pack.

Trina had decided the best way to flush out his ghost completely was to tackle his personal space and get it out of the way.

"I think so." She looked at the stack of suits all tucked into garment bags. "Let's see if there is something other than the Salvation Army or Goodwill to donate these to. I can't help but think a college student in need of a good suit would be more appropriate."

"Good point. I'll get online and see what's out there."

She looked at Fedor's tray of watches, all designer, all expensive. "Suicide prevention," she said aloud.

"What?"

"I need to donate the money earned from the sale of all this to organizations that help prevent suicide."

"That sounds very philanthropic of you."

Trina thought of the conversation she'd had with Wade about her future. Although the sale of the Hamptons home and all its contents was only one task, it certainly gave her something to occupy her time.

"It isn't like I need the money."

Avery snorted. "I might."

Trina shot a look at her friend. "What?"

Avery shrugged. "I burned through a million dollars this year."

Avery was one year out from her divorce and the five-million-dollar agreement between her and her ex. The money should have set her up for life.

"A million dollars?"

"Well, nine hundred and forty-five thousand."

"How?"

Avery sat on the edge of the bed, hands on her knees. "There is the Aston."

The fancy car would account for a quarter of the million gone.

"Okay . . ."

"I shopped a lot. Shoes, handbags . . . jewelry."

"Three quarters of a million dollars' worth?" Trina couldn't imagine. And she had more money than God.

"I shopped in Paris, and London . . . and Rodeo Drive. There might have been a couple of chartered flights." Avery looked embarrassed.

"A couple?"

"Okay, five."

"At what, thirty thousand each?"

Avery glanced at the ceiling. "No, more like twenty K . . . each way."

"Two hundred grand on plane tickets." Trina did the math.

"Right, not including first-class tickets everywhere else I went. When I wasn't on Sam's jet."

Trina sat beside Avery on the bed. "Your money isn't going to last if you keep burning it like that."

"I know. I should probably invest some of it."

"You should probably invest all of it and put yourself on a budget."

Avery winced.

"Or get a job." Trina smiled.

"I like my lifestyle."

"Didn't you say you married Bernie to get your parents off your back and out of your life?"

"Yeah."

"What do you think is going to happen if you run out of money?"

Avery leaned her head on Trina's shoulder. "You're right. I know. I've been living in la-la land for a long time."

"Unless you want to shackle yourself to another sugar daddy, this time for real, I suggest you figure it out."

"I'm not good at anything other than shopping and spending."

"Don't forget partying and making everyone around you smile," Trina added.

Avery lifted her head from Trina's shoulder. "My marketable skills are zip. I hated school, never really held a job. I'm about as privileged as they come," she confessed.

Trina scanned the room full of Fedor's things. Expensive things. The desire to call a one-stop auction house or estate sale agent was huge. But they would want a big cut, and the money sent to charity would be less. An idea started to form in Trina's head.

She stood and crossed to the set of watches collecting dust. She picked up one she couldn't name and handed it to Avery. "What do you think this is worth?"

Avery took it, rolled it around in her hands. "It's an Omega . . . so somewhere between two and three thousand."

Seemed like a lot of money for a watch.

Avery put the watch back and pulled out a different one. "But this, this is a Piaget. You can't get out of that store for less than twenty grand." She peered closer. "This has constellations, I'm guessing it's one of their higher end models."

"How high?"

Avery shook her head. "I have no idea, as much as a hundred grand."

Trina squeezed her eyes shut. "For a watch?"

"Could be. I'll have to look it up."

"It was just sitting in his closet. I'm afraid to look in the safe."

"Is there a safe?"

"Yeah, a couple of them, the biggest one is in his office."

"Do you know the combinations?"

Trina shook her head no.

Avery looked around the room again. "This place is holding a fortune, not to mention the house itself. You sure you want to give it all away to charity?"

"Feels like blood money."

Avery lost her smile and Trina looked away.

"You didn't kill him."

Her eyes landed on their wedding picture. "I didn't save him either."

"That wasn't your job."

"I was his wife."

"Trina."

She placed both hands in the air as if to stop Avery's words. "I know it was in name only. I've still been dealing with that guilt for a year."

"I don't understand why you're feeling guilty. You didn't ask for this."

Trina squeezed her eyes shut and felt moisture gather. "Fedor started having feelings for me."

Avery paused. "Oh, no."

Trina's eyes started to mist. "At first I thought it was just our friendship. We seemed to be able to talk about anything. He was losing his mom, so we talked a lot about that. But he started lingering and looking at me differently."

Avery set the watch down and placed a hand on Trina's shoulder. "Did he say anything?"

"He started to one night, at dinner. I felt it coming and made a comment about how nice it was to have a male friend who wasn't trying to make more out of our friendship. He got the hint. Not that it seemed to stop his feelings. If I had let him talk, or maybe tried to feel something more for him . . ."

"Stop it. This isn't your fault."

"I know that, intellectually. Still doesn't stop me from feeling guilty."

"Why didn't you tell me earlier? We could have been working through this."

Trina started to cry for the man she never loved. "I pushed it out of my head. Coming back here reminded me of all the conversations and little things."

"We can close this down and come back another time."

Trina shook her head. "No. I need this behind me." She turned a full circle. "Who knows, maybe there will be something in this house to clue me in to why Fedor did this."

"Losing his mom and falling in love with someone who isn't feeling the same is a strong reason," Avery pointed out.

"I know, but Fedor wasn't that weak. Or at least I didn't think he was. He was a man who found solutions. Even with his overbearing father."

"There is a solution to Ruslan?"

"Yeah, ignore him."

"That didn't work for us last year."

No, it hadn't. Ruslan had researched Alliance, the company that arranged her and Fedor's marriage, and went after Lori. Not in a legal way, but by kidnapping her brother and attempting to hold him hostage for proof that their marriage wasn't completely real. By the time that unfolded, Ruslan's people were either dead or gone forever, and no ties to Ruslan had been kept intact. Which prevented any legal action against the man. Yet they all knew who was behind it. Since that day, Ruslan had dropped out of the picture. After six months, Trina shook loose the bodyguards and extra protection.

Fedor's estate had ended up in the company lap, which Trina said she would manage, and Alice's estate had ended up in Trina's bank. None of which Trina had wanted. Ruslan, on the other hand, wanted it all. There simply wasn't any way he was going to get it. Fedor hated his father, and from what Trina had figured out, the man had abused his wife before they divorced. So Alice and the entire Everson family hated him, too.

Avery picked up the expensive watch again. "I'm going to look this up and call a locksmith. I'd feel a lot better if all the six-figure stuff was somewhere safe. Just talking about Ruslan makes me feel like he's outside, listening and ready to try his hand at burglary."

"He would never dirty his own hands."

"Still." Avery tossed the watch in the air, caught it. "Hiding stuff in plain sight only works for so long. Once we get appraisers and movers in here, nothing will be hidden."

"Let's figure out what we're looking at before we hire anyone. Then maybe we should consider a guard."

"Sounds good." Avery started to leave the room.

"Oh, one more thing."

Avery turned.

"Five percent, or whatever the going rate is."

"Five percent of what going rate?"

"You need a job, and I need someone to manage all of this and sell it for as much money as we can get. It will be like reverse shopping. Considering you're the knower of all things high end, I think you're perfect."

Avery used the watch as a pointing stick. "You want me to work for you?"

"Why hire a stranger when you're right here and already doing the job?"

"I don't know anything about estate sales."

"Me either. But I need to learn. When we're done here, there is Alice's house in Germany I haven't even been to."

"You're not going to keep it?"

Trina shrugged. "I don't speak German."

Avery grinned.

"It gives us something to do," Trina said.

The air in the room felt lighter. "There is a lot here. More than just a closet to go through."

Trina agreed. They thought they'd only be there for a long weekend, but when you found a watch worth a hundred thousand dollars sitting in a drawer with a dozen of its brothers, the job became bigger.

"Five percent?"

"Or whatever the going rate is."

Avery smiled. "You're on. But if I screw up, or don't know something . . ."

"I would have guessed that watch to be a few hundred bucks. Probably sold it for thirty."

"Got it. The bar is set low for messing up."

"Go, find a locksmith. One that isn't named Guido."

Avery turned and left the room. "On it."

Chapter Eleven

The ranch had a state-of-the-art recording studio that sat separate from the main house. It made life easier when Wade wanted to work. No need to head into Austin, or even Houston, where he'd have to deal with hotels and fans. Right now was time for rest, reflection, and living. Although he wasn't sure what rest looked like.

He turned on the lights and walked past all the expensive recording equipment and into the studio he would eventually sit in completely alone to record.

Half a dozen guitars lined the wall.

A smile crept onto his lips. He remembered his first six string and sitting in the senior quad at his high school, writing his first song. The instrument was an extension of his fingertips. Or so he'd been told the first time he'd shared his music. It was like he was born to it. Considering he'd never taken lessons to play the thing, he couldn't argue.

Wade removed one of the guitars from its stand and walked over to a stool to perch his butt. He strummed a few chords and tightened a string to bring the instrument into tune.

He started the opening riff of a melody that had been drifting in and out of his head for over a month. Even though he'd been on tour and busy with sold-out arenas for the better part of eight months, he still found himself writing new music. He didn't think touring and creating were exclusive to themselves, so he always had new stuff in the works.

He hummed a note, changed the rhythm, and then repeated it again. "I'm gonna make you smile . . ." He changed a chord, sang the verse again. He did it half a dozen times more before he grabbed a piece of staff paper and wrote the music down.

Time slipped away, and in what felt like minutes, the door to the studio opened, and Ike sauntered in.

"Do you ever stop?"

Wade glanced up. "I'll stop when I'm dead."

"Not if Vicki has anything to say about it."

"What is my mother up to now?"

Ike leaned against the wall. "I'm not supposed to tell you."

Wade dropped his smile. "I pay you."

"Right. So . . . there may or may not be a Texas-size barbeque planned for this Saturday to welcome you home from your tour. A band—that doesn't include you in the headline—lights, dance floor, a side of beef, several chickens, and at least one pig is on the menu. Anyone you've ever met in your life that hasn't asked you for money was invited." He paused. "And some that have asked."

Wade put his guitar aside and narrowed his eyes.

"By anyone I've ever met, would that include a certain ex–female friend that Vicki still has lunch with whenever she's in town?"

Ike looked away without comment.

"C'mon, Ike . . . you're supposed to have my back."

"I told her it was a bad idea."

He and Jordyn had broken it off before he started his tour. Not that it had been that long, or deep, of a relationship. This was why he didn't date close to home. Too damn complicated when it ended.

"I need to shut this down," Wade said as he stood.

"That might be a little hard."

"Why?"

"Jordyn's band is the entertainment, and the invitations have already gone out. Caterers are set and paid for."

Irritation scratched his skull. "Why didn't you tell me about this?"

"I didn't hear of it until I came home."

"Then you should have called me."

"It wouldn't have changed anything."

That's where Ike was wrong. "I would have flown to Barcelona and drank sangria for a couple of weeks. Found a dark haired, Spanish speaking, salsa dancing cutie to spend my time with."

"Well, unless you can bring said cutie to the barbeque, I'd plan on a romantic intervention between your mother and your girlfriend."

"Ex-girlfriend."

Ike shook his head. "She doesn't seem to know just how ex that is. You might have to remind her."

Reminding women it was over had been the theme of his dating life since he signed with his first record label. Before fame, if he wasn't feeling it, he simply said so. Now, there was begging and pleading, which were sometimes followed up by screaming and yelling. Jordyn had begged and pleaded. She also kept in close contact with his mother. He couldn't take any blame for introducing them. No, Jordyn and her band were on a local circuit that played at Jo's tavern and dance hall. A place he often went to blow off steam and have a good time. It was local enough to have neighbors that saw him often enough not to act starstruck when he walked in the room. Most of the time he felt like just another cowboy, tilting back a beer with his friends. He'd had hopes that he could return and find Jordyn hooked up with someone else.

Guess that wasn't going to happen.

"Saturday, you said?" An idea started to form.

"Yup."

Three days.

ᒪᓂ

"You're chasing me," Trina said as she answered the phone. The thing rang at nearly the same time it had the night before. Wade's name popped up and made her smile. She'd thought about calling him twice during the day, and then life distracted her to another closet, and in this case, another safe for the locksmith to crack open.

"Guilty." His voice was pure southern charm.

"Why?"

He paused. "That's a complicated answer."

"Try." She sat looking out the second story window at the rain falling in steady sheets.

"Do you want the short answer or the long one?"

She wasn't looking for a compliment, and a long answer would seem as if she were. "The short one."

"Okay, then. You're *not* chasing me."

Not the answer she had expected.

"Oh."

"I have more reasons."

"No, no . . . I asked for the short version. I bet a lot of women chase you." As in hundreds.

"They do." That might have sounded cocky, but Wade said it with an exhausted sigh.

"That must make it hard on your girlfriends."

He chuckled. "Funny you should say that."

"Why is that amusing?"

"What are you doing this weekend?"

Trina stopped watching the rain and moved to the edge of her bed. "I'm still in New York, working my way through this massive house room by room, why?"

"Can I tear you away?"

"Are you asking me out?"

"Are you ready for that?" He sounded hopeful.

Maybe when she wasn't standing a room away from Fedor's bedroom. "I'm not sure."

"Then I'm not asking you out . . . I'm asking for a favor."

"What kind of favor?"

"I need a decoy date."

"A decoy what?"

"Don't say no. Just hear me out."

"I haven't said no and you haven't explained anything."

Wade blew out a breath. "Hear me out, don't interrupt until I'm—"

"I haven't interrupted you."

"You just did."

Trina grinned.

Silence.

"Are you still there?"

"I'm not interrupting."

Wade chuckled. "My mother has decided a welcome home party is in order since I've been on tour for so many months. Lots of food, people, a band . . . dancing. You still owe me a two-step."

She opened her mouth with only a peep.

"Eh, I'm not done," he cut her off.

Trina bit her lip.

"Lots of people. Good people. You'd like them. Mainly old friends and neighbors. A few of my staff and people I've worked with. Anyway . . . there is one guest I'm not very happy about Mom inviting."

Trina waited for him to finish. Her mouth closed.

"Jordyn and I dated last year for a brief time. We called it off before I left. I'm not completely sure how she convinced my mother that she should be at the shindig, but convince her she did, and now I'm in need of a decoy date to help me out."

This sounded all too familiar. Decoy wife, decoy date. What could possibly go wrong? Trina glanced at the adjoining door to Fedor's room.

"Are you there?" Wade asked.

"I'm not interrupting."

"I'm done. You can interrupt now."

Trina closed her eyes, shook her head. "No."

"You can interrupt, I don't mind."

"No, Wade. I don't want to be your pretend date. I'm sorry. I know I owe you a favor after running off to the Bahamas to give me a few days' reprieve from my friends, but lying to your friends and family about us . . . I can't do that again."

"Again?" he asked.

Trina caught herself. "At all. I can't do it."

Silence.

She choked another apology inside her mouth.

"Then come as my real date."

"Wade."

"I'll teach you the two-step. You'll meet people outside your circle that won't hit on you since you're my date. I have a very big house with plenty of rooms. No expectations. If you want to stay in town, I'll arrange it. Please say yes, Trina. I really want to see you again."

That last line caught in her chest.

She couldn't imagine a Wade Thomas party.

"When is this Texas-size blowout?"

"Is that a yes?"

"Do you always answer a question with a question?"

"Saturday. The party is on Saturday." He sounded hopeful.

Trina scanned her bedroom again. There was a whole lot of work to do, but maybe one day off wouldn't hurt.

She really hoped she wasn't going to regret this. "Fine."

"Is that a yes?"

"Yes, Wade. I will be your date. No expectations. Like I said, I'm not sure I'm ready."

Did he just whistle? Trina was certain she heard a high-pitched squeak over the line.

"I have never worked this hard for a first date in my whole life," he said.

"I think you've already said this. Besides, it doesn't feel like a first date."

"It sure doesn't. But it will, little lady . . . it will."

⁓

"Save his office for Monday," Trina told Avery. She stood in the foyer of the Hamptons estate with a small suitcase at her feet. Boxes filled the halls as a testament to the dent they had made in the short week they'd been at the house. Two safes, both found behind paintings, had been cracked, revealing a significant amount of dollars, euros, and rubles, along with a stack of gold coins. Why Fedor felt the need to have so much money on hand would remain a mystery. The locksmith had blown out a whistle when the first safe was opened, prompting Trina to ask the man to leave the room once the second safe was cracked so she could see the contents without an audience. The large safe in Fedor's back office was the only one left to crack, and Trina wanted to wait until there was a bodyguard standing by. Lori's boyfriend, Reed, was arranging just that for the early part of next week.

"Wade Thomas . . . really?"

Trina set her sunglasses on the bridge of her nose and smiled with sarcasm. "I'm a big girl, Mom, I'll be fine."

Avery narrowed her eyes. "You're vulnerable. Especially this week."

"Am I some kind of wilted flower, dying in the corner?"

"There have been tears."

"Not many. Besides, I need to stop by the office while I'm in Texas, and the cemetery. Wade's party will be a nice distraction from all of that."

"Can one 'stop by' Wade's home from yours?"

"It's actually not that bad. He's south of Austin, so about a two-hour drive."

"Just be careful."

Trina placed her purse over her shoulder. "I should say the same to you. I'd feel better if we had a guard around here now."

Avery blew her off. "Because so many people show up at the door trying to rob the place?"

"No, because Kevin, the key man, started salivating when he saw the gold in the safe."

"Which is already at the bank."

"Still . . ."

"You're being paranoid. This house has been vacant for almost a year with all this stuff sitting here."

Trina sighed. "Okay, fine. But watch your back when you leave."

"I won't have a neon sign over my car telling the world I'm carrying thousands of dollars' worth of watches when I take them to the auction house."

Avery had embraced her new job and had appointments all over Manhattan throughout the weekend. Normal business hours didn't apply when the two of them waved around the kind of money Fedor's estate would likely fetch. And that was just with the stuff filling the walls and closets. Shopping real estate agents was high on Avery's list, and what better time to check them out than during the many open houses that took place over the weekend?

"Go, enjoy your party while I slave away at the office."

Trina laughed and hugged her friend. "I'll call when I'm back in town so you know I'm walking in the door."

"You'll call when you finish with the party and give me all the details. Don't be afraid to name-drop if you see anyone famous."

"Fine." Trina pulled the arm of her suitcase and rolled it in front of her. "Oh, by the way, I left a message for Cindy, my housekeeper, to let her know we're in town. If she calls back, have her and a crew come in on Tuesday to start working behind us, cleaning the rooms we've already tackled."

"On it!"

"Thanks again."

"Go. I have stuff to do," Avery teased.

Avery stood on the steps and waved as she pulled out of the drive.

Trina opted to drive herself to the airport, again to keep the amount of people coming and going from the property to a minimum.

A weekend date at Wade's home, with an ex-girlfriend and his mother . . . what could possibly go wrong? There would probably be a dozen other women vying for his attention. Trina looked through her rearview mirror as the Hamptons home disappeared. She was fairly certain no one was going to die, so how bad could it be?

Chapter Twelve

Wade opted for sunglasses and a baseball cap in an effort to keep his identity on the down low. He stood in the back of the crowd, waiting outside of baggage claim, where he'd told Trina he would meet her. When was the last time he'd stood in an airport to pick someone up? He couldn't remember.

He scanned the crowd, watching for the telltale sign of a cell phone turned his way. There were the kind of fans that noticed him in a crowd and would snap a sly picture, and then there were the people who walked right up, asked if he was Wade Thomas, and then requested a picture or an autograph. Seemed the pictures were the bigger request than his name on a piece of paper. Although he had signed plenty of boobs in his career.

His phone buzzed in his pocket, and he reached to answer without looking at the name.

"Hello."

"Wade?"

He didn't recognize the voice.

"Depends on who is askin'."

"It's the blonde pit bull."

He winced. *Avery.* "Trina did not tell you I said that."

"She most certainly did."

"Well, Miss Avery, I meant that out of my deepest respect," he backpedaled. "Strong women run the earth."

"Keep kissing up," she said.

He laughed as he scanned the crowed exiting baggage claim. "What can I do for you?"

"I wanted to make sure you didn't send some flunky to pick Trina up at the airport."

"No, ma'am, I did not. I'm standing right here, waiting for her now."

"Huh."

"Anything else?" he asked, knowing full well Avery wasn't done.

"Yeah. Don't mess with her head."

He opened his mouth to respond, only to be cut off.

"Don't lie to her. Don't tell her she's the only one if she isn't. Don't be an asshole."

Wade didn't think *The Blonde Pit Bull* was a worthy enough title for the woman giving him sass on the phone.

"You're a good friend, Avery. Trina's lucky to have you on her side." He really did mean that. Much as he was the one on the wrong end of the woman's gun.

"Uh-huh . . . right."

"I'm going to go out on a limb and say you really don't like me, do you?"

"I know your kind, and I've warned her. But apparently there isn't anything else I can do."

From the crowd he saw a woman of Trina's height with sleek black hair . . . his heart did a little two-step of its own.

"I'll take good care of her. You can count on that."

Yup, that was her. Those dark eyes caught his, even through his sunglasses, and her lips spread into a smile. The feeling in his belly made his entire body warm.

This was good.

This was *very* good.

Avery was saying something that he didn't catch.

"Ah-huh . . . sure. Thanks for your advice." He hung up.

Trina pushed one small, round designer suitcase in front of her as she approached.

He wanted to kiss her. Wanted to throw his arms around her, spin her in a circle, and make her laugh with the silliness of it all.

He hesitated.

"Screw it." Four giant steps and he gave in to the desire. He lifted her surprised frame off the ground, pulled her body flush with his, and dropped his lips to her ear. "I can't believe you're here."

"Wade!"

He kissed the side of her head, opting for something less personal, considering he had yet to savor her lips.

Yet, God willing, *be the right word.*

Damn, she smelled good. Something exotic with a hint of floral. He pulled in a deep breath of her scent and savored it to memory.

"Put me down," she laughed.

His sunglasses had twisted on his face and fell to the ground when he let her go. Her spice colored eyes peered into his. "You came."

"I told you I would."

He couldn't stop smiling.

"Okay . . . ohhh kaaay! This is good."

Her chest shook with her laugh. "You're blushing."

"I'm a happy man," he admitted freely.

She looked to the side and back again. "Do you think we should get out of the way?"

Wade followed her lead, found his glasses on the ground, and reached for her bag.

"I can—"

"But I'm going to," he interrupted and placed the suitcase out of her reach. With his free hand, he reached for hers. Their first date was starting now, and he didn't want anyone who might be watching to think for even a second that Trina wasn't with him.

They made it within a yard of the sliding doors of the airport before three giggly girls cut them off.

"You're Wade Thomas!"

"Oh my God, I love your music . . . we, we love your music."

"Cassie and I were at your last concert in Dallas, so amazing!"

Three teenage girls, all talking at once, was enough to make anyone's head spin.

Wade squeezed Trina's hand.

Around them, people started to stare.

"I knew you lived here, but never thought I'd ever see you on the street."

"Girls . . ." He looked around, lowered his voice. "We're kinda in a hurry. How about we do a quick picture and you help block this door so we can mosey on out of here?"

The girl he assumed was Cassie pulled out her phone faster than a sheriff could draw a gun. Within two seconds he was sandwiched between three giggly girls in the center of a selfie. Before they could check the picture, Wade reached for Trina's hand and pulled her out the doors.

He didn't look back, he just kept walking. "Sorry 'bout that," he said as he zigzagged through the crowd and toward the parking lot.

"You look like you've done that before."

He managed to sneak a peek at Trina over the rim of his glasses as he crossed the parking lot in a slow run.

Lucky for him, Trina kept up.

"A few times." He scanned the lot, pulled Trina to the left.

"Do you know where you're going?"

"Yup." Damn . . . where was his truck? He didn't dare look over his shoulder to see if they were being followed. His ten-gallon truck was in a lot filled with ten-gallon trucks. Maybe if he got a little—*there it is!* He moved faster.

Trina's suitcase was in his hands and tossed into the back of the truck at nearly the same time he was opening the door for her to get in.

"What's this?"

Wade brushed the flowers he'd bought her aside and hoisted her inside the cab.

"For you." He managed a smile before closing the door and running to the driver's side and jumping in.

The rearview mirror didn't show a mob, so he took that as a good sign to draw in a breath.

Trina had picked up the simple summer bouquet and leaned down to sniff. That was when he saw movement out of her side mirror.

"Buckle up, little lady."

Trina shifted her eyes to the side. "Seriously?"

"I'm afraid so. Teenagers are harder to shake than anyone our age."

He turned over the engine and pulled out of the space before anyone could block his way.

One of the girls from the selfie was running toward a car.

He heard the click of Trina's belt and used that as his cue to push down on the gas.

For a big truck, it sure maneuvered through the lot with ease.

There was a line leading out of the parking lot where he needed to pay the toll, and that was where anyone following would catch up.

Sure enough, a four-door, light blue sedan found him in line and cut off a car to inch closer.

He rolled down his window as he approached the booth.

A middle-aged woman stepped out of the little door to collect his ticket.

"How are you doing today?" he asked with as much southern charm as he possibly could. He removed his sunglasses, hoping the lady recognized him.

"I'm doing fine. Glad the heat isn't killing us."

Nothing.

Wade took off the baseball cap, ran a hand through his hair.

She disappeared inside the booth and rang him up. "That will be five dollars."

Wade pulled out a fifty. "Ma'am, would you do me a tiny favor?" He handed her the money.

"Excuse me?"

He glanced over his shoulder at the carload of kids waving cell phones out of their window. "You see that carload of trouble back there?"

She looked and shook her head. "Kids today."

"Well, you see, they have in their mind to follow us, and I'd just as soon get a head start."

She peered closer. "Why would they wanna do that?"

From the passenger seat, Trina spoke up. "He's Wade Thomas. I'm not sure if you listen to country music—"

The light bulb went on. "Oh, dear, yes . . . you do look like Wade Thomas."

"*Is* Wade Thomas," Trina announced.

"Yes, ma'am. Those girls are having a hard time understanding personal boundaries. So can you maybe take a little longer to process their ticket? Maybe give me a few extra minutes to get on the highway?"

She stood a little taller and ran a hand over her stomach. "I'd be happy to help you out, Mr. Thomas. Let me get your . . . your . . ." She waved the fifty in the air, looked at it. "Change."

"No, no, that's for your trouble. Thank you, Miss . . . ?"

"Lou Lou . . . everyone here calls me Lou Lou."

"Thank you, Miss Lou Lou."

"Goodness, Wade Thomas." She stared, her cheeks flushed.

The person in the car between him and the teenagers honked.

Wade pointed at the gate.

"Oh, of course," Lou Lou said, ducking back inside to let them out.

Wade waved out the window once he saw the barrier arm go back down and the next car pull up.

"That was crazy."

"Welcome to my life."

"Whoa." Trina was staring out the back window.

"Is she holding them back?"

"Oh, yeah." Trina started to laugh. "No wonder you were shocked I didn't know who you were."

"It's not often I go unnoticed." He pulled out on the frontage road before speeding onto the freeway. Only then did he look in the mirror to see if they were being followed. He blew out a breath.

He glanced over to find Trina staring, the flowers he brought her sitting in her lap. "You really are famous."

He smiled. "Are you just figuring that out?"

"Apparently. Is it hard? Or do you love the attention?"

"I'd be lying if I said I hated every minute of it. The first time someone recognized me in public had me high for a month."

"So what keeps you grounded?"

He thought about that. "Not a lot. My mama makes sure to tell me to take out the trash and reminds me to muck the stalls when I'm home. Sounds crazy, but doing things I have to hire people to do for me when I'm not around brings me back to earth."

Trina was silent for a moment. "Your mom sounds like she's a big part of your life."

"She is. I respect the hell out of the woman. Raised me all on her own with only a high school education. Sacrificed her needs over mine, time and time again. A lot of parents don't do that."

"Does your mom live with you?"

"I built a guest house at the ranch. She insisted, even though I thought it wasn't necessary. She didn't want my girlfriends thinking I'm a mama's boy, even though I'm comfortable enough to tell the world I am."

Trina was silent.

That's when he remembered her conversation about her late husband . . . and his devotion to his mother being so deep the man couldn't deal with her death. "I'm not him," Wade said. The smile from his face fell slightly. "I love my mother, and the day she passes will be excruciating, I'm sure. But I will live without her when it comes."

Trina studied her lap. "I'm sorry."

"No, I am. I should have realized that might be a hard thing for you to hear."

"I'm okay."

He reached over and placed his hand over hers. "Let me tell you about my home."

Chapter Thirteen

Trina had inherited Alice's ranch. The sprawling home was a little over six thousand square feet, complete with a stable for the four horses, a corral, and a barn large enough for the tools and equipment someone needed to maintain the land. She'd been in Texas long enough to see a couple of impressive spreads that people called home.

Then she pulled through the gates of Wade's home.

The frontage of the ranch closest to the road was home to a six-foot, tree-lined cinder block wall, perfectly manicured and maintained, before it opened into a set of double iron gates. Wade pressed a remote and let them in.

On one side of the drive was a split rail fence with grass and trees that seemed to go forever. Horses almost looked like yard art sprinkled onto the landscape. "How many horses do you have?"

"Ten," he said. "No, wait . . . twelve."

"You don't know?"

"It was ten before the tour, but I seem to remember taking on two of the neighbors', who were having a hard time keeping them fed."

Trina scanned the fence line. "You have neighbors?"

Wade laughed and drove right by the modest house.

"Isn't that . . . ?"

"No, that's my caretaker's."

They drove around a corner. "That's my mother's home."

This one was a little less modest, more like a three-thousand-square-foot custom home that could be found on many tracts in Texas, only this one had a wraparound porch and a separate garage.

Trina swiveled around just in time to take in what had to be the grand finale.

"Wow."

It was sprawling, it was ranch, it was two stories . . . and it was huge!

"Being cooped up in hotels all the time makes me want to spread out when I'm home."

"This is monstrous, Wade."

Instead of pulling into a garage, he parked close to the steps leading to the front door and jumped out of the truck.

She was already halfway out the door when he reached for her hand. "Let me show you around the outside before we go in."

A deep breath of country air felt energizing. "Did you have it built?"

"Rebuilt. The bones of the original house were here, along with the small barn and grazing land. The land is what sold me, that and the lake and creek that feeds it."

"You have a lake?" Most of the places she'd been to had ponds or a man-made lake, not the real thing.

They walked around the east end of the home to take in the back of the property. Trina gasped. The home actually sat on a small knoll, and the land behind the house went on for miles. There were stables that looked like something belonging to prize Thoroughbreds that won big purses at the races. The corral could play home to a rodeo, except that the viewing area was a covered brick and wood structure instead of metal stands. Before the land sloped into acres, Wade had a swimming pool with waterfalls and hot tubs, as in two. Why one needed two hot tubs in a pool was beyond her. A massive covered freestanding patio for entertaining hosted an outdoor kitchen. And people. The place was brimming with workers setting up for the party the following day.

"You might not believe it, but this is a working cattle ranch."

"Seriously?"

"Just under a hundred head of cattle beyond the lake." He pointed in the distance.

Trina couldn't see the lake.

"I'll show you later."

"Why cattle?" she asked.

He put his arm over her shoulders and winked. "Because this is Texas."

"Ohhhkay," she laughed.

"Well, hello, and who do we have here?"

A man close to Wade's height and weight and swagger made his way to their side.

"Ike, this is Trina, the woman I told you about."

"You mean the woman you said you were picking up from the airport but otherwise I know nothing about?"

Wade looked pleased with himself. "Yup, this would be her."

Ike put out his hand and Trina took it. "If it makes you feel any better, he hasn't told me a thing about you either."

Ike laughed. "I do feel better."

Another man approached from the other side.

Big guy, half a head taller than Wade, and eyes that looked through you even when he had a half smile on his face. "You must be a bodyguard."

That half a smile fell.

Ike slapped the man's arm. "She has your number already, Jeb."

"What do you know about bodyguards?" Wade asked.

"I've had my share," she said, glossing over his question. "I'm Trina." She stuck out her hand for Mr. Muscle to shake.

"Jeb. Wade's personal bodyguard."

With a strong handshake. "I knew it."

"Incoming," Ike said under his breath.

Wade turned, his gaze falling on a blonde bombshell in blue jeans. The ex-girlfriend? She looked a little older than Wade, but who knew. Trina braced herself for confrontation and felt some relief when Wade placed his arm over her shoulders again.

Jeb and Ike stood aside, and Wade led her forward.

"Don't be nervous," he whispered in her ear.

"Too late," she whispered back.

The blonde eyed her with a cautious grin.

"Mama, I'd like you to meet a friend of mine."

Mama? This is Wade's mother?

Trina was certain she showed the shock on her face.

"Trina, this is Vicki, my mother."

"This is certainly a surprise," Vicki said. Her eyes kept shifting between Trina's and Wade's.

"It's a pleasure." Trina extended her hand.

Vicki moved forward a little too quickly. "Trina, did you say?"

"Yup. Trina and I met in Florida at the end of the tour."

"You're the reason Wade took his time coming home." There was a bit of ice lacing Vicki's words.

"I am."

"Let me guess, you met Wade after one of his concerts?"

"No, actually. I've never heard your son sing. Except for on the radio, but that would be hard to miss."

Vicki offered an unbelieving laugh.

Trina glanced at Wade, whose face sat stoic.

Vicki slowly stopped laughing. "You're not kidding."

"No, Mama, she's not."

Awkward silence filled the space around them.

Trina attempted to fill it. "This looks like quite the party you have planned."

"Yes, it is. I should get back to it. Will you be staying with us?" Vicki asked.

Trina almost said no.

Wade cut her off. "Yes."

Vicki lifted her chin, smiled. "I see. Welcome, then. If you need anything . . ."

"Thank you."

Vicki turned and walked away, leaving them alone.

"That was . . ."

"Uncomfortable," Wade finished.

"Yeah, a little bit."

They both watched the woman walk away in silence.

Trina cocked her head to the side when she saw one of the men unloading straw bales check out Vicki's ass.

"Don't take this the wrong way . . . but did your mom have you when she was twelve?"

Her question cut the tension. Wade pulled her close. "She wasn't quite that young."

"I thought she was your ex at first."

Wade shook his head as if her words stung. "Lord, no."

Trina turned her gaze away from Vicki and up at him. "If the chill from Mom was that cold, what will it be from the ex?"

Wade looked over her shoulder, offered another smile. "I have a bodyguard standing by."

Trina dropped her forehead on his chest. "Oh, great."

☙

Wade showed Trina the room he wanted her in, the one closest to his, and encouraged her to make herself at home. Their weekend date wouldn't be intimate by any stretch, but he did want to find a couple of hours for just the two of them. But first he needed a word with his mother.

He admitted that he didn't often bring women around his mother, but she'd never been cold in the past. Why Trina was different was something he was going to get to the bottom of before the party.

Vicki stood by an outdoor stage, a semipermanent structure Wade had sung on many times since he'd had the home rebuilt to his needs. He half expected to see Jordyn by his mother's side but was told by Ike that she wouldn't be arriving until the next morning for a sound check.

"Hey." He placed a hand on his mother's shoulder to grab her attention. "Can we talk for a minute?"

"Sure." She pointed to the side of the stage and spoke to one of the stagehands that worked on Wade's crew. "Be sure and secure those stairs. I don't need anyone falling down."

"I'm on it, Ms. Vicki."

"Thanks, doll." She turned to Wade and glanced behind him. "Where is your *friend*?"

No mistaking that snark. "Inside, unpacking."

"Who is she?" The smile was gone.

Wade pulled her away from the stage and out of earshot.

"She's a friend, and why are you being so cold?"

"I'm not—"

"Mama!"

Vicki clenched her jaw. "Jordyn's band is playing tomorrow."

"Yes, Ike told me. Why would you ask her to be here when you know we broke up?"

"Now that you're home from the tour, I thought you'd be getting back together. She said you two were on hold, that when you returned—"

"It doesn't matter what Jordyn told you. I wasn't on a break, we were broken."

"She's such a sweet girl, honey. Exactly the kind of girl you need. She understands your business, your life here in Texas."

Wade placed both hands on his mother's arms. "Broken, Mama. I will spare you the details since you don't need to know, but trust me, it was never going to work. Now, I appreciate the fact that you care enough to meddle, but stop. I can manage my own love life."

"With Trina?"

"With whomever I choose. You didn't pick my dates in high school, so please don't try and pick them now."

"What am I going to say to Jordyn?"

Wade narrowed his eyes. "Is that what this is about? You're embarrassed?"

Vicki answered by keeping her mouth closed.

"Tell her what you have to, or don't tell her at all and I will. Again. But please, keep the chill factor to a minimum with Trina."

She rolled her eyes. "Fine. Fine!"

He kissed her cheek and walked away.

Chapter Fourteen

Trina thought Wade was taking her on a predinner walk, but apparently, he had other plans.

They found the lake, which was hidden by a stretch of trees at the far end of the manicured portion of his property. "It's beautiful." And quiet, which was nice, considering the buzz of noise up at the house.

He pointed out the cattle grazing on the hillside behind the lake.

"Because cattle," she said with a laugh.

"When in Texas." He laughed with her.

He walked them up to an old log cabin. "This has been here since before the previous owners."

"Really?"

"Yup. I had it cleaned up and the roof repaired, but kept it original. No running water, no electricity."

He opened the door, and inside, someone had set a table for two.

"What are you up to?" she teased.

"Tomorrow I have to share you, but tonight I thought this would be better."

Relief, knowing she wouldn't have to sit across from Vicki, had her smiling. "First date worthy."

"I do have a few tricks up my sleeve."

He moved inside and reached for the bottle of wine on the table. He'd already pulled the cork. "You liked red, if I remember right."

"And you like beer."

"Yes, but I'm not so redneck that I don't enjoy wine once in a while."

She doubted that.

"I do. I've even been wine tasting."

"Oh, really? Where?"

"Uhm . . ." He blinked. "Napa."

"What wine did you like the best?" she quizzed.

"Expensive." He lifted the bottle of wine. "So if I spend a lot on the bottle, it's got to be good, right?"

"Not really, but that's okay. There might be something I can teach you." Wade making an effort to please her placed several coins in his goodwill jar.

"I like the sound of that." He handed her a glass and poured one for himself.

"To first dates."

"First dates after we've shared private planes and hotels in disaster zones together." She clicked her glass to his.

She sipped and lifted her eyebrows in surprise. "This is actually pretty good."

Wade puffed out his chest.

"See, expensive equals good."

Trina lifted the bottle to see the label and bit her lip. "Wade?"

"Yeah?"

"What do you consider expensive?"

He looked away. "I don't want to tell you what I spent. Ruins the whole feeling I'm trying to create."

She stopped him with a glare.

He shuffled his feet. "Wanna eat?"

"Wade?"

"A couple hundred dollars, I think," he said out of the corner of his mouth.

She placed the bottle down, sipped the wine. "If you paid two hundred dollars for this bottle of wine, I'd be careful of anyone trying to sell you beachfront property in Kansas."

"There isn't beachfro—" His charming smile fell. "Jeb said it was good," he confessed.

She started to interrupt but he kept going.

"But I have been wine tasting, in San Francisco . . . which is technically Napa . . . ish."

Damn, he was charming. Like a kid wiping his mouth clean of chocolate after being caught in the cookie jar.

It felt fabulous to have someone care enough to try so hard.

"Don't hold it against me. I wanted to impress you."

"I'm impressed."

"Really?" He stopped shuffling.

"I am. I don't know why you're trying so hard."

He put the glass of wine down. "Are you kidding me? I've been busting my nuts just to get you here. Now that you are, I don't want to blow it with the wrong wine or my mom doing her best iceberg interpretation."

She set her wine next to his. "You can't control your mother or how she's acting, and if you don't know about wine, it isn't a deal breaker. I'm here, whether I should or shouldn't be."

"You definitely should be."

Again with the charm.

He stared, his gaze moving to her lips.

Would he . . .

Wouldn't he . . .

"We should eat." He looked away.

Her heart dropped. "Or you could kiss me."

Apparently Wade didn't have to be told twice.

Two steps and he pulled her into his arms and didn't give her a chance to say she was kidding. Not that she was.

His lips were on hers like an exclamation point, his hand to the back of her head. It was as if he was shocked to be there, until he wrapped his arm around her waist and softened his hold.

With every ounce of breath, he moved into their kiss and let her know that this was something he was good at. It wasn't wine, it wasn't controlling his mother . . . it was seduction.

He moved slowly, like there wasn't a care in the world other than letting her feel their lips mingle, his tongue ask permission and then take possession. He was smooth, unhurried as he sparked fire under her skin.

This was good, probably too good.

He changed his angle, explored deeper.

And he held her. As if he never wanted to let her go.

She wasn't sure how long they kissed or if the lack of oxygen broke it off or the sound of a distant animal brought them around. But when Wade's lips left hers, he'd left a little of himself behind.

"Wow," she said in a hoarse whisper.

"I'm happy to hear you say that." His eyes peered into hers. "I want to take this slow, and I've never wanted to take anything like this slow before in my life."

"That's probably a good idea."

He took a conscious step back and pulled out her chair. "Let's eat."

∾୭

He couldn't sleep.

The memory of her lips, the taste of her heart . . . and she was one door away.

"No."

He had to say the word out loud to stop him from walking the few steps to her room. Wade Thomas was good at a number of things . . .

125

singing, charmin', seducing . . . and making older women wish they could turn back the clock . . . but he sucked at waiting. Holding back for Trina put him, and his body, in the most uncomfortable position he'd been in for a mighty long time.

What kind of masochist was he that he welcomed the feeling? If it wasn't pitch-black outside, he'd saddle up Black Star and take the stallion for a ride. He probably wouldn't survive it, but it would match the burning he felt all over.

He had it bad.

The woman had found a way under his skin, and he had no intention of scratching that itch to make it go away.

He'd written enough love songs to identify what was going on inside of him. This wasn't lust, although that was part of his needs . . . no, Trina was more. The part of a song that brings meaning to the chorus. She hadn't looked off in the distance once since she'd been there, which gave him hope she wasn't considering her late husband. In fact, it was her that initiated their first kiss.

He smiled into the memory.

Sweet . . . tasty, and a hint of spice.

His thoughts made his body tighten even more.

"Go to sleep, Thomas . . . that ain't gonna happen tonight," he whispered into the night, to himself.

He rolled onto his side and forced his eyes closed.

All he saw was Trina.

～⑨

It wasn't hot.

The breeze flowing into her second floor guest room cooled the space without an artificial air conditioner, but she still couldn't stop the steam oozing from her skin.

It was a line . . . it had to be a line. No one said they wanted to take things slow unless they were about to call the whole thing off. Only Wade hadn't done that. He'd held her hand throughout their dinner and told her about how he had dreamed one day of owning a cattle ranch. He'd read a book when he was a kid about a man following his dreams, one prize steer at a time. He'd told her that owning as much land as he did in Texas almost required him to either have cattle or an oil field. He would leave the oil to her.

And they talked.

Wade Thomas, famous singer that he was, started out poor. More so than she had. Her parents had both worked hard to put her and her older sister through school. High school! Trina had put herself through a few years of community college and eventually worked her way into a job with the airlines. She'd met Samantha on a chance flight, where she'd learned about Alliance, and next thing Trina knew, she was married to Fedor Petrov and standing in a graveyard.

So why was she in Wade Thomas's home, wishing he didn't want to take it slow?

Trina flipped her pillow over, pounded it a few times with her fist, and growled.

&

The East Coast wasn't a place Avery ever wanted to live.

A night of tossing and turning due to the deafening silence left her comatose throughout the next morning.

How Trina thought she could endure this for almost two years of her contracted marital life, Avery didn't know. Who was she to pass judgment? At least Fedor liked cool tones and open space. Bernie had been all about dark wood and hunter green on the walls.

Still, Bernie lived in a place close to other people, where she could walk outside and see them.

All Avery noticed was a stray cat that ducked under the shrubs the second she approached.

Stupid cat.

Avery held her cup of coffee as if it were the answer to life, and crossed through the space between the main house and Fedor's office. Most homes like this had interior offices, but not Fedor Petrov's. He had to have a separate space, as if it would make a difference in his eventual outcome. Like what, sharing your space with your family, your wife, would make your wealth half of what you could accomplish in a separate space? Lotta good that did when you offed yourself.

Avery cautioned herself on her thoughts as she clenched her coffee and crossed the lawn.

Trina was avoiding the room, putting off the last memory she had until the bitter end. To Avery, it was just another room in a massive house that needed a set of eyes to see what held value and what could go at a garage sale for pennies on the dollar.

It was just stuff.

A dead rich man's stuff.

She opened the locked door, expecting a ghost to jump out.

Instead, she smelled paint and new carpet.

The large office had a desk in the center, minus the chair. There were two chairs positioned in front of the desk for visitors, and the walls were lined with bookshelves. Large windows were hidden behind floor to ceiling drapes, which Avery opened. She forced one of the windows up and moved to another one on the other side to capture a breeze and push out the stale air.

"Okay, dead guy, let's see what you have hiding in here."

She didn't start with the desk, which might seem like the obvious place. She started at the top shelf in the office. There were plenty of books, none of which looked very old or valuable. Still, she climbed a sliding ladder and removed a handful and set them on the empty desktop. Someone had gone through the effort of dusting the room, making Avery's job spider free, which she was incredibly thankful for.

She flipped through the books, making sure there weren't any papers, or money, stuck within the pages. As she went through each shelf, she stacked the books against a bare wall and reached for another. The third shelf over revealed a locked safe behind the books. Instead of a dial combination, this safe was locked with a key.

She rifled through the desk in search of a key. Strangely, the middle drawer was completely empty. The left top drawer held neatly placed pens, and not the Bic kind . . . no, these were of the Montblanc variety. Avery pushed the books she'd stacked on the desk aside and lined up the pens. One was so impressive she stopped rummaging and spun the thing between her fingers. Diamonds, tiny bits of glitter sparkled. "Just sitting in a drawer," she said to herself. All the Petrov treasures hidden in plain sight. Apparently it worked, since the pricey stuff didn't disappear by the sticky fingers of the staff hired to clean the vacant home. Or maybe the staff didn't think someone was stupid enough to leave valuables lying around.

Avery didn't so much as leave a twenty-dollar bill on the counter when the cleaning ladies were due at her condo. Perhaps there was a lesson in Petrov's thinking.

She set the pen aside and kept searching for a key.

Nothing.

She dropped to her knees to look on the underside. It wasn't uncommon to have hidden doors in desks, especially if the desk was as ornate and heavy as the one she was probing.

She considered running her fingers along the edges that she couldn't see, but she doubted the maids had dusted away the cobwebs. Making do without a flashlight, Avery used a lamp and plugged it in close to the desk before climbing back underneath.

The desk had been cleaned on the underside, at least at some point. She peered closer when she noticed a color difference in the pattern of the wood. "How can someone spill liquid on the underside of a desk?" Avery no sooner asked the question to the universe when her mind cleared and she realized what she was looking at.

A cold chill raced up her spine and had her scrambling out from under the desk and to her feet.

Apparently the cleaning crew missed a few spots after they removed Fedor's body.

Avery scrambled into the office bathroom and scrubbed her hands. Even then, she looked at the soap dispenser and wondered if the last person to use it was a dead guy.

Yeah, she was officially creeped out.

She gathered up the pens and left the office with a slam of the door.

The rest could wait until Trina came back, and even then, maybe they should elicit someone with a stronger backbone to deal with that room.

Chapter Fifteen

Trina had frequented enough Texas barbeques to know the event wasn't a formal affair. She donned a pair of tight jeans and a button-up silk blouse. Her cowboy boots were at home, so her two-inch wedges would have to do. A hat would have been overkill, not that she had one.

She spent a little extra time messing with her hair and added another layer of eyeliner to help her best feature pop out. Even though it had taken her some time to fall asleep the night before, she still felt more rested than she had in a couple of weeks. Being in the Hamptons home had placed more stress on her shoulders than she'd thought it would.

Thinking about New York prompted her to give Avery a quick call. She answered on the second ring.

"Hey . . . how is Texas?"

"Am I on a speakerphone?"

"I'm in the car on the way into the city."

"I thought that wasn't until this afternoon?" Trina glanced at the clock on the wall: it was just after nine in Texas, and ten in New York.

"I found some pens in Fedor's desk that I'm taking in to have checked out before I go to the watch guy."

Trina stepped out onto the balcony of her room. "You went into the office."

"Yeah. I didn't think you wanted to tackle it. Actually, I'm glad you didn't."

"Oh?"

"I'll leave out the details. Let's just say the cleaning crew didn't do a perfect job . . . after."

Trina squeezed her eyes shut. "No."

"Yes. No worries. After a little mental breakdown, I'm all good and en route to Manhattan."

"I'm sorry."

"Don't be."

"Has Cindy called back? I'll have her bring in a better crew."

"I haven't heard a thing."

"I'll try calling her again."

"How is the party?" Avery asked.

"It hasn't started yet."

"And *Wade*?" she said his name like it hurt.

"Give the guy a break, Avery. He's being a complete gentleman." She paused. "His mom doesn't like me, though."

"What? How can any mom not like you? You're perfect. Sweet, beautiful . . . not to mention the zillion dollar part."

Avery was good for Trina's ego. "Sweet and beautiful wasn't a winning point, and I doubt she knows about Everson Oil. Doesn't matter, I'm here for Wade, not her."

"Thanks for cutting me off, asshole!" Avery shouted. "Sorry. Everyone complains about LA drivers, but they hold nothing on these nutjobs."

Trina laughed. "I'll leave you to it, then. I'll call you tomorrow when I'm on my way to Houston."

"Still planning on coming back here on Monday?"

"Yeah, we have the art auction people coming. Reed is sending one of their guys out to keep an eye on things Monday, too." Reed was part of the security firm that worked with Alliance and many of their rich clients. They monitored the security system at her ranch in Texas and had wired the Hamptons home as well. Although, the camera system in New York was limited to the front and back doors and a burglar alarm. No need for them to go overboard when no one was living there.

"Perfect. Maybe we can get whoever shows up to do some of the dirty work in the office if we can't get ahold of your maid."

"Thanks for the visual."

"Sorry. Okay, I'm going. This drive requires my full attention."

"Talk tomorrow."

"Ciao." Avery hung up.

Trina went ahead and plugged her phone in by her bed before she left the room.

She found Wade in the kitchen with a cup of coffee in his hands.

"I thought I slept late," he said when he saw her.

"I was up at five," she teased. "I'm still not sleeping right since Italy."

"I tossed and turned a lot myself." His eyes traveled her frame and he grinned. "Good morning."

She stepped closer.

With a sly smile, she reached for his cup and tilted it to her lips. "Mmm."

He chuckled. "I can get you your own."

Trina shook her head. "Yours tastes better." It felt good to flirt.

Wade reached for his cup and moved it aside. He stepped even closer and lifted her chin with one finger. "Good morning, little lady."

She licked her lips. "Good morning."

He kissed her, just like the night before . . . slowly, sweetly. The taste of coffee on his lips and the scent of the soap he used was a lethal combination.

"Goooood morning," she said again, slowly.

"I could get used to that," he said, only inches from her face.

That made two of them.

"Coffee?" he asked.

"Please."

He crossed the kitchen and poured her a cup. "Anything in it?"

"Black is fine." She took a sip. "When does this party get started?"

"The caterers will be here in an hour, food goes on the grill by noon, and people will start showing up anytime."

"Am I dressed okay?" She opened her arms and invited his comments.

"You show those curves off any more and I might have to fight off a few of my friends."

She took that as a yes. "You'll have to point out the people I should know but probably don't."

"The only one you should know is me. I'll introduce you to the rest. Ike and Jeb, you've already met, and they are the men to go to if you can't find me and feel overwhelmed. Not that I plan on leaving your side."

"It's a party. I do know how to mingle."

"I have no doubt you'll hold your own, but people can be a bit possessive and downright nosy. Possessive about me and my time and nosy about you."

"You mean us," she said.

"Probably," he agreed. "I don't expect anyone to step out of line, but if they do, come right to me, and I'll take care of it."

"Like the ex?"

He frowned. "I wouldn't be surprised if she takes one look at us and leaves."

Trina could hope. "I've been warned."

He set his empty cup aside and slid a little closer. "How do you feel about public displays of affection?"

She blushed. Damn if he didn't notice and brush the back of his hand against her cheek. "As long as the people displaying their affection don't look like they need a room . . ."

He slid the hand from her cheek to her shoulder. "Darlin', every time I look at you, I feel the need for a room."

Okay, yeah . . . the heat factor leveled up with the sparkle in his blue eyes.

They stared, Trina with heat tingling up her spine and Wade emitting some kind of pheromone, willing her to step closer.

"There you are!" Vicki's words broke the spell.

Trina stepped back.

Wade chuckled.

"Mornin', Mama."

Vicki bounced in, wearing a black midcalf western skirt, a tank top that barely covered her breasts, and a fringed light jacket. She ended the ensemble with blinged out cowboy boots. Trina was fairly certain a hat would adorn the woman's head by the time the guests arrived.

Wade greeted his mother with a kiss to the cheek.

"So good to have you home." Vicki turned to Trina. "Did you sleep well?"

"I did, thank you."

Vicki's smile matched Wade's. "I don't think we got off to the right start, and I wanted to apologize if I came off as standoffish. It's just that I wasn't expecting Wade to bring a friend."

An apology with a *but* was never sincere. I'm sorry, *but* I have a reason.

"I didn't take offense."

"Any friend of Wade's is a friend of mine."

That sounded a little better.

"Thank you, Vicki."

"I would love to know how you two met."

"Hotel bar, actually." The minute the words came out of her mouth, Trina knew they sounded seedy. "Which isn't as bad as that sounds."

Vicki held her smile.

Wade stepped closer, placed his hand on the counter behind Trina's back. "It was midnight and we had both missed dinner. Trina had ordered a meal fit for a small village, and the kitchen had closed before I could order a beer."

"It wasn't that much food," Trina defended herself.

"Yes, it was."

Trina pushed against his chest to shut him up. "It wasn't. Okay, it was more than I was going to eat, which turned out well for your son."

Vicki's gaze bounced between the two of them.

"Then after I told her who I was she said the craziest thing I ever heard," Wade told his mom while looking at Trina.

"What's that?" Vicki asked.

"She said, 'Am I supposed to know that name?' At first I thought she was pulling my chain."

Trina watched Wade's expression when he told his mother the story.

"I wasn't interested in pulling a chain, I was hungry."

Wade laughed.

They were lost in the memory and smiling at each other when Vicki said, "Well, that's nice. I suppose it's good for you."

"It sucked for my ego," he said. "Here I was, trying to impress her, and nothin'."

"Yet here we are," Trina said.

Wade inched his hand on her waist in the slightest touch.

"That's sweet." Vicki broke the spell. "So what is it that you do?"

Trina held her breath. Revealing who she was sparked an entire conversation she'd just as soon avoid.

"Trina is—"

"A flight attendant," she interrupted Wade, placing a hand on his arm, hoping he'd get the hint. "Was . . . I'm in the process of building a business around attendants for private charters."

"That sounds very ambitious. Are you looking for investors for this start-up company?"

"No. I have that figured out." Which was true if she actually went through with it.

"Uh-huh." Vicki glanced at her son, doubt on her face flashing for only a second before her smile returned.

That's when Trina realized the fuel behind Vicki's fire.

"So you're technically unemployed right now."

"I have a pretty good savings," Trina told her.

Wade laughed under his breath.

"Well, good for you. There needs to be more women in business. Depending upon a man can often be disappointing."

"Mama."

"Present company excluded, of course."

She glanced out the kitchen window, toward the back of the house. "Looks like some of the help have arrived, I should get to work."

"Can I do anything?" Trina offered.

"Oh, no. I've got it, hon. You take care of you. Take all the time you need to change before the party."

Oh, God . . . *I'm not wearing the right outfit.* "I didn't bring . . ."

Vicki backpedaled. "You're fine."

"I came from New York."

Vicki narrowed her eyes. "You live in *New York?*" She made the state sound like a disease.

"No. I live close to Houston . . . where I have the right outfit, but I didn't have time to stop by—"

Wade squeezed her waist with his hand.

"Darlin', you're fine. Don't think another thing about it. You'll blend right in. Don't worry."

Sure.

Right.

Don't worry.

Chapter Sixteen

There should be a special license one needed to drive on the streets of Manhattan. One Avery never wanted to obtain. She ditched the car at the first available parking garage and shouldered her oversize mom bag. New York was one of the safest cities in the world, in her opinion. It might not feel that safe if she announced the fact her purse was loaded with some pretty pricey stuff. But to the average person watching her walk by, she was just another smartly dressed woman on a mission.

Outside the garage, she checked her phone for the direction of the building she needed and started to walk. Fall was sneaking into the air but not strong enough for big coats or fur-lined hats. With a brisk pace, she traveled several blocks through a crush of New Yorkers and tourists alike.

She found the address and ducked inside the building through glass doors. Braum Auctions specialized in items many of the larger houses didn't. Since Avery liked the idea of finding the perfect platform to sell the different mediums of collectables, she was willing to do the legwork.

Avery marched up to the reception area as she removed her designer sunglasses from her face. The perfectly polished woman behind the desk greeted her with a painted-on smile. "Good morning."

"Good morning, I'm here to see Mr. Levin, I'm Avery Grant."

"Miss Grant, welcome. I'll let him know you're here."

Avery decided to look at the art on the walls instead of sitting. Offices like this one reminded her of her father's. Whenever she had been summoned to his office, he kept her waiting in the lobby for hours as a form of intimidation. By the age of thirteen, the time spent in high-rise lobbies no longer brought sweaty palms and itchy anxiety. No, she recognized her father's tactics and didn't show up for her monthly meetings until the very end of his day. Her antics frustrated him even more than whatever offense he was mad at her for to begin with. Her rebellion started at thirteen and didn't end until after she married Bernie. Needless to say, her father was frustrated for a good many years.

"Miss Grant?"

Avery turned to find exactly what she expected, a balding, middle-aged, five-foot-seven man in a three-piece suit and a smile. She reached out her hand. "Mr. Levin?"

Men looked at her. It was something she'd grown used to the minute she put on a bra. Mr. Levin wasn't any different. She pretended not to notice.

"Come on in." He turned and walked them past the reception desk. "How was your drive into the city?"

"Excruciating, as always," she teased.

"Traffic is a fact of life no matter where we live, eh?" His corner office had plenty of sunlight, but no real view since they were only on the fifth floor of the building. Still, the office was large enough to tell Avery that Braum Auctions wasn't a basement operation where the merchandise she brought in was at risk of disappearing.

"Sit," he offered. "Can I get you something to drink? Coffee, water?"

"I'm fine, thank you. I appreciate you seeing me on such short notice."

He took his seat behind his desk. "When you described the pen you found, I couldn't wait to see it for myself."

Avery lifted her purse, careful not to show him all the other trinkets she had inside.

Mr. Levin removed a black cloth from inside his desk and a jeweler's eye loupe, along with a pair of white gloves.

"Here are the first few pens I found." She handed him a small box with three designer examples of Fedor's taste.

Mr. Levin picked each of them up, one at a time, and inspected them slowly and silently. "Very nice."

"I wasn't able to find these exact pens anywhere online."

"That's because they are limited editions . . . well, these two, in any event." He lifted the third one with gold trim and some kind of black onyx strips adorning the length of it. "I'll have to research this one," he told her.

From her purse, she removed a jewelry box she'd found in Trina's room to place the blinged out pen in. "Here is the one I told you about."

Mr. Levin blew out a whistle.

Avery leaned back while he studied the pen for what felt like ten minutes. "This is spectacular."

She actually thought it was gaudy. "Any idea *how* spectacular?"

He kept spinning it around in his gloved fingers. "High quality diamonds, and the rubies are exceptional . . ." For the next fifteen minutes he explained who the designer of the pen was and how few of this type of pen were in existence. No two were exactly the same. Blah, blah, blah . . . finally, the dollar amount trickled out of Mr. Levin's lips, and Avery felt her fingers buzz. She knew the watches in her purse were worth some serious money, but a pen?

"That much?"

"At auction, it could go for even more. Collectors will line up."

"For a pen?"

He smiled. "For a pen."

Avery had considered taking the pens to more than one auction house to see if the appraisals would differ, but the thought of walking around Manhattan with those in her purse had perspiration welling on the back of her neck.

She glanced around his office. "I assume you have security for these kinds of items?"

"Of course. We have not lost any of our consignments, nor ever had any stolen."

"I'd like to leave this with you, then, and when my friend is back in town, I'll have her come in and determine if she really wants to sell."

After an inch of paperwork and an hour of her day, Avery was back on the street and walking toward Park Avenue.

The desire to find a safe place for the watches sitting in the bottom of her mom bag burned in her head.

⁓

As Wade had predicted, guests started showing up before Trina finished her second cup of coffee. There were friends of Vicki's who didn't linger after Wade introduced her to them. Gus was part of Wade's band and one of the first members that he toured with after he cut his first album. Then there was Jerry. The only man at the party not wearing denim or boots. Jerry had a couple of inches on Trina, was probably in his early forties, and still had all his dark brown hair. He was an attractive man, and from the way he looked around the room at other people, and especially her, he knew it.

"Who do we have here?" Jerry asked as he nudged Wade and peered at Trina.

Wade placed a possessive arm over Trina's shoulders as he made his introductions. "Watch this one, Trina, he'll try and turn you into one of my backup singers."

She laughed. "Good luck with that, I only sing in the shower."

Wade lifted a flirty eyebrow. "This, I wanna see."

"Uhm, hello?"

"Sorry, Jerry." Wade wasn't sorry. "This is Trina. Jerry is my agent."

Jerry shook Trina's hand with a telling squeeze. Trina kept a smile on her face even though she wanted to pull her hand away as soon as she could and wipe it on her jeans.

"How come I've never heard of this beautiful creature?"

"You're hearing about her now," Wade explained.

"A pleasure," she lied.

"Smooth and slightly exotic voice, are you sure you're not a singer?"

Wade nudged her. "Told you." His gaze went over the top of Trina's head and his smile waned.

She followed his gaze.

Vicki was across the lawn, talking to a tall, leggy, stunning blonde. Big hair, huge smile, and boobs that would do Dolly Parton proud. She wore the boots, the hat, and the short denim skirt that not many women pulled off well. And she was staring directly at Wade.

Jordyn.

He placed his lips next to Trina's ear. "I should talk to her first, before I introduce you."

"Go. I'm fine here." Trina didn't turn when she felt eyes burning into the back of her skull.

"You sure?"

"I'm a big girl."

He kissed the side of her head and left her with Jerry.

"You know what the best part about country music is?" he asked as he took a giant step closer.

"What is that?"

"Songs about love triangles always race up the charts."

She tried not to look toward Wade and failed. He'd approached Jordyn, and she'd leaned in for a hug.

Trina looked away, not wanting to watch.

She found Jerry staring at her.

"I think you're going to be good for our Wade."

"'Our'?" He made Wade sound like a possession.

"For his musical muse. Perfect timing, too."

Trina wasn't following him. "How is that?"

"Between albums, between tours. Soak up a little love, a little heartache."

Trina stopped pretending to smile. "You want his heart to ache?"

Jerry seemed to catch himself, and he shook his head. "Oh, you know what I mean."

Yeah, she did. Wade Thomas was a meal ticket to someone like Jerry, and the man didn't even try to hide it. Trina didn't want to spend another minute at the man's side.

"There is something I need to do," she said as she took a step back.

"Nice meeting you," he said.

She just smiled and walked away. "Asshole."

∽

Avery could finally breathe. She'd dumped the six-figure watch along with several of its five-figure brothers with an auction house on Madison Avenue and searched out lunch with a view of Central Park. The crisp morning blossomed into a balmy afternoon. The temptation to stay in Manhattan the entire afternoon and spend some money tickled her shopping bone. Then she remembered her last credit card bill and the amount of money she'd spent on things that were sitting in her LA condominium, collecting dust.

She sat at the top of Bergdorf Goodman, sipping her chardonnay, playing with her salad, and considered it a compromise. Eating in one of the most expensive and famous department stores would have to do. Maybe when she returned to collect the money after the sale of Fedor's trinkets, she would indulge. But for now, she would try her hand at a budget. Her parents had tried to teach her money management since she was in college . . . well, her father attempted, her mother told her to marry a rich man. Her thirty-first birthday had passed the month before, so maybe a new leaf was in order.

The waiter returned to her table. Early twenties, tall, camera ready . . . he was yummy in all the right places. "Another wine?"

"I shouldn't." She was driving.

"How about some fresh bread to go with the second glass?" He flirted with his smile.

"If you insist."

She checked out his ass as he walked away.

He returned a couple of minutes later and poured from an open bottle. "I'm sorry about the cork."

She glanced at the glass. "What cork?"

He winked. "The cork that accidentally managed to slip into your drink. I'll have to comp this for you."

"Ah, that's very nice . . ." She glanced at his name tag. "Norman . . ." She tried not to laugh. "Your name is Norman?"

"Blame my parents."

"Well, thank you."

She nibbled on the bread, drank the wine, and checked her e-mail while lifting her gaze every once in a while to see if Norman was watching her.

The next time he came to the table, he didn't ask if she wanted another glass of wine. "I get off at six."

Damn it . . .

She needed to get back on the highway. There was still so much to do at Trina's house. This was a job. One she was actually going to get paid to do.

Norman, the booty call, wasn't on the schedule.

"I'm going to have to pass." Adulting sucked! "Work."

"What if I gave you my number?"

She smiled. "I don't live in town, but I do visit often."

"Sounds perfect to me."

Avery waltzed out of Bergdorf Goodman with an energy she didn't have walking in. She'd spent the morning conducting business. Real business. Had a little mostly liquid lunch that resulted in a phone number and a promise. Apparently she could be a proper adult and pick up a hottie, even if his name was Norman.

She buzzed through a portion of Central Park in an effort to work off any of the liquor she'd consumed. She hadn't finished that last glass of wine, even though she'd been tempted to do so.

Adulting.

She was adulting, damn it.

The hour to hit the freeway and avoid the bulk of traffic fast approached, so she made her way to the parking garage. As she did, she checked her phone for messages.

Nothing.

Which had started to bug her. With all of the male attention she found, there wasn't anyone who took the effort to check on her just to see if she was okay. Even her parents didn't bother with any real consistency. Only her new friends filled that void. Lori would call when she was in town, or stop by for a glass of wine. Avery knew she was the one to most often sneak up on Lori and Reed and invite herself over for a drink or dinner. The advantage of living in the same building.

Shannon had started calling her on occasion, although the two of them didn't hang out as much as they probably should. Maybe the conservative nature of Shannon would rub off on Avery if she spent more time with the woman. If anyone knew how to adult, it was Shannon. The woman still played the part of political wife several years after the marriage was over.

But Trina was Avery's go-to. They were alike in so many ways.

She clicked on her messages and pulled up Trina's name.

I know you're in the middle of the big party, just dropping a note to say that everything in NY went well. Fedor liked really expensive things.

She glanced up, saw her car, and fished for the keys in the bottom of her mom bag while she texted with one thumb.

En route to the house so call if you need to talk. Texting and driving in NY is just asking for trouble.

Avery pressed send at the same time something huge smashed into her side and threw her onto the pavement.

Her first thought was that she'd walked into something, or because she was on her phone, she'd become one of those YouTube videos of distracted people walking into a pond. But then she saw a boot coming toward her face, and she realized this wasn't an accident.

She tried to move, covered her head.

Never in her life had Avery been kicked. The pain was unimaginable. She tasted warm salt in her mouth as she cowered on the ground.

Roll away!

Do something!

She tried, only her body was a heavy, solid mass that needed to lose a hundred pounds. When the next hit came, she lost the ability to think about anything.

Chapter Seventeen

"There you are." Finding his way back to Trina's side was like swimming through a sea of fans that found the exit door from the stage to his limo. Even his friends didn't understand that he wanted his attention somewhere else.

As for Jordyn, the woman didn't understand the words *we're over*.

"There is someone here with me," he'd told her.

"I heard," Jordyn had said, looking over his shoulder.

Wade attempted to block her gaze in case Trina felt it.

Jordyn leaned in close . . . too close. "It's okay, baby. We all have to have our diversions."

"That's not how it is."

At that point, his mother joined the conversation to discuss how Jordyn was talking with a record label of her own, and wasn't that exciting?

Wade stood there for a solid five minutes, trying to keep things nice, and when he turned around, Trina was out of his sight.

It took thirty minutes and a dozen conversations before he found her. At that point, he beelined in her direction to find her sitting on a straw bale, talking to Jeb.

He waved off a distant cousin and sat on the straw beside her.

"Hey," she said with a genuine smile.

"Do you have any idea how hard it is to walk across this yard with this many people?" he asked.

Trina shook her head. "Wasn't hard for me . . . Jeb?"

"Never an issue."

Wade reached over and took the beer Trina was holding and tilted it back.

She smiled but didn't comment.

He realized two things at the same time. First, he liked that they had the comfort of sharing a coffee, or a beer, and second . . . the beer was nearly full and kinda warm. Trina had grabbed the beer to blend but had no intention of actually drinking it.

Somehow, that made him grin even more.

He scooted closer and didn't bother handing the beer back.

"How did that go?" Jeb nodded toward the direction of Jordyn and his mother.

"Fine . . . it went fine."

Trina lowered her chin and didn't blink.

Wade coughed up the truth. "She's having a hard time letting go."

"Not surprising," Jeb offered.

"Why is that?" Trina asked.

"She's a singer wanting a record deal. Wade has a reputation with plenty of influence. There's a lot of people wanting something out of him."

"Like Jerry?"

Wade turned toward Trina.

"Sorry," she retracted.

He sat up taller, narrowed his attention.

"He's my agent, he's invested."

"Of course."

Yeah, there was something in her eyes that told him there was more to her statement.

From the other side of the yard, the amplifier on the small stage let the crowd know that the music was about to begin. Up until that moment, a mix track of popular country music had been playing. Everything except Wade's music, which was always his request when his mother planned events like this one.

"Welcome, everybody." Vicki stepped to the microphone and grabbed the guests' attention. "I just wanted to give a big thank y'all for joining us. It's seldom my famous son is home and even more rare to have his attention when he is. Where are you, Wade?"

"Oh, geez."

Trina took her beer back and pushed him off the straw.

People around them parted so that he could have a direct route to the stage.

He stood and reached out his hand to Trina.

She started to shake her head but he didn't give her a chance. He took her hand and helped her to her feet. "C'mon. They won't bite."

"There you are," his mother said.

He started up the stairs to the stage, and Trina dug her heels in. Instead of forcing her up with him, he lifted a finger, asking her to stay close, and let her go. He kissed his mother's cheek and took the mic. "Howdy."

A chorus of similar greetings were shouted back at him. "It sure is nice to be home, did y'all miss me?"

Familiar faces laughed and a couple of his older friends shouted out no.

"I heard that, Ike."

Two of Wade's stage crew patted Ike on the back.

"I have such a blessed life to have the opportunity to go on tour and see so many places in this big, beautiful world, but coming home is always the best. Especially when I know everyone here is going to let me be myself and not try and get something out of me."

"Except the free beer," someone shouted.

Lots of hands went up, waving bottles in agreement.

Wade laughed.

He caught Trina smiling up from the steps of the stage.

"I'd like y'all to say hi to my friend Trina."

She offered a timid wave to the crowd.

"She looks a little fancy for you," someone yelled.

"Oh, she is. Trust me. I'm the lucky one."

Trina's face turned bright red. Her eyes pleaded with him to stop. His mother wasn't as subtle. "We should probably let the band play, don't you think?"

Wade turned his head toward his mother. "Thank you for coming. Eat, drink, and have a good time."

He hopped off the stage and didn't let anyone stop him until he was back at Trina's side. His lips moved close to her ear again. "Now everyone will know not to hit on you."

"That wasn't a problem."

Behind him, his mother introduced Jordyn and her band. There were several sets of eyes that moved between Jordyn and Wade expectantly. He even saw his mother holding her breath when Jordyn took the mic.

She smiled sweetly in his direction, her gaze never drifting to Trina.

"Let's all welcome Wade home once again, where he belongs, with the people that know and love him." Jordyn blew him a kiss that would have been innocent enough a year earlier.

Used to the attention of a crowd, Wade waved and smiled and hoped that was the end of being onstage for a while.

"C'mon, let's find you something you actually want to drink and me something cold."

Wade kept to his word and stayed by her side as much as he could throughout the party. He laughed at the amount of food she managed to put away, even though he ate twice as much. When she was ready to find a rocking chair, or a bed to let the meal put her into a food coma, Wade pulled her out on the dance floor.

"Just follow my lead," he said in her ear. "Two fast steps, two short steps."

Trina felt judgmental eyes watching them. "I'm going to embarrass you."

"Not possible, little lady."

She doubted that.

One arm wrapped around her waist as the other one took possession of her shoulder.

Trina started to sweat.

He shook her arm. "Relax. This is easy."

He started to move her on the dance floor.

Two fast, two slow, two fast, two slow.

Around them couples were doing the same dance, only they were pushing forward and backward, and men were dipping the women and spinning them around.

She miscounted, and Wade corrected his step and spun her around.

"Oh, lord."

"See, not hard at all."

Trina sucked in the beat of the music and tried not to think.

"There ya go. You're a natural."

"Yeah, right!"

He pulled both of her hands up to his shoulders and used his hands to guide her hips.

The smile on his face lit up the yard. "We just need to get you some boots." He spun her around.

She giggled like a schoolgirl. "So I can dress the part?"

"Yup." He winked and took one hand away, while keeping the beat, and placed his hat on her head. "Much better."

Trina tilted it back. "I might not give this back."

He looked at the hat, looked in her eyes. "I might not take it back."

The last time she'd worn a man's anything had been at her high school prom. Every date after that, she'd brought her own sweater to keep warm, and using a man's jacket hadn't been necessary. Wade's hat on her head took her back to a simpler time, when hand holding, dancing, and kissing were the cause of butterflies in her stomach.

They laughed as he spun her around, and never once did he mention the times she stepped on his feet. He just kept dancing like he was born to it.

When the music switched pace, he maneuvered them toward the back of the dance floor and paused. His finger grazed the side of her jaw, and she shivered, despite the fact it wasn't cold.

"You are so damn beautiful when you smile."

She bit her lip.

"C'mere." He swept in and placed his lips on hers.

Trina tilted her head back, holding on to the hat to keep it from sliding to the ground.

He was smooth, pressed her frame flush against his, from knees to chest. He tasted like hops and barbeque. Just when she thought he would deepen their kiss, he pulled back enough to talk against her lips. "You're killin' me."

"You started it," she said with her lips a breath away from his.

He kissed her again, short, meaningful.

Wade hummed something under his breath. She wasn't sure if it was a song or a mating call. Either way, it made her smile. Then he broke away and grasped her hand.

Next thing she knew they were back on the dance floor.

The afternoon slowly drifted into dusk. Lights strung out all over the yard kept the party lit up. The band took several breaks, but that didn't stop the music or the dancing.

Pies of every shape and flavor were added to the banquet of food, giving Trina another reason to hold her stomach.

At one point, Ike pulled Wade away, and she took the opportunity to find a restroom and freshen up.

Vicki found her inside the house on the way up the stairs. "It looks like you're having a good time," she said.

"I am. Your friends and family are very welcoming."

Vicki glanced at Wade's hat. "My son seems to like you quite a bit."

Again, Trina wasn't sure if that was a good or bad thing, coming from her. "You've raised a charming son."

"Oh, yes, he does know how to charm the ladies. Usually women are crawling all over him at these parties. This time there seems to only be one."

They'd kissed twice the whole night, and certainly no one was climbing on anyone. "I can't imagine he'd invite me here and ignore me to flirt with other women," Trina told her.

"He wouldn't mean to, but sometimes his polite nature won't let him stop a woman from trying."

Trina wasn't sure what hidden message Vicki was trying to tell her. If she wasn't high on the endorphins from dancing and Wade's attention, Trina might have just flat-out asked her. She pointed toward the stairs. "I was going to grab a jacket."

"Of course. Go on. We can chat another time."

Trina didn't like the sound of that.

On the landing up the stairs to her room, Jordyn stood poised against the wall, almost as if she were waiting for someone.

Her gaze snapped to Trina's, and she looked behind her before she started talking. "Hello. We haven't met."

"That doesn't mean we don't know who each other are," Trina said without pretense. "I hope this isn't awkward for you."

Jordyn flashed lots of teeth. "For me? Oh, no. I'm fine. I've known Wade long enough to know what he's all about."

Again with the hidden messages.

The woman was looking for a conversation that Trina didn't want to have. "If you'll excuse me."

Jordyn lifted up her hands. "Don't let me stop you."

You already did.

Once in her room, Trina took a long, deep breath. Laughter from outside reached the balcony. She walked to the door and watched the party from above. Wade was easy to spot, or maybe her radar had already dialed him in. He was laughing beside a few friends while over a hundred other people stood in small groups, socializing. It surprised her that there weren't more people vying for his attention. A celebrity of his standing almost always had a crowd trying to interrupt. This was obviously not that group of people.

She turned away from the open balcony door to use the bathroom before gathering her sweater from the back of a chair. She sat on the edge of her bed and removed her lip gloss from her purse. Two swipes of the tiny brush, and she tucked it away and placed her bag back on her nightstand. As she did, she knocked her plugged-in cell phone to the floor.

When she picked it up, the screen turned on and caught her attention. Three messages lit up.

All of them were from Lori.

Call me!

It's urgent!

Left a message on your voicemail. I'm flying out now, call Sam.

A chill ran down Trina's spine. Lori never cried wolf. The woman was always calm and collected—cold, even. Trina fumbled with her phone until she found Lori's message. She'd called six hours ago.

"Trina, it's Lori. Don't panic." Only it sounded like Lori was unnerved. "It's Avery. She's okay . . ." Lori cleared her throat. "Call me as soon as you get this message."

Trina started to shake.

She dialed Lori, ended up on her voice mail. Without leaving a message, she called Sam. When she picked up, Trina jumped on her. "What happened?"

"We've been trying to get ahold of you for hours."

"What happened, Sam?"

Sam paused. "Avery was attacked . . ."

∽

Wade saw Trina cut through the crowd, her eyes scanning everyone. Her smile was gone, as was his hat that he'd placed on her head hours before. She had her purse tossed over her shoulder and she held a sweater like she was leaving.

Something was wrong.

"Excuse me." He stopped the conversation midsentence and hustled to Trina's side.

She noticed him several yards out and met him halfway.

"What's wrong?"

Her lip quivered. "I gotta go. I need a ride to the airport." She was close to tears.

He placed both hands on her shoulders. "Slow down. What happened?"

"I need to leave now, Wade. It's Avery. She's in the hospital. I'm sorry. Can I borrow your truck? Or Jeb can drive me to the airport. Anything . . ."

"Take a deep breath, baby." He grasped her hand and started toward the house.

Jeb intercepted them at the back door.

"I'll explain on the way. Get the car," Wade told Jeb.

He left Trina on the driveway long enough to grab his wallet and a coat, and when he returned, she was already in the car, with Jeb at the wheel. Instead of jumping in the front seat, Wade took the back with her.

Trina was on her phone. "How long?"

Jeb took off. It appeared that Trina had already told him they were going to the airport.

"Okay. Do we know anything else about the person who did this?"

Wade started to draw a picture in his head.

Trina hung her head and sniffed. "I knew we should have had Reed bring in a bodyguard. She was taking stuff to the auction houses . . . No, watches and pens. I don't know, Sam. Expensive crap. Nothing worth hurting Avery over."

Wade placed his hand on Trina's thigh in an effort to comfort her.

"Of course this is my fault. She wouldn't have been there if I had just walked away from that house and let someone else deal with it."

Trina looked up and out the window, unshed tears in her eyes. "How long until we get to the airport?" she asked Jeb.

"Thirty minutes."

Trina told the person on the phone her timeline. "I'll be there."

She hung up the phone and punched the seat beside her.

Wade didn't ask, he just waited for her to talk.

"She was found in a parking garage, dragged between two cars. They beat her up, Wade." Trina started to cry.

He pulled her into his arms. "It's okay, honey. We're getting there as fast as we can."

She cried on his shoulder. "Sam is sending a plane. Just get me to the airport. You don't have to—"

"We're not having this conversation. I'm going. Jeb?" he asked, even though it was understood that where Wade went, Jeb went, unless otherwise arranged.

Jeb caught his eyes in the rearview mirror with a look of *Are you kidding?*

"You don't—"

Best way to get a woman to stop arguing was to get her talking about something else. "Tell me everything you know."

She sucked back a breath and started at the beginning.

Chapter Eighteen

A car waited for them at LaGuardia. She tucked into the back of the limousine with Wade while Jeb took the front seat, next to the driver. It was late and traffic was light. They arrived at the hospital well after visiting hours, but that never mattered when you knew someone in the ICU. Trina walked into the waiting room to find Lori and Reed.

Trina fell into Lori's embrace. "My fault."

"Stop."

"She was there because of me." Guilt would sit in Trina's soul for eternity.

"Avery has never done anything she didn't want to do. So stop!"

Trina pushed back the darkness inside. "How is she?"

"She woke up."

The fact that she hadn't been awake all this time wasn't lost on Trina.

"And she's talking . . ."

Chills. *God, please.*

"She's going to be okay, Trina."

Trina shook as she broke down.

Lori embraced her until the sobs ebbed.

Slowly . . . ever so slowly, the room came into focus.

Reed and Wade stood side by side.

"Can I see her?"

"For ten minutes at the top of the hour. Hospital rules."

Trina looked at the clock on the wall. They had half an hour to wait.

The door to the waiting room opened and Jeb walked in.

Wade turned to Reed and extended his hand. "I'm Wade."

"I'm sorry," Trina said.

"It's okay, Trina," Lori told her.

Trina sat beside Lori, and Wade made himself comfortable opposite the two of them. Jeb hovered by the door and watched the other people in the waiting room.

"Do the police have any leads?" Wade asked quietly, once they were sitting down.

Reed answered, "No. They're getting the surveillance tapes of the garage as we speak. Hopefully by morning we'll have some information."

"Has Avery said anything about her attacker?"

Lori placed her hand over Trina's. "They're able to wake her, but she's sedated now."

Reed sat forward. "Do you know where exactly she was going?"

"Christie's, I think. The other one I don't know. Avery had found Fedor's pens after I'd left for Texas, the expensive kind. She was all excited about them, said they were worth a ton of money." Trina swallowed hard. "I was going to give her a percentage of what was sold at auction." She turned to Lori. "Avery's burned through a lot of money this year and wanted a job. I thought, perfect. She knows all about high-end stuff that I'm clueless about. She was excited."

"Did she take the stuff to New York with her?" Lori asked.

"Yeah."

"At least we have a motive," Reed said with relief.

"What do you mean?" Trina asked.

"Burglary. Her purse was dumped out, but whoever did this didn't bother to take her wallet. There weren't any watches or pens on her either, so they must have taken those."

Trina shook her head and brought her purse to her lap. "I don't think she had any of it on her. Here, this text came through before all of yours. I didn't notice it until we were on the plane."

Trina turned the phone over to Reed, and he read it out loud. I know you're in the middle of the big party, just dropping a note to say that everything in NY went well. Fedor liked really expensive things. En route to the house so call if you need to talk. Texting and driving in NY is just asking for trouble.

Reed ran a hand through his hair. "Oh, shit."

"What?"

"We need to find out what she had on her, if anything."

"I don't care about the stuff—"

"This is about motive. Someone mugging her for a purse, a wallet, a fifty-thousand-dollar watch . . . that makes sense. Someone beating her up for nothing . . . and then dragging her behind a car so she wasn't quickly found by the first person to walk by . . . that feels too calculated for me. Or worse, they wanted her dead and were interrupted before finishing the job."

"You don't think this was random?" Wade asked.

"I used to be a cop. So no. I never think anything is random. But the motive of a thief is a hell of a lot easier to sleep on than a motive of someone wanting to harm Avery just to see her battered and bruised."

"Who would want to hurt Avery? She makes friends, not enemies." Trina looked at Lori.

"Someone wasn't happy with her."

The door leading into the patient rooms opened and a nurse peeked into the waiting room. Trina sat taller and gave the woman her full attention.

"Ms. Cumberland?"

Lori and Trina both stood at the same time.

"She's asking for you." The nurse looked around the room. "Three visitors at a time," she said to all of them.

Trina looked over her shoulder at Wade.

"Go, I'll stay out here."

Reed, Lori, and Trina followed the nurse back. In complete contrast to the waiting room, the ICU was lit up like it was one in the afternoon and not one in the morning. Nurses walked in different directions, the machines beeped and moaned, and the smell of human suffering oozed from the walls. The scent was unique to a place that saw the body in all stages of decay and trauma but was kept sanitary by antiseptic soaps and cleaning solutions. Trina hated it.

Lori squeezed Trina's hand. "She looks really bad. Try not to react with her watching."

The nurse led them into Avery's room and pulled back the curtain.

Trina bit her lip to keep from crying out.

Avery's head was completely bandaged, her face covered in gauze with the exception of her eyes, mouth, and chin. All of which were swollen and bruised to the point that Trina wouldn't have recognized Avery if she didn't know it was her. Her right arm was in a splint and her right leg was sitting outside the blanket and elevated on a pillow. It, too, was covered in some kind of wrap.

"Hey . . . ," Lori said softly, and Avery opened her eyes.

Avery licked her lips like it took serious effort to do so.

Trina stood at the end of the bed, not trusting herself to speak.

Lori took the chair on the side and pulled it closer to the bed.

"W-what happened?" Avery asked.

Lori looked at the nurse.

"You don't remember?"

Avery moaned.

The nurse spoke up. "She's amnesic to the event. The concussion isn't letting her remember anything you tell her. She'll ask the same questions over and over."

Trina squeezed her hands into fists. "Is that going to go away?"

Reed placed a hand on her shoulder.

"Most of the time it does. It's early. Try not to worry. Just answer her questions."

"Trina?" Avery pulled her drugged gaze toward her.

"Hey, honey."

"Weren't you gone?" Avery asked slowly.

The fact that she remembered gave Trina hope. "Yes, I was."

Avery closed her eyes and asked again, "What happened?"

Lori cleared her throat. "You were mugged in the parking garage."

"I was?"

"Yes."

"I'm in the hospital?" Avery opened her left eye, which seemed to be the less swollen of the two.

"You are."

"Avery, do you remember why you were in New York?" Reed asked.

Her gaze floated over to them again. "Hi, Reed." She moaned. "My head hurts."

Reed shook his head. "You rest and get better."

They all stood there staring for five minutes. Avery opened her eyes again. "What happened?"

❦

Wade stood when Trina and her friends returned.

Trina had lost a year off her life in the span of ten minutes. She was white as a sheet and holding back the pain that screamed through her eyes.

Wade opened his arms and she fell into them.

"She doesn't remember anything. I'm not sure she will by morning either," Reed told him.

"If ever," Lori said.

"Might be for the best," Jeb said.

Trina lifted her head from Wade's shoulder and turned around. "We were keeping a list of contacts on a spreadsheet at the house. She would have written down who she was seeing and where. I should go and get it so we can make calls when everyone opens in the morning."

Reed nodded. "Good idea, only I'll go. You stay here for Avery."

"You shouldn't go alone," Lori told him. "We've been up for hours. It's a long drive."

"I'll be fine."

Lori's stare said *Don't argue.*

"I'll go with you," Wade said. He glanced over his shoulder. "I'm drawing a little attention." He'd noticed the stealth selfie followed by two more people that arrived and didn't stop staring.

"Okay, but someone needs to stay with the girls."

"Oh, please," Lori said.

"Not negotiable, Lori. If this wasn't random . . ."

Lori stopped smiling.

"I'll stay," Jeb offered.

Reed sized Jeb up and down. "Okay." He turned back to Trina. "Where exactly was this spreadsheet?"

෴

"Do you really think Avery was targeted?" Wade asked once they were alone in the rental car.

"I hope I'm wrong about that."

Wade watched the lights of the opposing cars as they drove by. "According to Trina, Avery's the flirty, fun girl. In my experience, the only people that have a hard time with that are other women, and only if a man is involved."

"Avery probably has many of those enemies, but I doubt a woman did that to her." Reed concentrated on the road.

"How bad is she?"

"Broken wrist due to a size twelve kicking her. It appears that she tried to block multiple blows to her face. She didn't do a good job, however, as evidenced by the broken nose that they will operate on later, when she's stable. Sprained ankle from the fall, maybe. The hit to the head left her out of it for hours, and whether the hits to her face continued after she was out, or before, we won't know unless she tells us. For Avery's sake, I hope she never remembers it."

Wade noticed Reed's knuckles turning white on the steering wheel. "Who does that to a woman?"

"I don't know. But I will find out."

"I'm glad we left Jeb behind."

"Me too."

They drove in silence for several miles.

Reed glanced over with a slight smile. The only one Wade had seen on the man since they met. "You're Wade Thomas."

"Yes sirree."

"I saw you in concert in Vegas a couple years ago."

That surprised him. "At Caesars?"

"Yup. That was a fun night."

"I'm glad you enjoyed it." Wade had lived with his fame long enough to know how to accept a compliment without getting his ego in his armpits.

"I have a question," Reed started.

"Shoot." Wade leaned his head back, thankful he wasn't driving. The day had wiped him out.

"I've always wanted to know if the band makes money on the concessions."

Wade smiled. "Yeah. We do."

Reed nodded a couple of times. "Well, then . . . you owe me a beer."

It felt good to laugh. "You got it."

Chapter Nineteen

According to the navigation, they were fifteen minutes out from the house Trina had shared with her late husband. The closer they were, the stranger Wade felt about being there. How odd was it for him to be going there at all?

"Did you know Trina's husband?"

"No. I met the women after his death."

"The women?"

"Yeah, Lori, Trina, Avery . . . have you met Shannon?"

"Tall, thin, brunette?"

"Yup, that's her. No. I never met Fedor. I haven't formally met Fedor's father either."

"Why would you?"

Reed stole a glance, then turned back to the road. "Trina hasn't told you about Ruslan?"

"If that's the father-in-law, then no. Should she have?"

Reed shrugged. "You guys just started dating, right?"

"Yeah."

"Then no. I guess she didn't see the need."

"Is there an issue with Ruslan?"

"Not lately."

Wade turned in his seat. "Are you trying to be cryptic? If so, you're really good at it."

"None of it is for me to tell." Apparently that was all Reed was going to say on the subject.

He pulled off the main road and into a neighborhood of big yards and even larger houses. Reed drove up to a gate and put in the code.

The two-story house was dark, as any house should be at two in the morning. Even the porch light wasn't glowing. They both stepped out of the car at the same time and walked up the steps together. Reed used Trina's key to let them in.

Wade searched for the hallway light switch that every home seemed to have and turned it on.

The foyer looked as if the occupants were moving. Things were taken off the walls and placed in piles, and the two tables that Wade could see were home to unsealed boxes. Wade moved to close the door and Reed stopped him.

"What is it?"

Reed looked as if he were listening to the silence. "The alarm isn't set."

He walked to what looked like a home alarm system and looked but didn't touch it.

"Maybe Avery forgot."

"No, you heard Trina, they were both concerned about the contents of the house and had been setting the alarm, even when they were home at night."

Reed reached into his jacket and came out with a handgun.

"Whoa . . . I thought you said you were a retired cop."

He put a finger to his lips and shut Wade up. "Stay close," he said in a whisper.

Holy shit. This was far outside of his spectrum. Wade had shot a gun or two in his time, but mainly shotguns on his property. Handguns were home to men like Jeb, not Wade.

Wade followed Reed through the house and kept an eye behind them as they moved room by room. They swept the house and came up empty. Once Reed holstered his gun, Wade took a deep breath.

"Maybe Avery was in a hurry," Wade suggested.

Reed didn't look convinced.

Wade looked on the counter in the kitchen, where Trina said he'd find the spreadsheet.

It wasn't there.

Reed opened drawers until he found the one that held all the crap a junk drawer housed but that didn't belong in a kitchen. He shuffled through the pens and papers before slamming it shut.

"Should we call Trina?" Wade asked.

"No, Avery might have moved it. Let's keep searching."

They did, and nothing.

"Didn't Trina say something about a back office?"

Reed looked around and started toward the back door of the house. He switched on a light, and they both walked in the late night air to what looked like a smaller version of the house on the other side of the yard.

Reed stopped Wade midstride with a hand to his chest.

The door to the office was open an inch.

Reed crouched down, and Wade followed his behavior. With a lift of his hand, Reed told him to stay back.

Reed took a deep breath, paused, and kicked open the door before hiding back behind the exterior of the office.

Silence.

He started low and swung back into the room.

Nothing.

He turned on a light and Wade risked a look.

"Oh, shit."

Wade stood there and stared while Reed moved through the room, careful not to touch anything. He kicked open a door, ducked in, came back out. Then he put his gun away.

Everything was completely askew. From the desk to the chairs, the lamps. Papers were everywhere, pictures were off the walls and lying on the floor.

"Don't touch anything," Reed said as he reached for his cell phone.

Wade had seen this in a movie but never in real life. To say he was spooked was an understatement.

"Hey, Neil. Yeah, I know what time it is. Someone ransacked Fedor's office. No, I called you first . . . because nothing in the house was touched, just the office." Reed walked over to a crooked painting on the wall, and using his jacket instead of his fingertips, he moved it aside. There was a safe behind the picture. Reed tapped on it with the same covered finger. "No. It appears they were looking for something. We'll have to wait for Trina to get here to see if anything is missing. But the safe hasn't been opened. Check with the guys and find out if the alarm was ever set this morning, and if it was, when it was disengaged. Got it. Yeah, I'll call it in now."

Reed stepped around the mess and back out the door.

"This isn't good."

Reed dialed 911 on his phone. "The one thing I doubt even more than random acts of violence, it's any kind of coincidence." He turned away to talk to the operator while Wade stared at the quiet of the turbulent night.

⟋♙

Trina hated to leave the hospital, but Avery's parents had arrived, so at least she knew there was someone there every time she opened her eyes.

Jeb was a machine. The man hadn't slept at all, and he was the one driving them to the Hamptons house in the early morning light.

When Reed had called to say the office was vandalized, Trina knew, in her heart, that somehow the dots connected to Avery. As the night had worn on, it seemed Avery was a little more aware of where she was and had grasped why she was in the hospital. But there was still no memory of what had happened.

Trina closed her eyes for only a minute when they pulled out of the hospital parking lot, and the next thing she knew someone was waking her up.

Startled, she assessed where she was.

Jeb had pulled into the driveway, along with what appeared to be half of the Suffolk County police force.

"We're here," Lori said from the back seat.

"This is my house," Trina told the uniformed policeman who attempted to stop them at the door. "Bodyguard." She pointed toward Jeb. "Attorney." She moved her thumb in Lori's direction.

The officer stepped aside.

Wade and Reed were in the kitchen, along with two plainclothes police officers. Both of them wore badges attached to their belts.

Wade noticed her about the same time that Reed noticed Lori. They both stood and met them halfway.

"How is she?" Wade asked once Trina was in his arms.

"Tiny improvement. They said they were going to do another scan of her head this morning to make sure there weren't any changes overnight."

"Did you get any rest?" Reed asked Lori.

"In the car, you?"

He shook his head.

Trina turned to Jeb. "Jeb, there are plenty of guest rooms upstairs. Please make yourself comfortable. Get some sleep."

Jeb looked at Wade.

"We're good."

"I'll only need a couple hours."

"Mrs. Petrov?" One of the officers interrupted them.

She winced, no longer wanting to use the name. "Yes."

"I'm Detective Armstrong and this is Detective Gray."

"Good morning," she said on autopilot. She glanced around the kitchen. "I should make coffee. Anyone need coffee?"

Lori led Trina to a chair. "I'll get the coffee, you talk to these men." Then the questions started.

When was the last time she was in the house? Who had keys and who knew the security code to turn off the alarm system? Because the alarm was monitored by the company Reed worked for, he'd already told the police that it appeared that Avery did set the alarm when she left the day before, and sometime around two, the alarm was disengaged. The cameras on the front gate and front door didn't show anyone coming or going.

Lori pushed a cup of coffee in front of Trina.

"Thank you."

Wade rubbed the back of her neck as she answered questions. The touch did two things, it soothed the ache, but more than that, it filled her soul. The poor man picked the wrong woman up in a bar, and now he was sitting in her Hamptons dungeon instead of sleeping off what should have been a decent buzz from the night before. She apologized to him with her eyes and hoped he understood.

"As you may already know, we don't think anything was taken from the office, but you'll have to confirm that."

She closed her eyes, saw Fedor's lifeless body in her head. Trina took a drink of the coffee. "I doubt I can tell if anything is missing. I didn't go in there a lot, and it's been a year."

"Can you try? It will help quite a bit."

"Of course."

Wade rubbed her shoulders.

She held the cup with both hands, surprised at how cold they felt. "Is this related to what happened to Avery?"

There was silence in the room.

She closed her eyes and shook her head. "How? Why?"

Reed filled in the blanks.

"Your text from Avery came in at one thirty-five. The alarm here was deactivated at two, almost on the nose."

"You can't get from the city to here in twenty-five minutes."

"Right. Avery was on her way back here."

"How could anyone know that other than me? She sent the text to me, and I didn't even see it until after all this had happened."

"It could be any number of things. She told someone she was on her way home, maybe her phone was bugged. We might never know, since it was destroyed after a car ran over it in the garage. The working theory is someone wanted to keep her from coming home too early."

"They could have killed her . . . and for what?" Trina almost yelled her question.

"Has anyone ever threatened you, Mrs. Petrov? Anyone that comes to mind that is capable of this?"

She shook her head. "No."

"That's not true," Lori said in a quiet voice.

Everyone in the room turned at the same time.

"Ruslan," Lori said, looking directly at Armstrong. "Fedor's father stood in the front door of this house and threatened to get back at Trina for the death of his son. There were half a dozen witnesses."

"Not to mention him threatening you," Reed reminded them.

"What?" Wade asked.

"Ruslan blamed the women in Fedor's life for 'ruining him.'" Lori made air quotes when she spoke. "He's a big, scary man, but he hires people to do his dirty work. I'd be shocked if you found anything you can pin on him, including a traffic violation."

"This is your father-in-law?" Wade asked Trina.

"There was no love between Fedor and his dad. The two never spoke," Trina told him.

"That gives us something to go on," Armstrong said.

"Let's find out if anything is missing from the office. Forensics will be here in a couple of hours to start dusting for prints."

Trina pulled herself out of the chair and turned toward the door. God, she was tired.

The backyard buzzed with officers, most of whom stopped and moved aside when they walked by.

Her legs started to shake.

Wade stopped her. "You okay?"

She closed her eyes, opened them. "The last time I was in that office was when we found him."

"You don't have to do this." He looked at the police officers. "She doesn't have to do this."

Trina placed a hand on his arm. "I'm okay."

"You're shaking."

"Yeah, I am. But I'll survive."

Wade kept an arm around her waist when she continued walking.

She took the final steps through the door and cringed. It would have been harder to see the office in its normal state and imagine exactly how she'd seen Fedor. This way, with the desk sitting in the wrong place and the chairs in places they never were . . . it was easier, somehow.

Wade squeezed her shoulder.

"I'm okay." Yet as she said those words, she saw the wall behind the desk and remembered the blood splatter.

She swallowed hard.

"Can you tell if anything is missing?" Detective Gray asked.

"I wasn't in here very often. Uhm. His desk. A chair, only I think the original chair was removed with him. The wall was painted . . . after." It had been a lighter color, the whole room. But that wasn't what they were asking. "He liked pens, there was an old inkwell set on his desk." Not that they could see it under all the clutter. "I don't know if it was here after they cleaned up the room."

"Do you have a cleaning lady?"

"Yeah, Cindy . . ." Trina looked at Lori. "You remember her?"

"I do."

"She comes twice a month. She'd probably know if anything was missing more than I would."

Detective Armstrong wrote something down. "We'll need her number."

"It's in the house. I've been trying to get ahold of her the past few days, but she hasn't returned my calls."

The detectives exchanged glances. Armstrong wrote a note in his small pad of paper.

Detective Gray pointed to the safe behind the tilted painting on the wall. "Do you have the key?"

"No. I didn't have any of the safe combinations or keys."

"Really? That's odd."

She shook her head. "Not necessarily. We'd only been married for a year. I didn't see the need for that kind of thing."

The detectives were silent. "Your husband was a wealthy man."

"He was. He had everything to live for, it made no sense for him to kill himself."

"So why do you think he did it?" Armstrong asked.

Lori interrupted Trina before she could answer.

"The investigation that followed Fedor's death determined that he was distraught over his mother's impending death. They were very close. She passed shortly after Fedor's funeral."

While all that was true, Trina felt the hair on the back of her neck stand on end when Lori delivered the information in her lawyer voice.

Armstrong scribbled in his notebook.

"Gentlemen. If that's all, I think it would be good for all of us to get some rest. We've been up for over twenty-four hours." Lori cut everything off.

The officers exchanged looks.

Trina was too tired to figure out what had gotten up Lori's butt.

"You're Wade Thomas," Detective Gray said as if he was just figuring it out.

"Yeah, we talked about this a few hours ago," Wade said.

Trina looked up at Wade, then back to the officer talking.

"So you two are . . . dating?" he asked.

Wade opened his mouth and Lori stepped in front of him.

"Are you a fan, Detective?" Lori asked.

Gray tilted his head. "No. I'm more of a Guns N' Roses guy. I just, ah . . . I don't know. The man who owned all this is dead for only a year." His eyes traveled to Trina.

"Okay, that's enough!" Lori pushed Trina and Wade out of the room.

"You're out of line." Wade pointed two fingers at the detective.

Reed moved to stand beside Lori.

"Okay, everyone, relax. We're just doing our job." Gray looked at Reed. "You of all people should know that."

"Yeah, I do. If you're thinking what I think you're thinking . . . you're digging in the wrong hole."

Trina's head spun while she tried to catch up on the hidden conversation running all around her.

"We're going to go upstairs and get some sleep. If you gentlemen have any more questions, you make sure and wake both of us." Lori pointed between herself and Trina.

Gray started to grin . . . and not the kind of grin that made you smile, but the kind that made you worry. "You're a lawyer."

"Very perceptive, Officer. And he's a famous singer," she said, pointing to Wade. "And he's an ex-detective, and before the end of the day, you might meet the former first lady of California and a duke. Friends in this circle are seldom the gardener."

Detective Gray stepped back. "Yes, ma'am."

They were several feet away when Trina turned to Lori. "What the hell was that all about?"

"They were questioning you like a suspect," Reed answered for Lori.

"What? Me? Why?" She started to turn around.

Wade redirected her toward the house. "Another time, darlin'. You need to sleep."

Within half an hour, Trina sat curled in her bed, with Lori sitting beside her.

"I'm not guilty of anything, Lori."

"I know that."

"Other than not loving my husband."

"I know that, too. But keep that to yourself, Trina. It will only raise suspicion."

"This is all so wrong. Everything about this is just wrong," she cried.

Lori patted her knee. "Get some sleep, even a few hours will clear your head."

"We should be at the hospital." Yet even as Trina said those words, she knew if she didn't get a few hours of horizontal time, she'd only make herself sick.

Lori grasped Trina's hands.

"What room did Wade take?"

"Across the hall. He left his door open, so if you need anything . . ."

"This is so unfair to him. We barely know each other."

Lori smiled. "Maybe, but he doesn't seem to be itching to leave. Which says a lot about his character."

"I told you he was a good guy."

Lori patted her hand. "Get some sleep."

She didn't have to be told twice. Lori left the room, and her head hit the pillow and she was gone.

Nightmares startled her awake almost as quickly as she'd fallen asleep.

Her door shot open and Wade crossed the room in a pair of boxer shorts.

"What was that?" She looked around the room, expecting to see that something had crashed to the floor.

"It was you," Wade said while he sat on the edge of the bed.

"How long have I been asleep?"

"Not long enough, hon." He brushed her hair from her eyes and smiled.

"I'm sorry about all this . . . you don't deserve—"

"Shh, stop, stop." He crawled on top of the covers and pulled her head to his chest. "Go back to sleep."

"This is all wrong."

He stroked the side of her hair, and the heaviness of her eyes pulled her under.

"Shh, I'm right here. It's okay."

Chapter Twenty

Wade booked several suites at the closest hotel to the hospital where Avery was recuperating. He'd called Ike and asked him to pack a bag and get it to the hotel as soon as a plane could fly it out. While Trina was at Avery's bedside, Wade took a moment and called his mother so she wouldn't worry.

She was already beside herself.

"You left in the middle of your own party, that isn't like you. I don't like what this woman is doing to your head."

"Did you miss the part about how her best friend was beaten within an inch of her life and is in the ICU?" It was unlike his mother to be so cold.

"No, I didn't miss that, Wade. And don't take that tone with me. I'm not heartless. I just don't see how any of this is your problem. How long have you known this woman, a couple of weeks?"

Wade was starting to see the end of his rope with the conversation, and they had only been talking for five minutes. "Someone I know very well once told me to follow my gut when I was hungry and my heart when someone made me smile. Well, Trina makes me smile."

"I didn't say that, I said follow your gut when it came to women and leave the heart out of it, that organ only gets you into trouble." Ahh, there his mother was.

He chuckled. "Spoken like a scorned woman."

"Your father left for cigarettes and never came back."

"I've heard the story. I even wrote a song about it."

Vicki sighed. "I worry."

"I'm fine."

"Women have always wanted to get at your money."

He switched his cell phone to his other hand and turned away from a group of people that were walking out of the elevator. "I promise you, Trina isn't like that."

"Oh, and who paid for the emergency flight to New York?"

His mother was trying hard to find fault. "Neither one of us. She knows someone with a private jet."

"Oh, that's right . . . she's a flight attendant."

He didn't see this conversation ending until he gave his mother enough to nibble on.

"You know how much I hate it when people name-drop to get what they want?"

"W-what? Yes, and what does that have to do with this conversation?" she stuttered.

"Everson Oil, Mama. Trina is worth more than I am. She isn't using me. We met, we're both attracted and would like to see where this goes. There is nothing for you to worry about, so I'm going to ask that you end this entire conversation."

The line was silent.

"Mom?"

"Fine."

When a woman said *fine*, it was never fine. "I love you for your concern. Hold down the ranch a little longer without me."

"If I must."

Wade wanted to laugh. "Bye, Mother."

"You know I hate it when you call me *Mother*."

He chuckled. "Well, stop acting like a mother and more like my mama."

"You always were ornery when you had your mind set on something."

"Yeah, remind you of someone you know?"

"Wade Michael Thomas!"

Ohhh, the middle name.

Wade laughed.

"Bye, Mama."

She backed down. "Love you."

"Love you, too."

The waiting room had started to fill with nearly a dozen of Avery's friends and family. Trina was back in the unit with Avery's parents for the brief visit until they were all kicked out again. Wade poured himself his fifth cup of coffee for the day and was walking back toward his seat next to Lori when a short, balding, middle-aged man nearly knocked him over to get to Lori. Coffee splashed on his hand.

"Oh my God, how is she?"

"Bernie . . . what are you doing here?" Lori stood when the man approached.

"I got here as fast as I could. Is she okay? What happened?"

Lori glanced around before she encouraged the man to walk beside her as they left the waiting room.

Wade watched them disappear before taking his seat next to Shannon.

"Who is that?" Wade asked.

"That's Bernie . . . Avery's ex-husband."

Wade choked on the coffee he'd just placed in his mouth. Full-on spat the coffee onto his shirt like he didn't understand the concept of swallowing hot liquid.

"W-what?"

Shannon pulled a tissue from her purse and handed it to him. "Yeah, not shocking it didn't work out."

Bernie looked more like an older uncle, a father . . . maybe a brother from a different marriage. But Avery's husband? Oh, hell no.

The man was talking in hushed whispers to Lori across the room, but his eyes kept gravitating toward the door to the ICU. The man was clearly concerned. "Let me see what I can do," Wade heard Lori say.

Lori offered a polite smile when she picked up the phone to the nursing station inside the locked unit. Within a few minutes, Avery's parents, a pretentious couple if Wade ever met one, stepped out.

"We knew you'd come," Avery's mother said as she grasped Bernie's hands.

"I'd like to have some time alone with her," Bernie told them.

"Of course, of course." They stepped aside.

Wade expected Trina to funnel out once Bernie walked in, but she must have stayed behind.

Wade stood and offered Mrs. Grant his seat.

She took it. "He's such a good man. I don't know why they ever split up."

Lori offered a polite smile.

Shannon's smile was just as plastic.

All Wade could think was . . . *how on God's green earth did they ever get together in the first place?*

Reed walked back into the waiting room after taking a phone call and returned with a man approximately the size of a small house. He smiled, scanned the room, and then narrowed his eyes on Wade.

Because House Man was with Reed, Wade offered a nod as if to say, *Yeah, I'm him.*

Then the strangest thing happened. The man nodded and was like, *Cool.*

That was it.

For what felt like the hundredth time since this whole ordeal had started, Wade enjoyed the fact that the people in Trina's inner circle were not influenced by fame. Outside of acknowledging who he was, they didn't do the starstruck thing that so many others did.

He liked that.

Reed waved Wade and Jeb over to an empty corner of the waiting room.

Reed pointed to his friend. "This is Rick. Rick, Wade. Jeb is his bodyguard," he said.

"And friend," Wade made clear.

"Of course." Reed leaned in, lowered his voice. "Just making sure he knows who is carrying."

Which meant Rick was.

Wow, again with the armed response.

"Let's take this outside in the hall."

Wade followed Reed's gaze to find the same family that had been eyeing him all night, snickering as they watched them.

"Good idea."

They were two steps into the hall when Reed launched into his monologue. "So here's the plan. Someone is on Avery at all times. I'm arranging it with the hospital that one of us is in the room with her regardless of their stupid rules. Someone is with Trina like a shadow. Easy with you here"—he pointed to Wade—"but one of us three will be a breath behind you. We have reinforcements coming in to allow for rest. With the exception of you, Wade. We expect you to be on Trina like white on rice, and if that's a problem, you need to tell us now."

White on Trina's rice had a very nice ring to it. "Not a problem," he started with. "Mind telling me why this is necessary?"

Reed looked at his friend, his expression shifting from *I'm on a mission* to *This part sucks*.

"Forensics didn't find *any* prints in the office."

Wade felt a little lost. "Okay?"

"As in *any*. Not one. Not Avery's, not Trina's, not Fedor's . . . not the maid. None!"

"Oh, hell," Jeb said.

"Exactly," Rick said to Jeb.

"I sing songs for a living, mind helping me catch up here?" Because it seemed the three of them were talking in a different language.

"Have you ever heard of the term 'a cleaner,' Wade? That would be someone hired to come in and clean up a murder scene and not leave a trace. They miss nothing. Nothing! So when something looks like a burglary and ends up without a single print . . . that means there's something big at play," Rick explained.

"Whoever ransacked the office at Trina's house wasn't there to take anything, they were there to clean up," Reed added.

"Clean up what?"

"Only one person died in that house," Rick said. "And it's been closed up ever since. Now two women come in, they start shuffling through things, next thing you know one of them is in the hospital and the house is broken into. There is no way of knowing if whoever did this found what they wanted and are gone, or if they'll be back. Until we know who hired the cleaners, we have to assume the two women shaking up the dust need protection."

"You believe someone murdered Trina's late husband," Jeb concluded.

That was the moment that Wade caught up. "Trina said it was suicide."

"Which is how it looked," Reed said.

"Does Trina know this?"

Reed and Rick exchanged glances. "Not yet."

Trina had never seen Bernie in person. He was even shorter in real life.

Yet the lack of height was made up for by the dread-filled concern in his eyes. "Oh, dear lord, no. Who did this to you?" he asked the second he entered the room.

Avery had opened her eyes for a short time while her parents were there and then closed them after a few seconds. "What are you doing here, Bernie?" she asked slowly.

"Oh, thank God you're talking. Oh, darling."

Bernie sat on the edge of the seat Avery's mother had just vacated; his hand moved to grasp Avery's and ended up resting on top of the exposed skin of her upper arm.

"Who did this to you? Tell me and I'll put a hit out on them."

For the first time since Trina had walked into the hospital, a smile started to peek out from under the bandages covering Avery's face. "You won't kill spiders." A slight chuckle came from her and resulted in a cough that brought a grimace.

Trina brought a cup of water with a straw to Avery's lips.

Bernie's worried eyes met Trina's.

Avery finally opened both eyes and tried to smile a second time. "Who told you I was here?"

"Adeline called me."

"My mother should have left you alone."

"For once I'm grateful for her meddling. Oh, Avery . . ." He said her name with a sigh. "I know you're not mine anymore, but I do still love you."

Bernie glanced at Trina before focusing on Avery.

"Bernie . . . Trina knows. You don't have to pretend."

Trina felt her heart skip a beat. "The nurse just gave her more pain medication. I think it's working," Trina told Bernie in hopes that he wouldn't question what she knew and didn't know.

"Oh, please, Trina."

"No matter," Bernie said. "I care, and I'm here if you need anything."

Avery's eyes started to close and stay that way. "I'm okay."

Bernie huffed in disbelief. Before he could say another word, Avery's mouth slacked open and her breathing evened out as she fell fast asleep.

Trina nodded toward the door and encouraged Bernie to follow. He did, but not before he kissed Avery's exposed cheek.

Once they walked out of the room, Trina reached her hand out to shake his. "I'm Trina."

"Bernie, Avery's ex-husband."

"It was sweet of you to stop by."

He shifted from foot to foot. "I'm not sure what she told you about me, but—"

Trina interrupted him. "That you were both hasty in getting married and realized a long-lasting romantic love wasn't going to work."

Bernie looked relieved. "I would imagine that bump to her head has her saying strange things," he offered.

"Nothing I haven't expected."

Bernie paused and nodded. "It's probably best not to leave her alone with her parents until she's less . . . medicated."

"I agree," Trina said. "Lori and I are taking turns."

With those final words, Bernie's understanding seemed to come into focus. Alliance had a strict code of silence, but their unstated conversation became perfectly clear to both of them.

He reached for Trina's hands and squeezed them. "I do care deeply for her. Please keep me informed."

"I will."

Trina watched Bernie's back as he walked out of the ICU. When the door opened, she saw one of the detectives from the previous night standing in the doorway.

The hair on her neck stood up. There wasn't any way of knowing what Avery would say to the police in her drugged state. If word got out about Avery's fake marriage to Bernie, and someone followed that bouncing ball, it stood to reason that the police would question her about Fedor.

She turned to Doug, the nurse who had been taking care of Avery since the early morning hours. "Excuse me."

Doug looked up from the chart he was working on.

"I'm going to step out for a while." She glanced behind her at the approaching detectives. "She's really tired and could take a break from visitors," she told the nurse.

Doug stood. "I'll check on her."

Trina headed Detective Gray off. "Good afternoon, gentlemen."

"Mrs. Petrov."

"We'd like a few words with Ms. Grant."

"She's exhausted."

Armstrong looked over his shoulder toward the closed door to the ICU. "It appears she's had plenty of visitors today."

Maybe it was luck, or perhaps Doug caught on to Trina's need, but the nurse left Avery's room and stopped the men from entering.

"Trina?" Doug approached. "She's finally sleeping. I'm going to ask that everyone leave her alone for a few hours."

Gray removed a badge from his back pocket. "I'm Detective Gray, this is Detective Armstrong, we only have a few questions for Ms. Grant."

"Those will have to wait."

"We'll be back later, then," Armstrong said.

"I would suggest you call before returning. The neurologist has ordered a few tests . . ."

"We'll wait."

Doug stepped closer, lowered his voice. "How about tomorrow? Her family and friends visiting to tell her she's loved is helpful. Questions about what put her here are traumatic at this stage."

The detectives exchanged glances. "We'll be back."

Trina sighed her relief when they left. "Thank you, Doug."

"Nothing I said wasn't true."

"I'll step out for a while."

He stopped her. "I heard Wade Thomas was with all of you."

"He is."

Doug tilted his head. "I'm a huge fan."

"I'll be sure and drag him back the next time Avery wakes up to say hello."

"Really? That would be epic."

If Wade's name could keep the police away until Avery was alert, Trina would use it.

Chapter Twenty-One

"White on rice," Wade said as if he was in the middle of a conversation instead of walking Trina outside the hospital doors and onto the wet streets of Manhattan.

"Excuse me?"

He draped his arm over her shoulders and tucked her close to his side. "I've never played bodyguard before. I think I'm going to like it." He'd heard Reed bring Trina up to date on the lack of fingerprints found in the office. She seemed less concerned with that than everyone else involved.

"What does role-playing a bodyguard have to do with rice?"

He chuckled and leaned close to her ear. "Your bulky friends said I needed to be white on rice with you. I like potatoes more than rice, but I'll give it a shot," he teased.

They walked toward the hotel.

Trina stiffened and slowed her pace. "I'm sorry you've been dragged into all this. Please don't feel obligated to—"

"Oh, no . . . don't start that. I don't feel obligated, nor do I have some kind of hero complex that you're scratching. I might not prefer how we are spending time together, but I thoroughly enjoy the company and wouldn't dream of leaving."

"You have a love for hospital waiting rooms?"

A crowd of people huddled around them as they waited for traffic to clear to cross the street.

"I have a deep regard for right over wrong and being a friend in more than a Christmas card fashion."

They joined the masses and jaywalked to the other side of the street.

"If you need to get home, I completely understand."

He stopped in the middle of the sidewalk, causing a dam for the people rushing by. Wade pulled her to the side of a building and stood in front of her.

"Okay, darlin'. I'm going to say this once." He placed both hands on the sides of her face and stared her in the eye.

She opened her mouth, and he brought one finger over her lips to stop her. "Nobody needs me at home more than you need me here. I'm taking the charge of white on rice and I don't plan on leaving until the police find out what's going on. If they don't, then I'll just have to follow you back to Texas, where it appears you belong. So no more guilt about keeping me here or dragging me into anything. Got it?"

Trina tried to smile. "You're pretty demanding," she said quietly.

"Oh, darlin', I'm one hundred percent demanding, which is probably why I'm still single. I'm also determined to get that half-empty look out of your eyes and replace it with sparkling lights."

There her smile was. Seeing it warmed his heart.

"Now we're talkin'."

"Are you always this charming?"

He shook his head. "No. I saved it for you."

Trina snickered. "That's a line," she called him out.

"Guilty. But this time I mean it."

She narrowed her eyes.

He brushed his thumb over her jaw and gave in to the desire to kiss her.

The more often he brushed his lips against hers, the more he wanted to make her his next addiction. Even the busy streets of New York City couldn't keep his heartbeat out of his head as he tasted her.

When she opened her lips, he ended their public display and promised to deepen that kiss as soon as they were alone.

"Hey, Wade!"

The sound of someone calling him from several feet away, followed by a flash of lights, ruined the disco ball spinning in his head.

Sure enough, the paparazzi had found him. Instead of causing a scene, Wade pulled Trina alongside him and started toward the hotel.

"Who's your friend?" The flash of a camera followed the stranger's question.

People started turning to watch.

The man backed into people as he moved in front of them to get the image he wanted.

New Yorkers weren't all that friendly when being plowed into by a distracted pedestrian.

Wade tried moving around the man. "We're in a hurry. If you don't mind."

"Just one smile," he asked, the camera up to his eye.

Wade didn't oblige. Instead he pushed around the man, careful not to touch him, and doubled his pace to get away.

Trina kept up as if she'd done the paparazzi dance before.

When they approached the hotel, the man at the door sensed their plight, opened the door, and then cut off Mr. Camera Happy.

Wade took a deep breath when the elevator doors closed.

Trina twisted to stand in front of him, placed her hands on his chest, and pushed him against the wall. Without words, she pressed her body against his and demanded his lips.

It took him two seconds to catch on before his eyes closed and his body gave in to hers. Her lips were open, hungry, and not like any kiss he'd had from her before. He hardened in an instant.

The elevator dinged loud enough for Wade to put a tiny distance between the two of them when the doors opened.

A couple with a teenage son stepped onto the elevator, eyeing them. It had to be obvious what they'd interrupted. It was to Wade, in any event. Trina diverted her gaze from the other couple, her chest heaving as she sucked in silent breaths.

The kid watched them as the elevator made its way up. The parents looked away in silence.

Trina licked her lips.

Wade felt the need to wipe his.

The door opened on the floor of the hotel's view restaurant and let the family out.

It was Wade's turn to twist Trina into the wall of the elevator.

Her hands were in his hair, her body molded to his, their lips fused together.

This time, when the elevator announced an arrival to a floor, Wade glanced up to see the penthouse suites level. Instead of breaking her off, he lifted her up and encouraged her legs to wrap around his waist.

He felt her purse slip from her shoulder and catch on her arm as he walked her to the door of their room. Trina's teeth caught on his neck like a vampire searching for fuel. He pressed her against the door, probably too hard, but she didn't stop.

Wade found his wallet and slid the electronic key from behind his credit card. It took two swipes for the door to unlock. Once behind the private door, he dropped his wallet, she dropped her purse, and he filled his palms with her ass as he carried her to the bedroom.

His mind focused briefly, wanting to ask if she was sure of this moment, but her teeth grazed against the lobe of his ear as she moaned.

The bed caught his knees. Wade controlled his fall on top of her as the bed cradled her back. The stability offered Trina the ability to push her hips into his. God help him, he saw bright sparks of pixie dust at the thought of sliding into her. The warmth inside his belly reminded him of his teenage years and the inability to control his body.

Ice.

Cold.

Aunt Mavis.

Jesus, he needed to get this together.

He sucked in a breath and slowed everything down.

Trina sighed with him; her fingernails ran up his back and tugged at his shirt.

Wade captured her lips and tasted the mint of her morning tooth-paste before he let them go. She lifted her chin, and he kissed her neck until her shirt stopped him.

The smooth texture of her waist was warm against his palm as he inched higher. He was about to ask if she wanted this when she leaned forward and helped him remove her shirt.

She wore a plain white bra, her olive skin a stunning contrast he could sample forever.

"Sorry," she muttered. "I wasn't planning . . ."

He kissed the top of one breast, silencing her protest; his thumb traced the edges of her bra.

"Oh, God."

Her head fell back.

He was kissing her, caressing her, and already she was lost . . . he felt like the God she was calling out to and wanted desperately to deliver everything she needed . . . wanted.

Wade pushed her nipple from her bra and pulled it between his teeth until the hardness resembled a large nut.

"Wade," she called and her hips jolted.

Ice.

Winter.

Texas was hot in the winter.

Her hands found his ass and squeezed.

The moisture at the top of his cock told him to slow down.

Wade captured her hands and pulled them above her head, holding them there. "Stay," he demanded.

His eyes met the golden depths of hers. "Please," he added.

Her hips surged, but her hands stayed.

Wade used his lips and tongue to trail a way to her pleasure.

She was wearing cotton pants that slid off easily when she lifted her hips. Wade tossed them to the floor, along with his shirt, as he kicked off the sneakers he didn't normally wear. He was never so happy to not be fighting with a pair of tight boots when he returned his tongue and lips to Trina's hip.

"Sorry," Trina said, her hips reacting to his touch.

"You have nothing to be sorry about." He could sense her need as his own.

"Granny panties. I didn't think . . ."

Wade wanted to laugh, didn't dare. Plain white, nothing special, yet everything he could ever want. "Hello, Nana."

Trina chuckled and relaxed once he shifted her undies aside and said hello with his tongue.

He liked this part, and yet seldom had the opportunity to linger for long . . . until now. She tasted like honey. As much as he knew that was a metaphor, he couldn't help but think it was true. Trina opened to him, her back arched, her foot pressed into his spine as he searched for the part of her that drove the sadness from her eyes. When he found it, he worked it, ignoring his own body until long after her nails left marks, and her honey changed and tasted like sangria. She pulled his hair, forcing him away.

Even as she caught her breath, her hand searched him out.

"Please," she breathed. "It's been too long."

Artic.

Ice.

Her hand cupped him through his jeans.

It took two seconds to kick them off and feel her beautiful fingers taking in the length of him.

She chuckled. "Do they grow everything big in Texas?"

He used her laughter to slow things down as he buried his head in her shoulder. "That's a line."

"Guilty," she said as she bucked her hips and rolled him onto his back.

The levity was his short reprieve before he felt her hair cascade against his thigh.

He was smiling, confident, and then the warmth of her mouth covered him, and Wade's eyes rolled to the back of his head.

Yes . . .

He was going to lose it . . .

Ice.

Aunt freakin' Mavis has a really warm . . . oh, God.

He pushed her away. "Not yet."

Trina chuckled as she crawled up his frame and straddled her hips with his.

"Wade?"

He opened his eyes.

The heat of her hovered over the length of him.

"I have an IUD. I'm clean since—"

He broke off her words with his lips.

Wade pushed her away when she started to melt. "I have a condom in my wallet."

"Are you not . . . ?"

"I'm good, darlin'. I just don't want you to worry."

Even though the shift in thought dampened the mood, Wade twisted Trina to the side and rolled out of bed.

He grabbed his forgotten jeans off the floor to find them devoid of his wallet before he remembered the fumbling of the room key.

Trina lay sprawled on the bed in the middle of the day, one leg bent in a pose worthy of any skin magazine he'd ever used as a kid, while Wade scrambled from the room to the front of their suite in search of his wallet.

He half expected her to be asleep when he returned.

Instead, she sat up on her elbows like a goddess, with her granny panties half on and half off the bed, the sparkle in her eyes.

What a beautiful goddess she was.

Trina's gaze washed him up and down, lingering briefly at his cock. "I want to taste you again."

He twitched and all but jumped into bed.

They were arms and legs . . . lips and tongues, and no sooner did he manage to open the condom and cover the length of him than Trina was pulling him home.

She was tight. *Snowdrifts on the Alps or he was going to explode* tight.

She moaned, long and slow. Then, and only then, did she slow down and let him catch up.

Wade set the pace, his hips and hands . . . lips and tongue, everything moved in slow motion. "I have you," he told her, no longer having to think about Alaska to give this woman what she wanted. All he had to think of was her.

The glory of being the one to make her call his name stroked his ego in ways he hadn't felt before. When she moved faster, her nails digging deep, he kept his own tide back until the gentle squeeze of her pulsated and made him lose control one final time.

They were a heap of hot, sweaty, gasping flesh in the middle of the afternoon.

Wade held her tight and wrapped a free leg around her as he came to rest at her side. He'd like to say he hadn't had so many encounters in his sexual life to compare this one to the next . . . but he'd be lying. This one left him dazed. World-changing and life-altering dazed.

"Wade," Trina said, her breath slow and hot on his chest.

"Yeah, darlin'?"

"Was that—?"

He pulled the comforter over the two of them, felt his body slip from hers. "It sure was, hon."

She snuggled in, and God bless America, Trina fell asleep before he could close his eyes.

Chapter Twenty-Two

The glow of the setting sun spilled through the floor to ceiling windows of the penthouse suite. Trina's eyes fluttered open and reality seeped in. She wasn't alone. Wade slept soundly beside her, his arm was her pillow, her leg draped over his.

She smiled.

The memory of their lovemaking swirled like a hurricane in her head. She'd attacked him, flat-out threw him against the wall, and didn't let up until she was done . . . twice.

God, she felt good. Although she should be embarrassed by her behavior, she couldn't bring herself to care. She'd been reckless, and Wade had been responsible. She would have gladly accepted him into her body without protection, which was stupid when she stopped to think about it now, but he resisted.

What had he said again? Oh, yeah, so she wouldn't worry. And she would have. Wade "Country Star" Thomas had the opportunity to sleep with beautiful women all over the world. While he didn't seem the type to take advantage of that every night, she'd be crazy to think he didn't dip often.

Thanks to him, she wasn't worried. Besides, condomless sex was reserved for exclusive relationships. That wasn't something on the table this early in the dance.

She couldn't expect it of him, even though she knew there wasn't anyone else in her life.

Her stomach rumbled, reminding her that she hadn't eaten since the hospital cafeteria hard-boiled eggs and orange juice. She twisted her head far enough to read the clock. It was closing in on six thirty. They'd slept for three hours.

Room service was a phone call away.

Trina slowly disengaged her leg from Wade's to keep from waking him. Just when she thought she'd managed the hardest part, Wade wrapped the arm she was using for a pillow around her.

"Hmmm," he hummed.

"You're pretending to be asleep."

He shifted to his side, kept his eyes closed as he wrapped a leg over her hips. "I'm still dreaming."

She gave up trying to sneak away.

"Is it a good dream?"

His free hand traced the side of her waist as he spoke. "Action packed with a happy ending."

Trina relaxed her head and stared.

His eyes fluttered open and focused on her. "Hello," he whispered.

"Hi." She smiled.

"I have so many things I wanna say to you right now, but they all sound like lines in my head."

"Are they good lines?"

"Cheesy, giddy lines of *Holy cow, that was beyond the stars and back*."

Her chest rumbled next to his.

"I told you they were cheesy."

She rested her hand on his bare chest and played with the smooth, sculptured skin she found. "We were pretty spectacular."

He kissed the top of her head. "More than spectacular. Monumental. Epic. I think I wrote three new songs while you orgasmed."

"Three?"

"At least."

She liked the sound of that. She trailed her hand down his chest. His eyes widened when he realized where she was going.

"Maybe we can write another three before we get out of bed."

He stopped her hand.

"Darlin', I'm out of condoms. Something I will fix within the hour."

Trina couldn't help but feel disappointed.

"I just came off my tour and I'm not a saint. But as soon as I'm home, I'll have my doctor check everything out, and you can have your way with me anytime you please, latex or not."

Her smile widened. "That sounds awful exclusive, Mr. Thomas."

He traced her jaw, his smile grew more serious. "The desire to even think about another woman hasn't entered my head since we met."

"It hasn't been that long."

"Doesn't matter. I know what I want."

"That's sweet."

"I'm serious."

She lifted her head to stare into his eyes to see if he was. What she saw chilled her. "If what you want changes, you have to tell me. I'll understand—"

He placed a finger over her lips. "I don't want to give you that option, but I know it's too soon. So I'll make that deal. If something changes, I'll be honest, but I want the same from you."

He leaned up on his elbow and dropped his hand to her shoulder.

"I can do that."

Wade sealed their deal with a kiss that didn't go beyond a hand-shake with their lips. When he let her go, she turned to climb out of bed and paused. "What just happened here?" she asked more to herself than to him.

"You just told me you're going to be my girlfriend."

She glanced over her shoulder, her long hair falling over her bare breast.

"That's bound to tick off your mother."

Wade winced. "Do not bring my mother into this conversation, with you sittin' there naked and tempting."

Trina giggled when Wade leaned forward and took the back of her head in his hand and kissed her again. When she opened her lips to accept more, he moaned and broke it off. With a slight shove, he pushed her from the bed and patted her naked butt when she stood.

"You order food. I'm going to find a drugstore."

Trina smiled all the way to the shower.

∽☉

Wade had ducked out to follow up on the search for a value pack supply of condoms while Trina rinsed off.

Wearing a bathrobe and toweling her hair dry, Trina stepped out of the oversize bathroom in search of a room service menu. The second she walked into the living room, her stomach caught up in her throat and her heart jolted with fear.

Sitting at the dining room table was a long, lean woman dressed entirely in black. Her boot-clad feet were kicked up on an adjacent chair, and her right hand was playing with some kind of chain.

Trina backed up into the wall and caught her breath.

"Hello, Katrina."

"Who are you?" Trina took another step back, intending to run for the phone and call for help.

"What does your boyfriend not understand about white on rice? He speaks English, doesn't he?" The question unnerved her, especially since the woman spoke to Trina in Russian.

"Who are you?" Trina asked again, switching languages. She felt for the door behind her.

"I'm Sasha." She dropped her feet to the floor but didn't stand.

The name rang a bell in Trina's head, but she couldn't place her.

"Have we met?"

She shook her head. "No. But I know you. We have a mutual acquaintance."

Trina waited.

"Reed."

She felt her heartbeat start to slow. "You work with Reed?"

Sasha shook her head and stood. Even from across the room, the woman intimidated. A single ponytail held her hair back, the spandex pants and heeled black boots looked like something Catwoman would wear. The only thing this woman was missing was a mask.

"How did you get in here?" Trina wasn't ready to let her guard down completely with only the mention of Reed's name.

"Your boyfriend has one job . . ." Sasha looked her up and down. "Maybe two." The sly smile told Trina that Sasha guessed what she and Wade had been doing that afternoon. "I'm not here to hurt you, but the next guy will be."

Trina started breathing fast again. "What do you know?"

Sasha pulled a key out of her back pocket and tossed it in the air.

Trina dropped the towel she'd been holding to catch the key with both hands. "Interstate Bank on the corner of Penrose and Brooke outside of Houston, by the oil company's main headquarters. It's a safe deposit box in your name. I removed the contents from Fedor's safe three months ago. Information I'm sure you don't want to become public." She held up her hand. "Before you ask, no. I had nothing to do with the cleaners. People I would have hired wouldn't have trashed the place."

"Do you know who did?"

"I can guess. You can, too, if you looked hard enough."

Trina held her robe tighter. "You need to talk to the police."

"The police just get in the way and jump to the wrong conclusions."

A watch on Sasha's wrist made a noise. She glanced at it briefly and turned toward the door.

"Wait." Trina took a step forward.

Sasha stopped.

"Why are you helping me?"

She didn't answer. She shook her head and opened the door of the suite.

To Trina's surprise, Wade was standing there with a bag in one hand, the key to the room in another.

His eyes widened in shock.

Sasha walked right up to him and placed one manicured finger on his chest. "White on rice, Cowboy. Don't fuck up again!" Then she was gone.

"Who was that?" Wade asked as they watched her disappear down the hall.

Trina pulled Wade inside, locked the door, and followed up with the inside latch.

"I hope you bought a big box," she told him as she reached for her purse to grab her cell phone. "Because that woman reminded me how easy it is to break into a hotel room."

Wade's face turned to stone. "Did she threaten you?"

"No. I need to call Reed."

"I'll go after her," Wade said.

Trina grabbed his arm, stopping him. "She's not the problem."

Reed picked up on the second ring. "Hello?"

Trina stared at the key in her hand. "Who is Sasha?"

∞

By the time room service arrived, so had Reed and Lori from the hospital.

Rick was stationed outside Avery's room, and Jeb had taken up residence in the spare room in the suite.

"I told you about Sasha last year, that's probably why she sounded familiar," Reed said.

He'd asked her about the encounter over the phone but didn't explain anything until they arrived at the hotel.

"She worked for Alice . . . at least that's what she told me."

"Alice is dead."

"Some people are on payroll beyond the grave."

Trina held on to a cup of tea while Wade stroked her back.

"Do you know what she did for Alice?" Trina asked.

Reed glanced at Wade, then back to her.

"She was keeping an eye on you."

Trina's chest tingled. "Why?"

"I don't have the details. My guess is Ruslan."

"Ruslan hasn't been sighted in over a year," Trina reminded him.

"That doesn't mean he isn't out there," Lori said.

Wade spoke up. "Can y'all back up here a little bit? Alice is . . . ?"

"My late mother-in-law," Trina told him.

"Ruslan is the nasty father-in-law."

"The first person everyone in this room thought of when the police asked if anyone had threatened you," Lori said to Trina.

"Distraught words of a man who lost his son. We haven't heard anything from him or about him. Last time we checked, he was working on some new scheme in Munich, right, Reed?" Trina asked.

"That's what our intel told us."

"You have him being watched?" Wade asked.

"Have your friends close and your enemies closer. He isn't on a round-the-clock surveillance, but we do have people reporting in."

"People? What people?" Trina asked.

Reed paused. "Sasha."

"So she does work with you."

Reed shook his head. "No. She leaves a message, offers information, albeit brief, about Ruslan, and then disappears for weeks. She's virtually impossible to trace. The fact that she showed up here at the very moment you stepped out of the hotel . . ." Reed looked at Wade. "Tells me something is brewing."

Trina wanted to mention the key to the safe deposit box but decided it might be best to tell Lori when they were alone. Her guess was Fedor had his copy of their marriage contract drafted by Alliance. Papers Trina wasn't quite ready to tell Wade about.

"Do you think she knows who attacked Avery?"

"If she did, my guess is we'd know by now. Avery wasn't her charge, you are."

Trina felt her hands start to shake. "Are you telling me I've had a shadow all this time and didn't know it?"

"Maybe. If not physically, virtually," Reed explained.

"What does that mean? Virtually?" Wade asked.

"There are cameras everywhere. City streets, department stores, hotels, airports. All she would need is a tracker on you and the hacking skills of a second-year computer nerd at Caltech, and boom."

"That's scary," Wade said. His hand covered Trina's.

"What's scary isn't her tracking you, it's Ruslan tracking you."

Trina shivered. "How can they? It isn't like someone put a microchip under my skin like a dog."

Lori turned to stare at her boyfriend. "Oh, let's see . . . Reed snuck a pen in the trunk of my car, bugged the wine corks in my condo . . . what else was there?"

Reed growled. "That's it. Pens and corks."

"You tracked your girlfriend. Isn't that stalkerish of you?" Wade said with amusement.

"I wanted to keep her safe. Anyway, this isn't about me, this is about you." Reed changed the subject and looked at Trina.

"Bugging my houses or a single car would prove useless. I'm not at any one for any length of time. Bugging all of them doesn't seem possible."

"We have a trace on your phone. We talked about this last year," Reed reminded her.

"I forgot about that. I replaced my phone when we were in the Bahamas."

"It's attached to one of your apps. Finding friends, only it's encrypted. It's entirely possible that someone hacked into that, or placed their own."

Wade's hand squeezed Trina's arm. "Hey, remember I told you the guy at the phone store in the Bahamas said there was something glitching in your phone in a different language, suggested you check it out?"

"I completely forgot about that."

Reed put his hand out, palm up.

Trina stood and crossed to the table holding her purse. She removed her cell phone and handed it over.

"If someone is hacking my phone, why was Avery the one that was attacked?"

"We're working on that." Reed stood, pulled Lori to her feet. "So we're clear . . . no more drugstore runs unless you're together. If you need to leave for any reason, call me. I'm right down the hall." They reached the door. Reed turned. "What was so important, anyway?" he asked.

Wade shifted his eyes to Trina.

She tried to hold back a smile as she studied the floor.

Lori started to laugh.

"Stop," Trina said under her breath to her friend.

"You do look awfully relaxed, all things considered," Lori teased.

Trina shoved her arm.

Lori stopped giggling. "Oh, by the way, the nurse said they were going to get Avery out of the ICU in the morning and to a monitored room elsewhere."

Trina glanced at the clock in the room. "I need to get back over there. It's been over six hours."

"She's slept most of the day."

"Still."

Lori gave her a hug. "Don't stay all night. You need your rest, too."

"I won't. I want to be there when the police show up to question her, and then I need to track down Fedor's things she placed in the auction houses. Any chance your team has a trace on Avery's phone? That would make it easier." Avery still didn't have any memory of what happened since she left the house in the Hamptons. It was like she'd blocked the whole thing out.

"No. You, Lori . . . Shannon. Avery seemed the least likely to find this kind of trouble." Reed shook his head as if he were kicking himself. "I won't make that mistake twice."

Lori placed a hand on his arm. "We'll walk over with you tomorrow. I don't want you talking with the police without me there."

She kissed the side of Trina's cheek before they walked out of the room.

Trina leaned against the door, rested her head, and closed her eyes.

"Hey?" Wade brought both of his hands to her shoulders and gently squeezed.

She opened her eyes to stare at him. This was all such a mess. "Are you sure you want anything to do with all this? People around me get hurt."

"I'm a little bigger to take down than Avery," he pointed out.

She tried to smile but couldn't look him in the eye. She didn't want him to walk away but wouldn't blame him if he did.

Wade lifted her chin with his finger. "Hey. You didn't do this."

No, but she was responsible.

"People murder for the amount of money at stake. I never wanted any of this. Fedor and I were practical in our marriage . . . we had a prenuptial agreement that didn't amount to anything compared to what Alice left me. I haven't spent Alice's money, any of it. I use what Fedor and I agreed on, and that's it. If I could give it all back and make this go away, I would. Now Avery is in the hospital, you're stuck here with me, my friends need to be traced like stray animals . . . even my parents have a security system in their house now. The same house our neighbors would walk right into without knocking to bring a batch of cookies."

"Life only gives you what you can handle, and you're one tough woman, even with all the feels going on inside your head."

She let him pull her into his arms. "I'm selfishly glad you're here," she told him.

"Me too."

Chapter Twenty-Three

Wade entered the ICU with Trina for the first time. He'd stayed in the lobby during their previous visits, but since he was Trina's personal magnet, he wasn't letting her out of his sight.

Several of the staff did a double take when he walked in, and a few began to whisper to each other. He smiled and followed Trina.

Outside the door of Avery's room, Rick filled an uncomfortable chair, with a book in his hand.

"Oh, good," Rick said as he shook Wade's hand. "How long do you plan on staying?"

Trina walked into the room, leaving Wade behind. "As long as we need to."

"I could use half an hour. Jeb said he'd be back by ten for the night shift."

Wade looked around the busy unit. "They're okay with this?"

Rick nodded. "They're used to it. As long as you don't get in the way."

"They were strict the first night here. Ten-minute visits at the top of the hour."

"Avery's stable now, and we pulled several strings." Rick stretched. "I'll be back in thirty minutes."

Wade took a deep breath, walked into Avery's room, and forgot his smile.

"Sweet Jesus," he said under his breath.

Trina had warned him, but he didn't imagine the blonde pit bull could ever look this bad. The bandages on her face were pristine white, while her skin sported every color of the rainbow.

"At least pretend it's not that bad," Avery said as her one unswollen eye landed on him.

He painted on an instant grin.

Avery rolled that same eye.

"Oh, darlin'. What can we do?"

There was a male nurse in the room, putting something in Avery's IV.

Her voice was muted due to what looked like something stuck up her swollen nose.

"How about a hamburger?"

Wade was ready to call a personal chef.

"No can do. Surgery is scheduled first thing in the morning," the nurse told her.

"That means I can eat until midnight," she argued slowly.

"Jell-O and juice."

"Killjoy."

"What surgery?" Trina asked.

"I'm getting a nose job." Avery tried to smile.

"She started bleeding, which is why her nose is packed. The surgeon wanted to get it taken care of tomorrow."

"Is she ready for that?"

"No," Avery argued. "But blood tastes like crap, so bring on the fix. I want this over with so I can get out of here and find the bastard who did this and kick their ass."

Wade smiled at the fight in her.

"I think you're going to have to stand in line," Trina said before looking at one of her legs, which was propped up on pillows.

"That will have to wait, then."

"How is the pain?" Trina asked.

"Better now that they gave me this button." Avery lifted her one good hand to display said button. She pressed it several times in a row.

The nurse laughed. "You can press it all you want, it will only deliver a small dose every hour."

"Stupid thing is broken." Avery let it go in her lap.

"Someone is chatty enough to leave the ICU," the nurse said.

"As long as the nurses in the next unit are as cute as you," Avery teased.

"I told you I have a girlfriend."

"I told you I don't care."

Wade was laughing now.

The nurse glanced at him and then Trina. "Yup, she's not sick enough to stay here."

"That's really good news."

Avery sighed. "Man, I feel like shit."

"You're awake enough to tell me that, so I feel better," the nurse said.

"Masochist."

"Wade, this is Doug, by the way. I told him I'd introduce you," Trina said.

Wade stepped forward and extended his hand. The man had to be in his late twenties, maybe early thirties. "My pleasure," Wade told him. "Thanks for taking such great care of our girl."

"I'm a huge fan."

"You're a masochistic, hamburger denying, cute fan," Avery corrected.

"That's more than I got out of her when we first met," Wade told Doug.

Doug laughed. "I, ah . . . I had my girlfriend bring over my guitar. Any chance I can get you to sign it?"

"Absolutely, bring it out."

"That'd be awesome. I'll go grab it. Thanks, Mr. Thomas."

The professional nurse one minute, fan guy the next, hustled out of the room as if Wade would change his mind.

Avery turned toward Trina. "Did Bernie stop by earlier?"

"Yes, he did."

"Did I say anything bad?"

Trina patted her hand. "No. You were fine."

"Remind me to ask how you two met once you're out of here," Wade said.

"Strip club," Avery said without missing a beat. "I was the stripper, he owned the club."

Wade glanced at Trina. "Is she serious?"

"You're gullible and she's on drugs." Trina laughed.

"Sit down, you're making me nervous," Avery demanded.

"Yes, ma'am." Wade took a vacant chair on the opposite side of the bed from Trina.

"Rick said the police were coming back."

"Yeah," Trina confirmed.

"I don't remember anything. You went to a party . . ."

"Right, at Wade's house in Texas."

"I-I was . . . Fedor's watch."

Trina sat forward. "Right. You were taking the watches here to have the auction house appraise and advise. Do you remember which one you went to?"

"I barely remember driving in. God, this sucks."

Trina patted her hand. "It's okay. The doctors think it will come back."

"I hope so."

Wade wasn't so sure that was a good idea, considering the mess her body was in because of another human being. He couldn't imagine anyone beating a woman. Seeing Avery in that bed made him realize the threat against Trina was more than just show. He'd chuckled at *white on rice*, but now he got it. Really got it, and he didn't plan on giving anyone the chance of doing this to her.

Doug returned to the room, an acoustic guitar in his hand. Behind him, a couple of the other nurses stood by, watching. "You sure this is okay?" Doug asked.

Wade accepted the guitar and winked. "My pleasure. How long have you been playing?"

"A couple years. It's just a hobby. Helps me relax after a busy shift."

"Fenders are one of my favorites," Wade told him. He strummed the strings and tuned the A before strumming again. "They have a great sound." Wade moved his fingers over the strings like he was born to do. When he looked up to see Avery smiling and Trina beaming, he decided it wouldn't hurt to hum a few bars.

> I want a woman who tastes like whiskey and sips
>   like wine . . .
> A woman who smiles like sunshine and laughs
>   like spring . . .
> Everyone says you won't find love if you're search-
>   ing for her . . .
> I swear I'm not lookin' but you're not there . . .
> All I need is your heart . . .
> All I want is your love . . .
> Stop looking for me, darlin', I'm standing right
>   here.

Trina tilted her head and listened to him with a smile that angels blessed, and Wade kept singing.

> I want a woman who smiles at children and cries
>   in the rain . . .
> A woman who melts in my arms and calls out my
>   name . . .

Everyone says you won't find love when you're
searching for her . . .
I swear I'm not lookin' but you're not there . . .
All I need is your heart . . .
All I want is your love . . .

He could see other nurses and visitors gathering outside the door,
but all Wade saw was Trina's glittering eyes.

I want to stand there with you in the morning
light . . .
Fall asleep beside you after talkin' all night . . .
I want to find you, darlin', and give you all of my
heart . . .
I need to find you, baby, and share all of my
love . . .
So please stop searchin', honey, and let fate have
a spin.
I'll stop lookin', sweetheart, and we'll let love
slip in.
Cuz everyone says you won't find love when
you're searchin' . . .
All I want to give you is all of my heart . . .
All I want from you is all of your love . . .
Stop searchin' for me, baby . . .
And I'll stop lookin' for you . . .
I'm standing right here, honey, starin' at you.

He let the last chord fade off as he ended the song. Moisture gathered behind Trina's eyes, and Wade's heart skipped several beats.
Applause snapped him out of his daze.

"Okay," Avery said as the clapping came to a close. "You can date her, but you can't marry her."

"Avery!" Trina scolded.

"He wrote that song forever ago. He has to write one for you first."

Wade slid the guitar to his lap and took the pen Doug handed him. "I'm going to have to write a song about my girlfriend's pit bull."

Trina laughed.

"Now we're talking," Avery agreed.

⁂

The phone in the penthouse suite woke them up at seven in the morning.

Trina had fallen asleep in Wade's arms after talking most of the night. Their afternoon nap had left them with more energy, which they put to good use. It helped that an early morning wasn't necessary, since Avery was headed for surgery before the first cup of coffee.

Wade rolled over, pulled the phone to his ear. "Yeah?"

Trina snuggled back on her bicep pillow.

"When did you get in?"

She couldn't hear the other half of the conversation and decided to close her eyes.

"Fine, yeah. Come on up."

Wade blindly placed the phone back on the cradle.

"Who was that?"

"Ike." He kissed the side of her head and rolled out of bed.

"He's here?"

"Yup. He brought me a few things from home. Take your time. I'll order some coffee."

Trina leaned up on her elbow and smiled at the display of flesh Wade provided with his naked butt.

Wade caught her stare. "Keep lookin' at me like that and Ike will hear more than I'd like him to."

"Is that a threat or a promise?" She let the blanket drop to her waist.

Wade's eyes glossed over. "That's just mean."

She giggled. It felt good to flirt and tease. "Go." She shooed him off and kicked away the covers to stand. "I wanna be there when Avery is out of surgery."

She walked around the bed and toward the bathroom.

Wade snaked his hand around her waist, and their skin touched from knees to chest.

"Good mornin', darlin'." He greeted her with a kiss and a squeeze to her butt.

He felt so right it hurt. "Mornin'." She used his Texan drawl when she pulled away.

By the time she made her way into the living area of the suite, Ike, Jeb, and Wade were drinking coffee and talking in hushed whispers.

They stopped when she entered the room.

"Don't let me interrupt." Trina crossed to the room service coffee and poured a cup.

The silence in the room made her pause. She moved the coffee cup to her lips and found three sets of eyes trained on her. "What?"

Wade offered a nervous laugh. "What are your feelings on the tabloids?"

She lowered her cup and glanced at the table the three men were sitting at. Even from across the room, she could see her image splashed on the front page.

"Let's see," she said as she moved to get a better look. "The tabloids tell entertaining lies attached to photoshopped pictures. They have one tiny truth in their web of deceit and bastardize the First Amendment. They get away with splashing their blasphemy to the world because dragging them into court is a colossal waste of time and money." The first magazine she picked up was a picture snapped by the photographer the day before, asking who she was as they ran into the hotel. Since they got her name right, they must have found out. It read: "Is Wade Thomas Off the Market?"

The second one was of her the previous year at Fedor's funeral. Wade's picture was of him onstage at a concert. The headline read: "Will the Black Widow Strike Again?"

The third one was a less flattering image of Wade and her holding hands outside the doors of the hospital, laid over a picture of her Hamptons home surrounded by police cars. The caption? "Tragedy in the Hamptons."

Trina put her coffee down and picked up the magazine with the two of them outside the hospital. "Is my butt really that fat?"

Wade started to chuckle.

Jeb sighed and Ike grinned. "Okay, then. You found a woman who understands the media."

"I wish I didn't."

"I don't like that they're calling you names," Wade said.

"I don't like how they made my butt big." Trina made an effort at looking at her own ass over her shoulder.

Wade swatted it with a playful smile.

Ike turned to Wade. "Corrine wants to know all about Trina."

"Who is Corrine?" Trina asked. How many women did Wade have in his life?

"My publicist," Wade explained. "Tell her she's my girlfriend."

Ike regarded them with a lifted eyebrow.

"Don't look at me," Trina said. "He started the whole girlfriend thing . . . I was just looking for a good time."

Wade turned toward her and lifted her off her feet, his hands firmly on her not-as-big-of-a-butt as the tabloid led others to believe. He twirled her around. "I'll give you a good time," he teased.

Smiling was starting to truly work the muscles in her cheeks and make them ache.

She liked it.

"You're adorable," he told her.

She wrapped her legs around his waist and let him hold her off her feet a little longer. "Do you really want to tell the world you've got a girlfriend?"

"What I want is to tell the world that you've got a boyfriend so no one else comes knockin'."

"I doubt I'll be good PR."

"I could not care less about any of that," he said.

Wade kissed her, briefly, and set her down.

"Tell Corrine, Trina is my girlfriend and we've been practically inseparable since we met." He tapped Trina's nose. "Including a secret trip to the Bahamas on a private plane."

"That was platonic," she said.

"No one has to know the details. Besides, the tabloids will find it if we don't reveal it."

She sighed. "Fine. Your mother is gonna be pissed."

"Again with my mother. I'll deal with her. Don't worry. What about your parents?"

Trina hadn't given it a lot of thought. "I should probably call them. They don't know about any of this as it is."

"You haven't told them?"

She shook her head. "If I told them about you, my mother would remind me that it's only been a year since Fedor's death. She's Catholic, and while she doesn't want me alone my whole life, I can guarantee she will think it's too soon for me to be dating anyone, let alone be in any kind of relationship. My dad will want to meet you as soon as a plane can fly him here."

"That's sweet."

"He will wonder if you're gunning for the oil money."

Ike laughed from across the room. "Sorry." He ducked his head when they both turned to look at him.

"When Daddy finds out about Avery, he is going to worry. I don't want to do that to him."

"Fathers are supposed to worry, darlin'."

"Yeah, well . . . he isn't getting younger, and I'd hate to be the one to add more stress to his life."

"That isn't your call. If you don't tell him, the papers will."

"You're right. I know you're right. It will have to wait until I get my phone back, though. I haven't memorized a phone number other than my own in years."

"So we have today's game plan. We let Corrine deal with the Wade Thomas PR, you'll get ahold of your parents while I prepare to meet your father."

"You'll deal with your mother," she pointed out.

"Yup. Anyone else?"

"I should make a call to Diane and Andrea."

"Who are they?"

"Fedor's aunts. I'm pretty sure they listen to country music, so you're safe there."

Wade smiled.

"All of this can happen from the waiting room at the hospital. I don't want Avery waking up without me there. You shower, and I'll call Lori's room and see if she's ready to walk over."

Chapter Twenty-Four

Avery was getting sick and tired of waking up with a new pain somewhere on her broken and battered body. Hospitals were not the place to sleep. Between doctors coming in every few hours, nurses waking you up every two hours in the middle of the night, tests, and visitors, she wasn't sure how it was possible to get better at all.

That morning she'd been wheeled into surgery before the sun came up, or so it seemed. In the fog of her brain, Avery realized that she'd gotten out of surgery only to wake up in a recovery room feeling as if the world had sat on her face and wasn't giving her any room to breathe without pain shooting behind her eyeballs. Someone had given her something in her IV and she'd fallen into a blissful haze again.

Now, the earth was still knocking her in the face, but the pain wasn't as sharp as it had been the first time she'd opened her eyes. Her back felt as if she'd been moved to a proper bed instead of being on a surgical gurney. She'd take her comforts any way she could at this point. A soft mattress on her ass was a start. She attempted to move her head and instantly regretted it.

She moaned.

"Hey . . ."

Trina.

"Water," she sputtered.

Trina was there with a cup and a straw. Since the bed was already elevated, Avery didn't attempt to sit up more. The first sip hurt, but the second sip soothed. Trina pulled it away. "The nurse said only a few sips to start. We have to do everything we can to keep you from coughing or getting sick to your stomach."

She imagined the pain with either task would equal walking barefoot on broken glass. Avery's face was covered in bandages once again and it felt as if someone had a party in her nose and had invited the entire state of New York.

Trina came into focus, the concern in her eyes making Avery want to blow off her pain.

"How do you feel?"

"Ready to party." Avery closed her eyes.

"There's a button for the pain medication."

Yeah, but the medication would just knock her out, and she wanted a few minutes of cognition before falling back asleep.

"How do I look?"

"Ready to party," Trina repeated her words with a small laugh.

She opened her eyes again. "No, really?"

Trina made a point to look everywhere but in Avery's eyes, as if studying her face. "There's more swelling, and a few new colors have been introduced to your complexion. I'd hold off on any new selfies for your Tinder profile."

Avery smiled and felt the packing in her nose even more.

"I'm so sorry any of this happened, Avery."

She held open the palm in her good hand, and Trina slipped hers in. "Not your fault."

"But if you weren't in the city for me—"

Avery tried to squeeze Trina's hand. "Still not your fault." She used only her eyes to look around the new room. It was a private room that looked less like a hospital room and more like a hotel. The darker color on the walls soothed her senses more than the stark white of the ICU.

There were flowers. Two bouquets sat on a shelf across from her bed and brightened the space. "What time is it?"

"Two thirty. Are you hungry?"

"No. Where is everyone?"

"Lori, Shannon, and Reed are grabbing a bite in the cafeteria. I told your parents I'd call once you're awake. Your mother doesn't like hospitals, apparently."

"Yeah, did she tell you why?"

Trina shook her head.

"Because they remind her of two days of labor with me . . . her greatest disappointment."

Trina looked at her as if she were joking.

"Fine, don't believe me. But if you ask why she has an aversion to hospitals, she'll tell you because of the time she's spent in them. Then ask my father when my mother was in a hospital the last time."

"I'm sure that's not it."

"I'm not feeling sorry for myself. I'm telling you the facts. Whatever, she stresses me out anyway. Now that I'm out of the ICU, I'm pretty sure I can get her to go home."

Trina patted her hand. "Bernie sent the flowers."

"That's nice. Do I still have a guard at the door?"

"Yup. Rick is right outside."

"That's good." And it was. There was comfort in the fact that no one could come in and finish the job. The pain in Avery's body was proof she was lucky to be alive. "Where is Wade?"

"Dealing with a few PR issues while I'm here with you. The police are coming by this afternoon."

She closed her eyes and tried to remember something, anything about that day. All that came to her was a fuzzy memory of walking by Central Park, and then she was waking up and feeling like she'd been run over by a bus. "I don't remember anything about what happened."

"The investigators of the assault asked us to call them if you have anything new to tell. The police I'm talking about are the ones dealing with the break-in at the house."

Avery blinked through swollen eyes. "What break-in?"

Trina opened her mouth and then closed it.

"Trina?"

"Someone broke into Fedor's office and completely trashed the place, after wiping it clean of every fingerprint, on the day you were attacked."

"Robbery?"

"We don't know if they took anything."

"They were too late. I took the pens to Mr. Levin." Even as she said the name, the memory unfolded in her head. "Braum Auctions. I remember that now."

Trina sat forward.

"He has the pens." It felt good to get that piece of memory back. She closed her eyes and searched for more. "The watches. I remember being happy to have them out of my purse. God, where did I take them?" Why couldn't she remember?

"Christie's?" Trina suggested.

"Yes! Oh, right. They were snotty but so excited about an auction and wanted to know if we had more." The hair on Avery's skin tingled. "I remember that now."

"Anything else? Do you remember anything else?"

She saw the garage when she closed her eyes. Only she was leaving the car . . . "I had a mom purse. I think it was one of yours. I needed a big one to put everything in."

"Yes." Trina seemed excited. "The black one."

"I remember leaving the garage. I don't remember going back in. That's where they found me, right?" She seemed to remember someone telling her that when she was in the ICU.

"Yes."

Avery shook her head slowly. "I don't remember anything else."

Trina smiled. "Well, it's more than yesterday, so there is progress. The doctors will be excited to hear that."

Her head started to throb, and instead of denying herself relief, she opened her palm. "Where is that button of fun?"

Trina reached over the bed and put the thing in her hand.

Avery pushed it and sighed long before the medication circulated in her veins.

～ා

Ruslan Petrov was a patient man with one impatient moment in his past. That moment changed everything. He was a man who had more plates spinning in the air than a circus performer, and one was slipping off his finger, and he'd be damned if he dropped anything now.

Across from him, Zakhar delivered unwelcome news. "Ms. Grant had already delivered the items to the auction houses."

"Did your man at least steal her wallet?"

"No."

Ruslan clenched his fist. "He didn't finish the job."

"He said he was interrupted."

"Let me see if I understand this correctly. I said to make it look like burglary, and now it simply looks like a vendetta. And she's alive to identify him."

Zakhar matched Ruslan's stare. "I have already taken care of the situation. Nothing will be tied to you."

That had Ruslan releasing the hold he had on his own fingers and rubbing the tension away.

"What about the other collateral damage?"

"She is scrubbed. No trace."

"I expect nothing was messy."

Zakhar smiled, a white line of a scar he earned in a street fight distorting his face, making his grin look like a threat. It was one of the many things Ruslan liked about the man. "Car accident."

It would be so much easier if he could just scrub the woman who destroyed everything. But that would only result in the wrong people looking his way. Instead of losing a fortune, he'd lose his freedom.

He used a remote control to reveal a monitor behind a picture on the wall. When the image flicked into focus, a map of the world emerged. With another button, the map focused on the state of New York. Several dots blinked, each a different color.

Katrina's bitch lawyer and their friend blipped in the same place. He knew without looking that they were at the Manhattan hospital where he'd put their friend. The redneck blipped a few blocks away, and it appeared Trina was by herself downtown. Which didn't sound right, considering she'd been flanked by security since he'd started his cover-up. A cover-up he had thought he'd taken care of the year before.

Ruslan pointed at the map. "Where is this?"

Zakhar moved behind the desk and clicked into the program tracking the players.

"Looks residential."

"Have our man on the ground find out. What about the house?"

"Police activity has pulled out. They didn't find anything."

At least that worked as he'd planned.

"I do have some positive news," Zakhar said.

"I'm waiting." Ruslan reached for a cigar on his desk.

"The tabloids are circulating speculation on your daughter-in-law. Indirectly pointing a finger at her for Fedor's death and questioning if she's unhappy with one man's fortune and trying to add to it with her new male friend."

Ruslan rolled the cigar between his fingers and held it under his nose. "That's helpful," he said before he reached for a lighter. Once the cigar was lit and the sweet smoke filled his lungs, instantly calming his nerves . . . he blew out the smoke slowly. "I think it's time for me to visit my son's grave."

"In Texas?"

If his Russian friend disagreed, he didn't express his feelings.

"I'll arrange it."

⁓

Two days later, Trina was arranging a hospital bed to be delivered to the Hamptons house for Avery's release. She wanted to take her back to Texas, but the plastic surgeon and neurologists felt that should wait for another week.

Lori argued to return to LA, but Trina pointed out the quiet of the country would give Avery the time she needed to heal. Ultimately the decision was one of practicality. They would stay in the Hamptons home for the next week and then fly back to Texas for the prolonged future. Considering the surveillance and bodyguards on them now, it would be easier to watch over them at the ranch.

Truth be told, Trina was a little anxious to get into the safe deposit box Sasha had given her the key for. But taking care of Avery was the priority, and the box would have to wait.

The only media was a lone car parked across from the Hamptons home with a camera pointed out the driver's side window.

They pulled in like a presidential motorcade. Three black SUVs, all rented, and all home to at least one armed bodyguard.

Wade jumped out of their car and opened the door for Trina and Avery. Jeb stepped in the second Avery poked her head out, reached in, lifted her out of the car.

The drive from the hospital had been slow, to avoid potholes and any unnecessary bumps along the way.

Trina walked ahead of everyone with keys in hand to let them all in. Once inside, she disarmed the alarm system and tossed her purse on the foyer table.

She turned to Avery, who looked comfortable in Jeb's massive arms.

"Do you want to go to bed or get propped up in the family room?"

"I've been in bed for days," Avery said.

"Family room it is." Trina pointed Jeb in the right direction and went upstairs to find a few pillows and a blanket while everyone else filed inside.

By the time she returned, the flowers from the hospital were brought in from the cars, as well as several pieces of luggage from the group.

Shannon took the blanket and pillows from her and went to Avery's side.

Lori was already in the kitchen, brewing a pot of coffee, and Wade and Ike were hoisting bags to the second floor.

"Good thing this is a big house," Lori told her as she removed coffee cups from the cupboard.

"It felt like a mansion when I was married. Then it was a place to rest between hospital visits and funeral homes."

Lori gave her a one-arm hug. "You survived it."

"Feels like I'm right back where I started." Her gaze drifted to the family room.

"Except that no one is ending up in the ground, and there's a big Texan winking at you every time you walk in the room."

Just thinking about Wade had blood rushing to her face.

"God, it's good to see that smile," Lori said.

"I can't believe he's still here. All this crazy and he hasn't even hinted at leaving."

"Nothing wrong with that."

Jeb and Reed walked in from the back door, with Rick close behind.

"Okay, ladies." Rick managed to get all their attention through the great room right as Wade and Ike walked in. "And gentlemen. The security system has been updated as of yesterday. Everything is being monitored remotely from our headquarters. Audio and visual. Trina, you'll notice the new cameras we have put inside." He pointed out two small fixtures that were in the corners of the great room and another in the kitchen. "There are more in the hallways and other common spaces. Bathrooms and bedrooms are not online. The backyard, and especially the back office, are live. The front door and gate are up, as usual. We have also placed a few cameras on the perimeter of the property for shits and giggles."

"That seems like a lot of work, considering we plan on leaving in a week," Trina said.

Rick let his usual smile lapse, and his gaze traveled to Avery, lying on the couch.

No one continued to question the need for more cameras.

"So keep that in mind if anyone wants a little touchy-feely in the kitchen. Not that my men will go out of their way to watch, but you never know." Rick was joking, his men weren't really like that, but then again . . .

Trina's eyes found the whites of Wade's, her heart skipped a beat. Since Reed and Lori already knew the drill of surveillance, and Shannon didn't have a man in the house that she knew enough to be touchy or feely over . . . and Ike and Jeb didn't seem to be into each other, that left the warning squarely on Wade and her.

"I think I'm safe there," Avery said from the sofa.

Oh, yeah . . . and Avery. Who probably wouldn't mind someone watching if she were up to doing anything other than sleeping and popping a pill every four hours.

Rick continued, "We have a team overhauling the ranch as we speak to get it ready for your return. Wade?"

"Yeah?"

"I assume you have a security system at your place."

"I do. Although not quite as extensive as what you seem to have here."

"There are always people around, anyway," Ike told him. "It's a working ranch."

"Which means you need more security, not less. Trina, do you plan on spending any time at Wade's?"

She glanced at Wade, then back at Rick. "Well, yeah . . . eventually. I mean, I hope—"

"Then we'll send in a team."

Wade held up a hand. "Whoa, wait just a minute."

Before Rick could continue, a call from the gate did a double ring on her phone.

Trina answered while Rick and Wade talked about cameras and alarms. "Hello?"

"Mrs. Petrov? This is Detectives Armstrong and Gray. We'd like to have a word with you."

Trina's heart started to pound in defining thumps. "Okay."

She pressed the button for the gate to open. She looked up to find everyone staring.

"Detectives Armstrong and Gray are here."

She noticed Lori's back stiffen, her chin come up. Reed and Lori exchanged glances, and Wade moved to her side.

"I'll let them in," Jeb offered.

"I still don't remember anything more from the last time I spoke with them," Avery said from the couch.

"It's okay, Avery." Shannon sat by her side.

Armstrong and Gray stepped into the room and did a quick scan. While both detectives weren't small men, they didn't quite compare to Rick and Jeb, with Reed close at their heels. "Sorry to bother you, Mrs. Petrov, but we had a few questions and a new development to share."

"Did you find the bastard who did this to me?" Avery asked from the couch.

Gray stepped around the kitchen island so he could look at Avery. The man seemed uncomfortable. "No, ma'am. But we do have a lead on a surveillance camera coming from the parking garage."

"We're following up on it," Armstrong added.

"What kind of lead?" Reed asked.

"Sometime after the cameras spotted Ms. Grant entering the garage and before the police and medics showed up, a known felon was seen leaving from a back door. The cameras from a Chinese restaurant adjacent to the garage picked him up."

"What kind of felon?" Rick asked.

Avery pushed herself up on the sofa as she listened.

"The kind that people hire to do the unthinkable. Which is why we are delivering this news, and not Officer Ferrero, who you spoke with the day of the assault. Our departments agreed to consolidate the cases, since we think they are connected."

"Do you have a picture of him?"

Everyone turned to look at Avery. It wasn't just the question she asked, but how she said it. Her voice was low and her words so slowly said, it didn't sound like her.

"Do you remember a face?" Gray asked.

"I might. A picture might spark a memory."

That was news to everyone in the room. So far Avery hadn't said one word about remembering anything, let alone a face.

Gray stepped over to the couch and removed his phone from his back pocket. Reed and Rick crowded in close to get a look.

Trina watched Avery's expressions while Shannon held her hand.

"This is the image from the back of the garage. It's poor quality, but we can still ID his face, since he is in our database."

Avery blinked a few times and lifted her good hand to the screen to zoom it in. "Is he wearing boots?"

"Yes, he is. Do you remember boots?"

She closed her eyes but didn't say a thing. "Do you have another picture?"

Gray turned the phone around and scowled through a few things before showing it to her.

Trina peeked around Rick's shoulder. With a haircut and a shave, the man in the picture would have been attractive outside of the acne scars on his face. But in this one, an obvious mug shot, as evidenced by the number he was holding and the plain background of the photograph, the man looked as if he'd been on the streets and either hadn't slept or had been taking drugs.

"Is this him?"

Avery blinked several times. "I don't know."

"It's okay." Shannon patted Avery's arm.

Gray didn't seem surprised by Avery's answer as he put his phone away. "We're looking for him and will bring him in for questioning when we find him."

Avery looked away. "Thank you."

"Mrs. Petrov?"

Hearing Detective Armstrong address her as a married woman rubbed her the wrong way. "My late husband cared about me so much he killed himself. If you don't mind, Detective, please call me Ms. Petrov, or Trina will work."

"*Ms.* Petrov," he obliged. "When was the last time you saw Cindy Geist?"

It took Trina a second to realize who he was talking about, since she never used Cindy's last name. "My housekeeper?"

"Yes."

Trina tried to remember the exact date. "It was after our trip to Europe last year." Her gaze moved to Lori. "About two months after Fedor's funeral. I came back to close up the house. She agreed to come in periodically to keep the place up and supervise the cleaning crew."

"She didn't come in while you were here preparing everything for sale?"

"No. I've been trying to get in touch with her since we got back. She never returned my calls."

"Why are you asking?" Reed asked.

The detectives looked at each other, and before they could open their mouths, Trina felt her skin grow cold. "Cindy Geist died in a car accident five days ago."

"Oh, God."

Wade moved closer and pulled her hand into his.

"Brake failure on a blind corner only a few blocks from her house."

Trina couldn't process the information before her mind denied it. "Brake failure? No, no, no . . . how can that be? Her husband is an auto mechanic. I met him once." Trina squeezed her eyes shut in search of his name. "Allen? Yes, Allen. He was proud of his work. Popped the hood of her Mustang . . . it was a Mustang, vintage year. I don't remember which. But he was passionate about the work he'd done on that car. He loved her. Sent her flowers on her birthday, asked me if it was okay that he surprise her with a midweek day off."

Trina felt tears spring in her eyes. "He wouldn't allow her brakes to fail." She shook her head. "That isn't right. That can't be right."

"We didn't like the sound of it either," Gray told her. "Her husband is demanding an investigation, not that he needs to. Cindy was the only one with the keys to the house, is that correct?"

"Yes."

"She came twice a month to clean?"

"That was the arrangement." Trina couldn't picture the woman dead.

Armstrong was taking notes. "When was she employed by you?"

"Fedor had her on payroll before we were married."

"She was the one who found your deceased husband . . . is that right?"

Her screams and Trina running in to find out why would live in her memories forever. "Yes."

Wade wrapped an arm over her shoulders.

"Was she the one who cleaned up . . ." Armstrong's words trailed off.

"No. The funeral home suggested a service. I didn't want anyone who knew Fedor picking up those pieces."

"They didn't do a good job." Avery's cold words from the sofa turned every head in the room.

"Excuse me?" Armstrong asked.

"I was searching for a hidden drawer in his desk. My dad has at least two, so I thought I'd find something. Since Fedor had a pen worth a quarter of a million dollars just sitting in the drawer, I thought it was worth looking. I didn't find any. But I did find blood. Dried blood on the underside of the desk. It's like the cleaning crew did half the job and figured no one would look. Gross."

"That's right. You told me that when I was at Wade's house for the party. Wait . . ." Trina turned to stare at Reed. "Didn't you say the office was spotless? No prints, no blood, nothing?"

Reed nodded.

Without words, Trina pulled out of Wade's arm and marched toward the back door of the house. She stormed toward Fedor's office, pulled away the caution tape the police had put there, and shoved the door open before flipping on the lights.

The place was still in shambles. In addition to the room being torn apart, there were smudges of black dust everywhere. She'd watched enough television to know what investigators left behind when looking for fingerprints. Without a beat, she moved to the desk, which wasn't in the exact place it normally was, but was still sitting upright.

Someone called her name, but she didn't look up to see whom.

She walked around the desk and ducked to look underneath.

The lighting didn't allow a visual of anything, so she stood, placed both hands on one edge, and pulled with everything she had.

No one was more surprised than she was when the desk fell over and crashed to the side with a noise that filled the room. She was pretty sure she'd pulled a muscle with her effort, but she ignored the pain in her shoulder and dropped to her knees. She ran her hand over the exposed wood of the underside of the desk.

Nothing.

She searched the legs of the desk, opened a drawer, and looked under it.

Nothing.

"Nothing! There's nothing here." Her blood started to boil. She punched the side of the desk once . . . twice . . .

Wade stopped her from doing it a third time. "Shhh."

"Why?" She felt tears again. "Why would someone come in here and scrub away his blood?"

Before her mind could come to the right conclusion, she heard Armstrong say, "We need to open up Fedor Petrov's file."

Chapter Twenty-Five

There was a rule when dating that absolutely everyone knew and most followed. Don't talk about your ex.

Unless the police were questioning you because the suicide of said ex had become a murder investigation a year after it happened.

Wade sat next to Trina while the detectives asked her questions about the day of Fedor's death. She didn't remember many details. She'd joined her husband on one of his many trips to the hospital. She'd left the hospital before Fedor, which wasn't uncommon. Since her mother-in-law was chronically ill, a twenty-four-hour vigil wasn't practiced. Although Trina had spent more time at the hospital that day, since Alice had slipped into a coma a couple of days before Fedor's death.

Fedor worked out of an office in the city and would often return there after seeing his mother, and then come home late to eat and hibernate in his home office for hours. Which explained why Trina and Fedor had separate bedrooms. A question Wade had had since he first walked into her Hamptons home but didn't want to ask.

The detectives left after what felt like hours of questions. The minute the door closed behind them, Wade expected everyone to take a step back and sigh. Only that didn't happen.

Rick's phone rang.

Lori reached for her purse and said she needed to call someone named Sam.

Reed turned toward one of the hidden cameras and said, "Did you catch all that? We need files on everything from that day."

It was as if the room mobilized, and the only people surprised by the activity were Wade, Jeb, and Ike. The three of them watched the others in silence.

"Are you okay?" Shannon had moved to Trina's other side.

Wade put his attention back on the woman who had stolen his attention since the day he set eyes on her.

"I should have known. Everyone painted Fedor as weak and capable of killing himself. He wasn't weak, he was losing the only woman who loved him with every ounce of her being. He was sad and distraught over not being able to stop it."

"Trina?" Rick had lifted the phone from his ear to grab her attention.

She swiveled her head.

"The security system you had before . . . were there cameras?"

"Only at the gate to see who was driving in. Everything else was basic burglar and fire alarm stuff."

Rick nodded and repeated what she said to whomever he was talking to on the phone.

Lori returned after making her call in another room.

Reed sat on the arm of one of the overstuffed chairs, and Rick concluded his call to join them. "We launch our own investigation," Rick told Reed.

"Follow the money," Reed said.

"The money ended up with me," Trina sighed.

"But it wasn't supposed to," Lori pointed out. "Fedor's trust placed his assets back into Everson Oil's hands. Fedor's private company was divided between the shareholders, with the controlling interest given to Everson Oil."

"He didn't leave it to you?" Wade asked.

"No. I told you, we had a prenuptial agreement."

Rick turned to Lori. "Is there any way we can get Alice's estate attorney to reveal what her original will stated, the one she had before adding Trina to it?"

"That's a hard push. Attorney-client privilege extends after death."

"Even in the case of a murder investigation?" Wade asked.

"Especially in the case of a murder investigation. It's part of the reason it was brought into law in the first place. A client needs to be honest with their lawyers, and the only way we can get that out of everyone is to promise to keep what we know to ourselves."

"But lawyers make mistakes. Sometimes they say things they shouldn't," Reed pointed out.

Lori and Reed stared at each other with unspoken words.

"So Lori has lunch with Alice's estate attorney while we're in New York and sees what she can find out." Rick didn't ask, he stated like his idea was a done deal.

"I don't know about that. Isn't that risky for you?" Shannon asked.

Lori blinked her gaze away from Reed's to look at Trina. "Only if he is hiding something to protect Alice and her name after her death. Since I represented you and Fedor in your prenuptial and following his death, it isn't uncommon for me to follow up. If it feels like he's hedging me away from a conversation, we know he is protecting her, if not, he'll tell me what he can."

Reed sighed. "I guess that means we're staying in town a little longer."

"I have Cooper flying in first thing in the morning to take my place," Rick said. "If word leaks out that Fedor's suicide is now a murder investigation—and news like that always drains through the cracks—there's going to be a lot more people with cameras at your gate."

Wade listened to the entire conversation going on around him in silence until Rick mentioned the media. Then his thoughts turned to his own mother, and his own home.

He looked at Ike and Jeb, who had remained silent during the entire exchange.

"About that security system at my ranch . . ."

Rick looked at Wade and smiled. "On it."

⁓

Jeb, Ike, and Wade volunteered to do a grocery store run before word got out. He used the alone time to hear concerns from the others.

"Let me get this straight," Ike started the second they were in the car. "The woman you've known for what . . . two weeks? Is the widow of a man who committed suicide, but now we find out he was murdered right before the man's mother dies . . . all the money ends up in Trina's bank. Her BFF has the holy shit kicked out of her for reasons unknown. Their friends rally together as if they are on some kind of military mission, with bodyguards and surveillance that rivals the White House . . . and you want to date this woman?"

Jeb drove, and Wade twisted around in the passenger seat to address Ike. "Do you read, Ike?"

"You mean books?"

"Yeah."

"Sometimes."

"Did you ever read that book *He's Just Not That into You*?"

"I saw the movie, why?" Ike asked.

"I didn't see the movie, but one of the guys in the band had the book on our tour bus. I started reading it, and at first I thought, well, hell, this just sucks that there is a book out there to tell every woman all the secrets a man has. You know, the things we do and don't do if we wanna keep a woman around, but we know it really isn't going anywhere. It's like a guidebook for women to wake up and realize when a guy isn't in for the long run."

"What does that have to do with this conversation?"

Wade held his hand in the air. "Hold up . . . I'm getting there. Then I kept reading, and I thought of myself and wondered if there was anyone out there that I was willing to be that man for. You know, the guy who always calls because he wants to, not because he's expected to. The guy who remembers important dates and the things a woman says because he actually listened."

Ike bounced in the back seat when the car hit a pothole. "That's Trina?"

Wade shrugged and smiled.

"Two weeks, Wade! You can't know that in two weeks."

"Maybe that's true. But I'll never get to three weeks to find out if that woman is Trina if I leave now."

Ike rolled his eyes and sat back in the seat and turned his head toward the window. "You have a hero complex. You see a woman you can rescue and you're putting on a cape."

Wade looked at Ike like he was crazy. "Did you see all the firepower in that room? That Rick guy makes Jeb here look like his scrawny stepbrother."

"Hey, watch it!" Jeb said without heat.

"I don't need to put on a cape for her when she's surrounded by Marvel superheroes."

Ike sat forward. "You know I'd do just about anything for you, but blowing smoke up your ass by saying she's worth it isn't in my capabilities."

"Good thing I don't need your smoky breath." Wade turned around to look out the window.

"How do you plan on playing hero when you have two nights in Vegas at the end of the month?"

He'd actually forgotten about that. "I'll figure it out."

"You hear everything she says, huh?" Ike asked after thirty seconds of silence.

Wade was starting to reach the end of his patience. "Yeah."

"Uh-huh . . . well, did you catch the part about her dead husband being distraught about losing the *only* woman who loved him?"

He had heard that and didn't know what to make of it.

"Married one year and the love was gone?" Ike asked.

Wade swallowed hard.

"None of this feels right."

Yeah, it didn't feel right. "Jeb?"

"Yeah, Boss?"

Wade glanced Jeb's way, noticed the tightness of his jaw. The man never called him *Boss*, even though Wade paid the man's salary.

"Let's head on over to the airport."

Jeb questioned him with a look, his hands tight on the wheel.

Ike hit the back of Wade's seat. "Hell, yeah. That's what I'm talkin' about."

Thirty minutes later, Jeb and Wade were pulling away from the airport drop-off as Ike grew smaller in the rearview mirror.

Wade took a deep breath, leaned back, and closed his eyes. "That's better."

∾

She hated Texas. Yeah, heat was a big part of the reason for her dislike for the place, but it wasn't the warm weather that really ate at her. It was the inability to wear her normal clothes without sticking out. Blending was something Sasha needed to do.

Wearing a floral print dress she'd burn at the earliest opportunity, she ducked under the wide brim of the hat on her head and scratched the blonde wig covering up her dark hair.

Sasha dropped on one knee behind a tombstone and made as if she were searching her massive bag for a tissue. From the side of the "purse," she slid aside a hidden cover from the camera inside and looked at the image picked up on the screen. She zoomed in and placed a hand to the side of her head, turning up the volume on her earpiece.

Ruslan stood to the side of Fedor's grave, hands folded behind his back. His three-piece suit didn't single him out of a crowd, but his stony disposition while visiting his son's grave did.

As soon as he blipped on the radar in the States, she'd been close enough to smell the bastard.

She snapped a picture and waited.

Zakhar, his hired thug, stood several paces away. Dark glasses covered his eyes as he scanned the cemetery.

As luck would have it, Texans mourned their dead instead of burying them and forgetting. So the cemetery had several pockets of people milling about, giving her the camouflage she needed.

She glanced at the stone she knelt in front of. Bess Ann Carroll, 1904–1965. Surely the woman had been dead long enough to avoid anyone stopping by and seeing Sasha pretending to grieve over the grave.

The camera caught Ruslan turning his head. With a clear picture, she snapped an image.

"C'mon, say something, you bastard."

The high-powered microphone pointed in his direction picked up the breeze, or maybe that was Ruslan's heavy breathing. He knelt down and spoke under his breath.

"Can you hear me, you idiot?" Ruslan spoke in Russian.

Sasha turned up the volume.

"You bring this nothing, your bitch, from nowhere, and fuck all my plans. Now I watch my back like a dog. You should know she will eventually go down for your death. And when no one can reach her but my people, I will see that she is properly taken care of, eh? Even if I never see a penny of what is mine, I will take great pleasure in her sorrow. I hope you can hear me."

Ruslan stood and made the sign of the cross over his body. The motion alone should have burned his skin, but it didn't.

He looked up again, as if sensing someone watching him.

With a step back, he signaled to the car waiting, with a man as big as Zakhar standing by. From the trunk, the man removed a floral wreath. Something one saw at the funeral, and not placed on a grave a year later.

The second man leaned it on the gravestone.

"Is the camera working?" Ruslan asked.

The man appeared to play with the flowers and stood back. "All is ready."

Ruslan turned his back and walked away.

His minions followed.

 ⁂

It started to rain when the sun set, and now there were steady sheets creating puddles on the windowsill's edge.

Trina studied the moisture that gathered at the top of the window, then dropped as gravity and wind drove it down. Every once in a while, the drop would slow and detour a little to the right or the left. It joined with another drop of rain and grew . . . but it kept going until it hit the bottom and collected in a small pile. She couldn't help but feel like her life was one of those tiny drops that kept pushing her off course. Like the raindrop at the top of the window, she was all alone, only each time her life went off course, she picked up another person to join her for the ride.

The door to her bedroom opened and one of those drops walked in. Her stomach fluttered.

"Do you have any idea how much I love that smile?" Wade asked.

She turned back toward the window and traced a drop with her finger.

Wade walked up behind her and slid his arms around her waist, pulled her close, and dropped his chin on her shoulder.

Her heart fluttered along with her stomach.

"What are you thinkin' about?" he asked.

"About the butterflies kicking around inside of me every time I see you."

He nuzzled her neck and she leaned into him.

"Today was a hard day for you."

"Every time I think the answers are just around the corner, I turn to find a labyrinth with dead ends and circles. Today I found more questions. It feels like I'm never going to have all the answers."

He hugged her harder. "Can I ask you something?"

She turned her head enough to look in his eyes. "Anything."

"Is it easier or harder to know your husband was murdered?" The soft question in his eyes told her he truly cared about her answer.

"I've been blaming myself for Fedor's suicide for a year. Now I'm kicking myself for not looking harder and seeing the truth. The trail to his murderer grew colder with every day that passed. Now I've let him down by not trusting my judgment."

"If the police didn't see a reason to investigate, how could you have known?"

"Because he was my friend. We talked every day."

The answer seemed to appease Wade.

"Can I ask you another question?"

This time, she was fearful of what that would be. "Yes."

He hesitated . . .

She turned around in his arms and looked him in the eye. "Ask."

He squeezed her waist with both hands. "Are you still in love with him?"

"Oh, Wade." The expression on his face told her he was torn up over having to ask, or maybe he was afraid of her answer.

She shook her head quickly. "No." Before he could ask anything else, she told him what she could. "I was never *in love* with Fedor. Not the kind of love you're talking about. He never had that place in my heart."

Now he looked confused. "But you were married."

She blinked a few times. "His mother was dying. He would have done *anything* to make that woman happy in her final days. Alice worried more than any mother on this earth that her son was going to be alone once she was gone. Fedor and I met through mutual friends . . ."

Understanding washed over Wade's face. "You married a stranger? A man you weren't in love with?"

She tried to smile. "I cared for him. I did. I sometimes wish I had loved him the way a wife should love her husband. There were times I thought he was falling in love with me, which makes me feel even more remorseful."

"But you both entered into your marriage as what, an arrangement?"

She shrugged. "I speak Russian. He talked me into it, said I could back out anytime. We both wanted his mother to pass without worry. We drew up a prenuptial, he wanted me to have more, said he would buy me a house after our divorce so I could start a new life without any financial stress."

"You married him for the money."

It made her sound like a hooker. "It was a business arrangement. He married me to give his mother peace of mind while cancer ate her away. I married him to make enough money to bankroll my private flight attendant endeavor I wanted to start."

For the first time since they met, Wade's eyes showed doubt.

"I know how it sounds, how it looks. It was mutual. I promise you. Ask Lori. She set up the agreement."

"I don't need to ask Lori." His gaze softened.

"I can count on one hand how many times Fedor kissed me, Wade. Three were in front of the cameras at our wedding, the other two were at the hospital in front of his mother."

Wade looked over her head and around the room. "You had separate bedrooms."

She nodded. "Of course."

"You never slept with him." It wasn't a question.

She shook her head.

He tilted his head back and closed his eyes and sighed, long and deep.

"Here I thought I was competing with a dead man and wondering how I was going to win."

Trina rested her hands on his chest. "You're not competing with anyone. I haven't had a boyfriend for five years, and the butterflies didn't last past the first few dates. It's one of the many reasons I said yes to Fedor's plan."

Wade lost his smile, but his eyes twinkled. "Who was this boyfriend?"

His grin made her smile.

He reached up with both hands and captured her head. "I guess I don't have to feel bad about doing this." His lips lowered to hers, and she melted into the wings fluttering in her belly. He was so very good at erasing everything in her world but the slow tingling of his lips on hers and the smooth transition of his tongue taking over hers.

Her knees began to buckle, but he simply held her tighter, changed positions, and kept kissing her like he had nothing better to do for the next year.

Wade came up for air and bent enough to lift her into his arms. "I don't have to feel bad about doing this either."

She smiled as he walked her into her bathroom and turned on a light.

It was too bright, so she pointed toward the one next to it. The one that left the room in a soft glow.

He struggled to turn switches off and on while holding her.

"Don't drop me," she said, laughing.

"I haven't let you go yet."

He managed to dim the lights without dropping her and then walked them to the shower. He set her down and turned on the water.

"Lots of people in the house, we should conserve water and shower together."

There was no way they were going to conserve anything. "Probably a good idea."

He reached into his back pocket and removed his wallet. From it he pulled a condom and waved it at her. "In case you can't control yourself."

Trina placed a hand on her chest. "Me? I can hold out longer than you."

He lifted an eyebrow, a smile in his eyes. "Did you just smack down a challenge, ma'am?"

"I think I did."

With a wicked smile, he reached over his shoulders and pulled his shirt over his head.

Her heart skipped a double jump rope and her mouth started to dry. He was so very well sculpted. Wide shoulders that slimmed at his waist.

She swallowed.

"Done looking?" he asked.

Right . . . this was a challenge. Her racing heart told her she was going to lose if she let her mind wander any more.

Wade watched her fingers move as she reached for the buttons on her shirt and slowly undid them.

She wore a lacy purple bra that Wade seemed to admire when he licked his lips. Before she let her shirt drop to the floor, she moved to her jeans.

Wade shifted his feet, but his eyes never left her hands as she stripped.

In a move more daring than she normally allowed herself, she let her fingertips follow the zipper down and passed a slow circle over herself through her clothing.

"Sweet Jesus," he muttered.

It was hard to miss the tightening of his jeans while he watched.

Because he had yet to move in and help her, Trina wiggled her hips to remove her pants until she kicked them away and stood in a loose shirt, panties, and a bra.

Wade shook his head and leaned down to grab one of his boots. He struggled with it and had to jump a few times to keep his balance while he removed it.

He kicked the second one free, and Trina let her shirt drop to the floor. She reached for the clasp of her bra, and he stopped her. "Let me."

Only he was struggling with his jeans and fell into the counter before he kicked them away. His underwear went with the jeans, and Trina knew she'd win this round of her challenge.

Steam filled the bathroom when he opened the glass door of the shower. Wade adjusted the temperature before he reached for her.

"I'm still wearing—"

"Don't care."

He was kissing her before she felt the water wash over her hypersensitive skin.

Trina's fingers had a feast as they followed the water over his shoulders and down his back. She didn't stop there . . . the curve of his ass was an hourly temptation.

Wade dropped his mouth to the top of her breast, his lips hotter than the water soothing their skin. Just when she thought he'd pull her bra away, he turned her to face the wall. He found the shampoo and poured a generous amount in the palm of his hand before rubbing it into her hair. He massaged her scalp, which should have distracted her from all the pulsating girl parts of her excited body, but his touch only added to it.

With soap-filled hands, he trailed down her neck, her shoulders, and over the bra he had yet to remove. She steadied herself on the shower wall. When his touch fanned out over her stomach, everything clenched, and when he reached over the scrap of material covering her, her knees wobbled.

Wade kept her upright by holding her with one firm hand right between her legs, his fingers teasing. She tried to give him more room, but he didn't linger. She whimpered when he returned to washing her body instead of making her cry out his name.

This was his tactic to win their challenge, and as much as she wanted to beg him to do more than pet her, she wanted to see how he would hold up when she turned him around in the warm, soapy water.

The strokes of his hands didn't leave any part of her untouched. When he moved back up her body, she turned and slid her hands down her waist and removed her panties. "Missed a spot," she teased. She lifted a leg on the shower step and washed the space he had missed. Then did the same to the underside of her breasts once she let her bra fall to the floor.

Wade placed both hands on the tile behind her, his breathing just as heavy as hers.

Trina didn't try to kiss him or even touch him when she reached for the soap. She did, however, let her hardened nipples brush against his chest before she moved to take his spot in the shower space.

She knelt down and, with both hands, began his bath on one of his legs. She used long strokes, each time reaching higher, until her fingernails grazed his tightened balls. The picture she knew she was teasing him with made her want to look, but she continued, ignoring his erection, which was inches from her lips.

His hips pushed forward when she switched to his other leg.

One of his hands reached for the back of her head.

She smiled, knew he wasn't going to let her stand without tasting him. But he was going to have to ask.

The globes of his butt felt good in her slick hands. She reached around his hips, moved her head to the other side of his cock, felt the tip brush her cheek.

His fingers tightened in her hair.

That was when she looked up, jaw slacked, the tip of her tongue dancing over her teeth.

"You win," he said, his voice hoarse.

Not losing eye contact, she gave him what he wanted, first with her tongue, then her lips, and eventually felt him hit the back of her throat. His legs quivered when she took him deeper and closed her eyes. She wanted to take all of him, but she also needed to breathe. She stroked what she couldn't take and looked up enough to know he was watching every move she made. She smiled around him, and then dove in for more.

"Stop, I'm going to—"

She didn't stop. And apparently he didn't have the will to pull her away. Her lips tingled with the taste of him. The siren in her stretched and purred with the power of her ability to make him lose control.

Her knees ached when she tried to stand.

Wade reached out a hand to help.

"You didn't stop." He wore a drunken smile.

"Oops."

The water started to turn cold. Trina glanced at the showerhead. "So much for conservation."

He shivered, grabbed the shampoo, and made quick work of finishing what she started.

Once out, Wade tossed a towel over her shoulders before grabbing one for himself.

With Superman speed, Wade dropped his damp towel and helped her with hers.

"I can manage," she said, her grin teasing.

"I'm sure you can, but I can't wait."

He dried her off. Even managed to wring out her long hair before wrapping her in a dry towel. With both hands on her backside, he pushed her out of the bathroom and straight to the bed. He turned her around and playfully nudged her onto her back.

"Now, where were we?" he asked as he dropped to his knees. "Oh, yes . . ." He picked up the edge of the towel with his teeth, dropped it to one side. "There we were."

Chapter Twenty-Six

"Good morning."

Trina blinked, hardly believing what she was seeing.

"Wade?" she called behind her.

"Just a second, darlin'."

"I see you weren't expecting me."

Trina looked at the two new additions in the room and then to Lori, who was huddled over her coffee cup.

"Hi, Daddy," Trina finally addressed her father.

Wade's footsteps stopped when he walked into the kitchen. His voice penetrated the back of the room. "Mom. What are you doing here?"

Vicki and Mauro sat at the kitchen counter, coffee cups close by. Neither of them looked like they knew how to smile.

Trina's father didn't start with any pleasantries. His gaze tracked Wade as he walked into the room and kissed his mother's cheek.

"Really? In your husband's house?" Mauro spoke in Spanish.

The euphoria Trina shared with Wade the night before shattered with her father's accusing words.

Trina lifted her chin. "It's rude to speak in Spanish, Papa."

"Do you want everyone to hear what I have to say?" He looked directly at Wade.

Wade placed a hand on her arm, sensing the heat in her father's words, even if he didn't understand them.

Instead of giving her father a private audience, she forced a smile. "Wade, I'd like you to meet my father, Mauro. Daddy, this is Wade."

She waited a beat and prayed her father hadn't lost *all* his manners.

Mauro puffed out his chest like he had for her first date when she was fifteen, and went toe-to-toe with Wade.

Wade put his hand out. "It's a pleasure to meet you, sir."

Mauro lifted his hand slowly before grabbing hold.

The room was silent while they shook hands.

Trina glanced at Lori.

Lori looked at their clasped hands.

Vicki glared at Trina.

Her father silently kept shaking for what felt like five minutes. "You're a musician?" he eventually asked, even though he had yet to let Wade's hand go.

"I am."

Lori cleared her throat and Mauro finally released.

"I'm surprised to see you here," Wade told his mother.

Vicki lifted her chin. "Ike returned without you. I was concerned. Imagine my surprise when I arrived thirty minutes after Trina's father. Both of us quite clueless about what is going on here."

"And my surprise when I learned the tabloids had the truth of the matter regarding your new *friendship*," Mauro said.

"The tabloids are full of lies, Papa. You know that."

"Are you two dating?" he asked.

Trina glanced at Wade.

"Yes, sir. We are."

Her father narrowed his eyes at Wade. "Then you should have respect for her late husband and take it away from this house." Mauro's words were harsh and meant to hurt.

"There have been a few unfortunate events that have prevented that."

Mauro looked unconvinced. "What could be so limiting that a man of your standing and wealth cannot overcome?"

"Is there a party in here?" On crutches, Avery hobbled into the kitchen.

Lori scrambled to her side to help, and Wade pushed a chair out of her way so Avery had a clear path to her perch on the couch.

"What are you doing up without someone helping?" Trina asked.

"Shannon doesn't need to watch me pee," Avery insisted.

"Oh my Lord."

Trina turned around to see Vicki's and her father's eyes tracking Avery.

"We will be leaving the house once Avery is ready to fly," she told her father. "I'm sorry to disappoint you. But it couldn't be helped."

"What happened?" Vicki asked.

Mauro had met Avery before, when she was visiting over the holidays. He seemed to lose much of his anger while watching her attempt to walk.

"Someone beat the crap out of me in a parking lot in broad daylight in the center of Manhattan. At the same time someone else broke into the office out back. No one thinks it's a coincidence. Oh, and the police are opening up Fedor's case as a murder investigation." Avery sighed once she was finally on the couch with her foot propped up on a few pillows. "Did I miss anything else?"

"No, that about covers it," Lori said.

"Who is Fedor?" Vicki asked.

"Trina's late husband," Wade told her.

"Murder?" Mauro asked Trina directly.

She answered with a single nod. "Whoever broke in didn't take anything, they just wiped the room clean of any fingerprints."

"And blood," Avery offered. "Don't forget the blood, and the house-keeper's mysterious accidental death. I forgot about that."

"Is this all true?" Mauro asked Trina in Spanish.

"Sadly," she told him.

"No wonder Ike suggested I come," Vicki said.

"Ike had no business dragging you into this. In fact, it's safer for you to be at home."

"Then you should come with me."

"Once Trina can safely leave, I'll be back in Texas." Wade moved beside Trina and placed a hand on the small of her back. "I'm truly sorry if that upsets either one of you, but that's how this is going to play out."

Jeb, Reed, and Shannon walked into the room and paused at the door.

Wade turned to Reed. "How soon will we have Rick's replacement here?"

"Couple hours."

Wade addressed Jeb. "When he arrives, I'd like you to accompany my mother home. Make sure she arrives safely. If I need ya back, I'll let you know. Otherwise, plan on helping out Reed's team in any manner they need to ensure the ranch is safe."

"You got it."

"And tell Ike he should start looking for another job."

"Wade, no—"

"He placed you in danger, telling you to come here. Now I need to get you home and remove some of the protection we have in place in order to make that happen. He was completely out of line."

"But—"

"No, ma'am. There are no buts in this situation."

"I'll take care of it," Jeb told Wade.

"How soon can you leave?" Mauro asked Trina.

"Five days. So long as nothing new happens."

Avery snorted from the couch. "With our luck, something new is bound to happen by lunch."

∽

Something new came in the form of an increase in body count.

Armstrong and Gray arrived at the house at two o'clock. Right after Jeb left for the airport with Vicki and Mauro. Their conversation was directed toward Avery.

"We found our suspect," Gray stated once everyone was seated.

"He's dead. OD in Central Park. He was found two days ago. Came in as a John Doe until he was identified through his tattoos."

Avery blinked. "What kind of tattoos?"

"Do you remember something?" Trina asked softly.

"I don't know."

"He liked his ink, but kept most of it off his face and forearms."

"Most?" Lori asked.

Avery stared off at the wall across the room, her fingers on her good hand scratching the inside of her wrist.

"Avery?" Shannon's calm voice seemed to focus her. "Do you remember something?"

She looked down at her arm before shaking her head. "No."

"If you do . . ."

"Yeah, I know. Call you."

The conversation moved to Trina. "Our investigation into Cindy Geist has taken a turn."

"Oh?"

"We found fifty thousand euros in a coffee can in her backyard. Her husband said she'd buried it a year ago as a time capsule. She didn't tell him what was in it. When he dug it up and found the money, he called us."

"Euros?"

"Strange currency for a woman who'd never been out of the country."

Trina felt her skin crawl. "Blood money. She knew something."

"That's our thoughts. She and her husband had applied for passports and were planning a second honeymoon."

"Or she was running," Reed said.

"She didn't run fast enough." Avery's stone-cold delivery of the facts chilled the room.

∽

Just after dark, Trina, Wade, and Reed were in Fedor's office, putting the place back together. There wasn't a chance in hell she'd see if anything was missing without seeing it as it had been when Fedor was alive.

Reed held a photograph he'd received from the crime scene pictures. How he obtained them, Trina didn't ask. She was thankful that she didn't need to see the ones that actually showed Fedor's lifeless body.

Although she knew exactly when Reed was looking at those particular pictures. He flipped them quickly when she walked around him to peer at his phone.

She pushed a plush chair to the far corner of the room, beside a bookcase, a lamp, and a side table.

Wade and Reed scooted the desk around until it was perfectly centered to the room and just past the three-quarter mark of the second set of windows. The curtains had been replaced . . . after. There was a fireplace on the north side of the room, the hearth clean of ashes and soot. She remembered how Fedor liked to have a fire going on cool nights. He didn't like the gas-fed options like they had inside the house. "Crackling wood and the smell of smoke is primal," he'd told her, laughing.

"You okay?" Wade asked as he came up behind her.

She blinked her gaze away from the fireplace. "Yup."

Reed picked up shards of broken glass and looked at the picture on his phone. "I'm assuming that this used to be this vase." He turned the phone around and pointed to it.

Trina shrugged. "Looks right. I couldn't really tell you."

Reed looked from his phone to the desk, and then tweaked the objects on the desk until he got them just right.

It took a couple of hours, but they finally had the room looking somewhat normal, minus the dark smudges left behind from the investigators searching for prints.

"Okay." Reed dropped his arm holding his phone. "We're done." He turned a full circle, looked at his phone, and repeated his action several times.

"It's all here." Trina didn't see one thing missing.

Reed flipped through a few pictures, tilted his head, and stared at where Fedor's body would have landed.

"Let's talk about what you would see when you normally walked in."

Trina pushed the last time out of her head and moved to the door.

"It was almost always late. Or around dinnertime, if he was home. Most nights he was at the hospital until late. At least toward the end."

Wade watched her from the corner of the room, something Trina was acutely aware of.

She offered him a reassuring smile, flipped her hair over her shoulder, and walked toward the desk.

The memory of Fedor sitting behind his desk, his eyes fixed on the fire in the hearth, filled her thoughts. Many times he didn't even realize she was standing there until after she called his name. Not that the office was so big that he could miss her walking in. It's just that he was so focused on his problems, it was easy to sneak up on him.

"... so he would jump sometimes, when I stood next to the desk." She stood there now, looking down and trying hard not to see him there dead.

Alive.

See him alive, she told herself.

She rolled her hands.

"When he wasn't whittling some new trinket, he played with two silver balls. Like worry stones. It was a habit."

Reed flipped through a few pictures. "Did he keep them in here?"

"This is where I noticed them. It wasn't something he did when he was at the hospital, so I doubt he kept them with him."

Reed pulled open drawers that they'd dropped the contents back inside in their haste to make the room look normal.

They didn't find them.

"They aren't here. The coroner report should tell what was found on his person when they brought him in. I'll see if we can get a copy."

"Seems like an odd thing to be missing," Wade said.

"Were they valuable?" Reed asked.

"I have no idea. No more than anything else in here, I suspect."

"Sentimental? Did they belong to a family member? His mother?"

Trina shook her head. "His grandfather gave them to him. That and this." She picked up the inkwell and fountain pen that sat on the corner of his desk. "It belonged to his grandfather on Ruslan's side."

"'To my pride and joy,'" she read aloud.

Wade moved beside her.

"So the grandfather called him his pride and joy. Not his own son," Reed mused out loud.

"I didn't question it. I just know that at some point Fedor pointed out the pen and showed me what was written on it."

Reed smiled and set the pen in question back on the desk. "So Grandpa loved his grandson more than his own son, and the only things missing in here are the silver worry stones."

"Shouldn't we tell the police?" Wade asked.

"We will . . . eventually."

"Eventually?"

Reed sighed. "There are always leaks in investigations. Just like me having the pictures of this office the night Fedor's body was found, someone else might be listening in on other facts. Two missing silver stones mean nothing unless we find them with someone who shouldn't have them. Then maybe we will have a direct link to our killer."

"I would think stealing anything like that would be a stupid mistake for a killer willing to go through all this effort to hide."

"Many perps collect trophies of their kills. In this case, there might be a personal connection. Considering Ruslan is the number one suspect, it wouldn't be a stretch to pin him for a man who wanted to be his father's pride and joy . . . and therefore, he grabbed the stones at some point. Could have been the night of Fedor's death, or maybe last week. It's hard to say."

"Why not let the information leak and sit back and watch? If it's Ruslan, he might try and get rid of the stones. Or bring them back here," Trina said.

Reed paused. "That's certainly an option, but not until this house is empty. Our murderer has been free for a year. Chances are they think they're home clear, but now that the police are opening up the investigation again, things will heat up."

"We need to get Avery out of here," Trina muttered.

"We need to get *you* out of here." Wade wrapped his arm around her waist.

She rested the side of her head on his chest. Leaning on him had become a habit, one she didn't want to break.

Reed's cell phone rang and he turned to take the call. "I'm afraid to ask why you're calling."

Reed looked at Trina and Wade as he spoke.

He didn't blink. "Is that so. Why?"

There was a pause while he listened.

"Can you tap that feed into our system?" Reed smiled. "Of course you can."

He nodded. "Where is Ruslan now?"

Trina heightened her attention to Reed's conversation.

"No, I have New York covered. Do you need backup?" Reed grinned again. "Of course not. You know how to get ahold of me if you do."

He hung up.

"Who was that?" Wade asked.

"Sasha."

"Catwoman?"

Reed smiled. "Yeah, her. Seems Ruslan had a need to visit his son's grave."

Trina narrowed her eyes. "What? Why?"

"To place flowers, of all things . . . flowers hiding a camera."

"He wants to see who is stopping by?"

"So it appears. Only we're attempting to trace the feed back to him."

Wade squeezed Trina's arm. "My mother is on her way back to Texas."

Reed held up a hand. "And Ruslan has already left."

"Where to?"

"The flight plan was Mexico City. Sasha is following."

Trina turned a full circle in the room. "Ruslan has to be behind this. Behind Fedor's murder."

"Why would a father kill his son?" Wade asked.

Trina lifted her head. "I don't know. But I know someone who would."

"Who?" Reed asked.

Trina scanned the room again. "Alice."

"But she's dead."

"That doesn't mean she's done talking." And it was high time Trina heard what she had to say.

Chapter Twenty-Seven

While Trina accompanied Avery to her follow-up appointments with the plastic surgeon and the orthopedist one last time before returning to Texas, Lori and Reed detoured to the law office of Dwight Crockett. Alice's estate attorney had been the one to say there would be letters arriving throughout the year, and since there had yet to be one such note, Lori decided to probe further.

With the help of her friends, Trina locked up the Hamptons home and packed all her personal belongings. Everything else would be dealt with later. If Trina had any say, she wouldn't deal with it ever again. The skeletons in the closets there seemed to come to life, and she was getting tired of jumping at her own shadow.

Shannon met Trina, Avery, Wade, and Cooper, the relief body-guard, on the tarmac. They arranged a jet large enough to accommodate their group through Fairchild Charters, a company Trina had once worked with and had one day hoped to equip with her team of elite flight attendants. Now she was using their services as a paying customer.

Strange how life worked out sometimes.

She recognized one of the pilots when she entered the jet.

They exchanged pleasantries before she introduced him to everyone. "We're just waiting for Reed and Lori."

Unable to help herself, Trina assisted the flight attendant serving and did a quick check to make sure they had everything they needed for the three-and-a-half-hour flight to Texas.

The surgeon had removed the bulk of Avery's bandages, leaving her with a small scrap of material over her nose. Most of the swelling had gone down, and the colors on her face were a nasty yellow green, but even those were looking better each morning.

The longest lasting effect was the haunted look in Avery's eyes. Trina saw it every time Avery didn't think anyone was watching her.

Social services at the hospital had suggested Avery see a psychologist or counselor of some sort to help deal with the aftereffects of the assault. At the time, Avery didn't want to hear it. But maybe in a few weeks Trina could talk her into it.

"We're here," Lori announced as she and Reed climbed the steps into the plane.

Trina met the whites of Lori's eyes. "Do you have the letters?"

Her smile waned. "Let's get on our way."

The hope in Trina's chest sunk.

When the pilot had the jet in the air, Lori relayed her conversation with Mr. Crockett.

"He had been instructed to send the letters to a mailbox in Arizona."

"Arizona?"

Lori nodded. "Starting six months ago."

"Who was supposed to pick them up in Arizona?"

"Dwight didn't know. He was assured the letters would get to you," Lori told Trina.

"I haven't gotten them."

"I told him that. He seemed surprised."

Reed unbuckled his belt and moved to the minibar, selected a bottle of water.

The flight attendant attempted to help him, but he waved her off. "I've already informed the team. We'll find out who has control of the box and if the letters are just sitting there, or if Alice had another party invested in getting them to you."

"Did he send out everything?" Trina asked Lori.

"He says there is one more letter in his possession. I asked him to hold on to it until he hears from me. In light of everything going on, he agreed."

"Well, that's something, at least."

"So what's the plan now?" Avery asked.

"I'll get you comfortable at the ranch, and then Lori and I will go to the bank, check out whatever is in that safe deposit box."

"I'm going to have to go home for a few days," Shannon interjected. "I don't want to miss any more appointments than I have to." She paused. "Unless you need me."

"We have it," Avery told her. "But take a bodyguard."

"I doubt anyone is after—"

Reed stopped her. "You've heard every conversation we've had. I'll have someone on the ground ready to accompany you wherever you need to go until we get to the bottom of all this."

Shannon frowned.

"Hey, at least you don't have to worry about Scarface taking you out. Since he's dead." Avery's off-color words made everyone pause.

She looked up. "What?"

"Whoever hired him isn't," Reed reminded her.

"Don't you have clients to see, Lori?" Trina redirected the conversation.

"This has been more important."

"I won't disagree, but you need to get back to your life, too."

"Trina—"

"I have bodyguards and Texas law behind me."

"And me." Wade reached out for her hand and laced his fingers through hers.

"Didn't I hear something about a Vegas show you're scheduled to perform?"

"I'll cancel."

Trina lost her smile. "No, you won't."

"Excuse me?"

"Wade. That's ridiculous."

He matched her frown with one of his own. "You are more important than a crowd full of strangers."

As much as she wanted to fall into the image he was painting, reality kicked her. "I don't know when things are going to settle down. You have a life, and I've taken you away from it since the day we met."

"My choice." He wasn't backing down.

"Vegas is a short flight. You have two shows scheduled, right?"

He didn't answer.

"Wade. Be reasonable."

"We'll discuss this later."

"There isn't anything to discuss. If things were calm, I'd go with you."

His thumb stroked the inside of her wrist. "We'll see."

"Your mother hates me enough as it is. If you start canceling shows on my behalf, I'll never get on her good side. If this is gonna work"— she pointed between the two of them—"then your mom has to tolerate me." Trina wasn't about to hope for more.

"What is your obsession with pleasing my mother?" he asked.

"Hey, my last mother-in-law left me a zillion dollars. It's important."

Wade cracked a smile. "My mother doesn't have any money."

"Great, then maybe I can leave her some of mine. The point is, you have a life. It isn't all about me."

Wade broke eye contact with her and looked around at all the faces staring at them.

"Let's have Jeb meet you at Trina's. We already have more security en route to your home. All I suggest is avoiding any after-parties or breaches in backstage security. Like everyone else here, you've been privy to all the conversations, and there is always a chance someone is watching you as closely as everyone else. But unlike the rest of us, you have a harder time blending into the background, and that will come in handy if you need help," Reed said.

"So we're all set." Trina grasped Wade's hand.

Wade grumbled but didn't argue again.

⌒⊚⌒

Trina's hands shook as she entered Interstate Bank. When she gave them her ID, she half expected them to tell her they didn't have a box with her name on it.

They did.

She and Lori were led into the locked room full of locked boxes.

Once the bank manager left the vault, Trina found the box number that matched her key. She slid the metal container from its slot and placed it on a table at one end of the room.

"Well . . . here we go."

Trina opened the box. Inside were two large envelopes. She opened the first and removed familiar paperwork. "Samantha's contract." The only proof that her and Fedor's marriage was secured even before they said *I do*.

"Sasha knows about Alliance."

Fedor would have placed the paperwork in his office safe, a safe that was virtually empty when they finally opened it just prior to closing up the house. There had been a stack of euros to the tune of fifty thousand.

Trina pushed the contracts aside and opened the second envelope. This one had several pieces of paperwork bundled together.

A photograph of Alice when she had to have been in her twenties fell out. She had a black eye and a battered soul. Along with the image was a copy of a hospital report. She used a fake name and said she'd fallen. Trina kept reading until she found a doctor's note saying that the injury didn't match the story, and that he suspected she was being abused.

Several other images through what seemed to be a couple of years followed. One had a social service referral, along with an agency in place to protect children.

"He was beating her."

Trina kept flipping until she found an even more disturbing image, Ruslan in midswing and a woman falling to the ground. Only this wasn't Alice, it was someone else. Tall, exotic. She couldn't be more than twenty, if that. It was hard to judge, since the image was faded and printed on plain paper. The next two pictures were of Ruslan standing over the same woman.

The last one was of the lone woman's lifeless body.

"Jesus." Lori blew out a breath.

"This had to be how Alice got away from him."

"She had something on him."

Trina turned the paper over, and on the bottom, there was a name.

Lori removed her cell phone and started taking pictures of the images and a close-up of the name.

"The fewer people who know about this, the better," Lori said before they left the bank.

"If I tell Wade, he might never leave."

"Avery has had enough trauma, and Shannon needs to distance herself."

"No texting, no phone calls. In person only and in secure places."

Trina glanced at her purse and thought about her phone. A phone that had a bug in it so deep, it took a week to find. She now had a new phone, and the one in question was sitting at the ranch, where she wanted whoever had tracked her to think she was.

"When will we take this to the police?"

"When we can prove something. Otherwise all we do is poke the sleeping bear. And Ruslan pokes back, as Reed keeps pointing out."

"Good thing I don't have anywhere to be for a while."

"Everyone vacating will give the illusion that we've found nothing."

"You're starting to sound like your boyfriend," Trina told Lori.

"I like to think he's starting to sound like me."

They exited the vault and signed out of the bank before meeting Reed, who stood by the front door. He didn't dare walk in with a side-arm attached to a holster.

"Well?" he asked once they joined him.

Lori opened her phone and showed him the pictures in silence. Reed's smile fell.

She pointed toward the camera at the door. "Nothing new," she said.

"Let's get you home, then." He ushered them into the car and out of the parking lot.

"This stays between us," he said without offering any other words on the subject of a dead woman at Ruslan's hand.

"We're one step ahead of you," Lori told him.

Trina glanced out the back window of the SUV and wondered just how many eyes could possibly be on her at that moment.

Chapter Twenty-Eight

"I don't want to leave." Wade stood on Trina's porch, holding her in his arms. Jeb sat in the car with the engine running to keep it cool in the Texas heat. Even though fall was nipping the air in the rest of the country, Texas didn't get the memo.

"I know. I appreciate the thought of you wanting to stay, but it isn't practical, Wade. My life is complicated, and it isn't fair that I've monopolized yours as much as I have."

"That's my choice."

"Is it? Wouldn't you rather have taken me out dancing, made love to me out in a field somewhere, and sent me flowers in the morning instead of spending all our time in hospitals and talking to the police?"

Wade blinked a few times. "Sorry, I'm stuck on the image of you naked in a field."

She playfully slapped his chest. "None of this, of us, has been normal."

"Yeah, and I'm usually the cause. It's kinda nice to have the crazy on the other side of the relationship."

Trina smiled. "Glad I could help with that." She slipped her hands around his waist.

He pulled her closer. "I miss you already."

Her eyes grew misty.

"Hey . . . no tears."

"Sorry." She looked down.

"Don't be. A woman crying over me is wildly exciting. But if it hurts too much, I'll unpack my bags now."

Trina swallowed back her mist and faked a smile. "I'm good. Besides, you need to stock up on supplies while you're gone." Supplies meaning condoms. They'd talked about it the night before when they burned through the last of them.

"Nawh, I'm going to see my doctor and ditch the need."

She liked the sound of that.

He looked over his shoulder at the car before pulling her as close as two bodies could be with their clothes on.

"I'm going to miss you," he whispered as he leaned down to kiss her.

The tears were there again, fueling her response and making her cling to him. What if he walked away and realized he didn't want the drama anymore? What if he found Jordyn more appealing when he got home? What if his fans reminded him of all the things he would give up by having an exclusive girlfriend?

What if he didn't come back?

She clung to him for one last taste before he broke away.

"I'll be back," he said against her lips.

"I wouldn't blame you if you ran off and never looked over your shoulder," she said but didn't mean.

"That isn't going to happen."

"Good. Because I was lying. I'll hunt you down and make you fall in love with me." Where those words had come from, she wasn't sure. But she didn't regret them when they fell out of her mouth.

"Will you?"

"I can be very persuasive when determined."

"This I can't wait to see."

She reached up to kiss him again.

He pulled away and leaned his forehead on hers. "If I don't leave now, I'm not going to."

She would never know if he would come back if she didn't let him go.

She rubbed her hands on his chest one last time and dropped them to her sides.

"I'll call when I get home."

"Okay."

He turned and jogged down the steps.

She watched his backside as he walked to the car.

"Your eyes are burning a hole in my ass, little lady."

"Get used to it."

He tossed his head back and laughed as he climbed into the car.

She watched as he disappeared down her driveway, and clenched her shirt over her chest. "He'll be back," she told herself.

"He'll be back."

Traffic sucked, and it took three hours to drive from Trina's home to Wade's ranch. It took four hours to talk his mother off the ledge. Five minutes to tell Ike one final time that he no longer needed him and remind him of the confidentiality clause in his signed contract if Ike planned on ever working again. Ike was reminded to keep anything he'd heard or seen in regards to Trina to himself. Saying goodbye to a man Wade thought was his friend wasn't as hard as he thought it would be when he noticed how quickly Ike reminded him of the financial severance they'd agreed on if they ever parted ways.

The letters of recommendation, however, weren't something Wade was willing to deliver.

The inner circle that included his agent and publicist was quick to smile and tell Wade whatever he wanted to hear. Which only left Jeb and his mother to tell him the truth about anything. Considering his mother's take on things, that really only left Jeb.

"I'm counting on you to be up-front with me," he told his bodyguard and friend.

Jeb looked around the great room. The new cameras and extra bodyguards on the ranch couldn't be ignored.

"I trust her and her friends," Jeb told him. "I'll let you know if that changes. As for matters of hearts and sunsets . . . you have to determine if she's the right fit."

Wade didn't skip a beat. "She already fits."

"There is one thing I like about Trina above anyone else who has been in your life."

"Oh?"

Jeb made eye contact and didn't break it. "She doesn't need anything from you other than you. Not your money, your fame . . . your connections, your music. Just you. That's a rare gift in your world. Even I need your money." Jeb's smile had Wade laughing.

"I appreciate your endorsement."

"Honey?" His mother walked into the room, a familiar face following behind. "Dr. Kushman said you called him. You feeling okay?"

"Hey, Charles, thanks for coming on such short notice."

"Anything for you, Wade."

"Sweetheart?" His mother was all syrup and smiles once he put an end to her rant about Trina.

"I'm good, Mama. Just a checkup. No time to go into town." Wade blew past his mother and shook the doctor's hand. "Let's step into my office."

House calls were a nice perk of his fame.

By eight o'clock that night, Charles had called with a clean bill of health, and Wade was on the phone, saying good night to Trina.

"You sound even sexier over the phone," he told her.

"I've been practicing all day."

"My doctor just called, and I'm all checked out."

"That was quick."

"Important things are taken care of first."

Trina laughed.

"I'll be happy to stock up on more supplies for when I'm back from Vegas." He secretly hoped she wouldn't encourage him to glove up. He hadn't forgotten what unlatexed lovin' felt like, even though it wasn't something he did very often in his life. Especially since he'd broken the top one hundred on the charts.

"Like I told you, I have an IUD. I'm happy to get a copy of my last bloodwork if you want to see it."

"I trust you." More than anyone else he'd been with. "But why the IUD, if you weren't sleeping with Fedor?"

"I was a flight attendant. Periods got in the way."

"That makes sense."

"I'll let you decide," she told him. "I might be provoked to hunt you down if you didn't come back, but I would never trap you."

He shivered. "That was both exciting and a little terrifying, all in the same sentence."

"How so?"

"Exciting to see you hunting me down. Would you dress like that woman in the hotel room, Catwoman?"

"Sasha?" Trina laughed. "I don't think I could pull that off."

"I disagree. I might buy you the outfit just to find out."

"Harboring fantasies about her, are you?"

"Just the outfit. Not the woman." Wade propped his stocking feet up on his bed and relaxed against his headboard.

"So what's the terrifying part?"

He gave his head a quick shake. "The reality that I wouldn't mind you trapping me."

He heard her suck in a breath. "Wade . . ."

"Too soon?"

"No, I just . . . I'm not taking you up on that. There will be no accidents that force us together. You're gonna have to want it and stick around to see if it works."

"Should I get in my truck right now and show you just how much it works?"

"When you're back from Vegas."

Vegas couldn't come and go too soon.

⤙⤚

Ruslan threw a crystal glass across the room and took brief satisfaction in it shattering into a thousand pieces on the floor.

He looked at his phone again. Saw an image he knew was out there but had been told was destroyed.

Now they had it.

They . . . the collective clusterfuck that was on him like maggots on rotted flesh.

Natasha had tried to blackmail him.

Him!

In Natasha's attempts to blackmail him, Alice had gained her freedom by catching him in the act of removing that *pizda* from this earth. His wife was wise enough to know that she, and her son, would be dead if she said a thing to anyone. So when he'd gone to Fedor's that night just over a year ago to sway him to his side, he'd learned that not only did Fedor not know about Natasha, he'd also turned into a *tryapka*.

No son of his could be that weak.

He'd put up a fight. Even had a gun, which Ruslan had put to good use.

Everything had been sewn up.

All the ends neatly tied.

Until his daughter-in-law came back.

Now everything was falling apart, and if he didn't get his hands a little dirty, everything would be destroyed.

"The woman in the pictures was Natasha Budanov, the same name written on the back."

"Russian." Trina now had a name to go with the face of the dead woman whose killer was still free. "How was she connected to Ruslan, outside of the fact he killed her?"

Reed spoke to her on a secure line.

"They were lovers, from what I can tell. She lived in Germany. He would visit her when he was there."

"She didn't look old enough to acquire a taste for a monster like him."

"He had money, and she was just short of a hooker."

"What do you mean?"

"She had a prior of burglary while she was servicing a man."

"Servicing?" Trina winced.

"Prostitution isn't as frowned upon in other parts of the world as it is here. Have you been to Amsterdam?"

"Yes."

"Okay, so you know. Jacking the john for his wallet is a bigger deal. Natasha was pretty enough to avoid the streets, but she liked money. I can only assume Ruslan paid her well enough to keep her as a mistress."

There wasn't enough money in the world.

"Did her death go unnoticed?"

"Virtually. But then, Ruslan was a mist in her bedroom that faded when the sun came up. The only person willing to part with information was a friend in the same field as Natasha that still lived in the same town."

"How on earth did you find her?"

"We have boots on the ground where Natasha lived. With a picture of the woman and a wad of euros, people talk. Our source had a picture of Natasha and herself back when they were both working on their backs. Natasha's friend gave up the profession after Natasha's death. We dug a little deeper and found the prior in the database and connected the dots. Miss Budanov was found dead on the rocks off a cliff. It was labeled a suicide."

Fedor's image flashed in Trina's head. "That sounds all too familiar."

"We thought so, too. One more thing."

"I'm listening."

"Natasha had a child."

The blood fell from Trina's face. "Ruslan's?"

"We're not sure. Locating her is proving more difficult than finding the mom."

"A girl?"

"That's what our source told us."

"Fedor had a sister?"

"Maybe, maybe not. Natasha wasn't an exclusive woman. We would need a paternity test to prove it. With Fedor dead and Ruslan unavailable to swab, we may never know. But we are looking. The question really needs to be, Did Alice know about the child? Did Fedor? Sasha said she found the papers in Fedor's office, but did she find all of them? Or did Alice give them to her?"

"Why don't you just ask her? Doesn't Sasha contact you?"

"Whenever she's damn good and ready, she will. Until then, I'm out of luck."

Trina hung her head, gripped the phone. "Let me get this straight. You can find a woman who is what, dead twenty years?"

"Twenty-five."

"Twenty-five years," Trina continued. "But Stealth Woman in a black leotard remains elusive?"

"Yup. Pretty much." Reed held no guilt in the tone of his voice.

"Should I be impressed?"

"Hell yeah. I am. So is Neil, and you know that man never cracks a smile."

Neil never talked, let alone smiled.

"What about the box in Arizona?"

"Empty."

"Who is it registered to?"

Reed started laughing. "Buddy Nash."

"What?"

"You heard me. Buddy Nash. Move the name around, take away a few letters . . . sounds a whole lot like Natasha Budanov, doesn't it?"

Trina squeezed the bridge of her nose. "You know, I really wish I had known Alice longer."

"I can do you one better. I wish I had known her at all."

∽∾

Following Ruslan in Mexico City was a hell of a lot easier than in a graveyard in Texas. With her dark hair, dark eyes, and the ability to speak the language, she fooled the locals. She added a fake mole to her cheek and made sure it matched the one on the bogus passport she carried, and waltzed around in big sunglasses and red-hot lipstick on her lips.

She lost Ruslan inside the hotel but followed him with her bug on his phone. She was making herself comfortable in the lobby when Zakhar walked past her and out the doors of the four-star establishment.

Zakhar was on a mission.

Instead of holding back, Sasha followed.

He stayed on foot, walking through the city and around the backs of buildings that had seen better days. At one point Sasha reached into her bag, swapped out her sunglasses, and tossed on a hat. A second glance behind him and Zakhar wouldn't be any wiser to her presence.

He made his way down an alley that would have proved she was following him had she trailed behind. So she walked by and then crossed the street. He ducked into what looked like a building where she could find a replacement passport and the people associated with the trade.

She waited for thirty minutes, all the while keeping an eye on the app showing Ruslan's location. He hadn't moved.

When the door opened to the alley, Zakhar walked out with two extra men.

They were big.

Recruits, she immediately thought. Ruslan was hiring help.

She'd seen this before.

Zakhar walked them to the center of the city and into a store that specialized in big and tall suits.

For a moment, Sasha's thoughts flashed back two years.

She stood inside one of the most expensive department stores in New York, Alice at her side.

"You don't need to buy me clothes."

"I don't need to do anything," Alice said. "But I'm setting up your accounts and want to make sure everything is taken care of."

Alice had hired her, flown her to the States, and funded the way for Sasha to watch over and protect an army instead of just her son and his wife.

"I won't say no, but this is overkill."

"Is it? I've been told you're the best. Does the best not deserve the pay of kings?"

Sasha knew at that moment there was more to Alice than the woman was letting on. But she held back and played out the woman's game. "How many people in this room have a weapon?" Alice had whispered.

Sasha had taken half a minute to scan the room. "The doormen, the man at the jewelry counter . . . but those are obvious. The man over there, in the suit, with his wife." He looked like an ordinary customer, but she noticed the way he made sure his jacket didn't slide open. "I'm guessing an off duty detective."

Alice smiled.

Sasha reported three more "customers" that she would consider armed and dangerous.

By the time they left the store, Sasha was overloaded with bags, and an account in her name was filled with more money than she'd spend in a lifetime. Alice had insisted that Fedor and Katrina would frequent many social circles, and Sasha needed to blend.

For a brief moment, Sasha felt as if she'd found her fairy godmother.

Before she let herself open her heart, she looked into the drawn eyes of a dying woman and shut her emotions down. No need to get attached to someone on their way out.

Still, as Sasha watched Zakhar and his now well-dressed thugs leave the store, she felt a little kinship to them.

They were hired and dressed the part.

Too bad they were working for the wrong side.

Chapter Twenty-Nine

Summer had yet to lose its grip on Vegas. It helped that the bright lights of the never-sleeping city warmed the Strip. Not that Wade had much of an opportunity to explore the city.

He remembered touring the city with Gus, Sebastian, and Luke early on in his career. The other members of his band didn't have quite the name recognition as Wade, since he'd branded himself as a solo artist, but his bandmates had enough claim to fame to warrant a following of their own. Something Wade encouraged at every turn. Truth was, the music they played was Wade's. From lyrics to composition. Gigs like the one here in Vegas were bread and butter to his band. While they did make some money off the albums, it was the venues that filled their banks.

Wade was prepared to cancel for Trina but couldn't help but feel happy he didn't have to, for the sake of his guys.

"Mind telling us what all the Blues Brothers are doing, standing around?" Gus, his bass player, asked while looking toward the closed greenroom door.

"Extra security."

Sebastian pulled a longneck from the table to his lips. "Have someone stalking you?" he asked with a grin.

Wade adjusted his hat and turned away from the mirror. "More like the girl I've been seeing."

"The one from your party?" Gus asked.

"Yup, Trina."

The three of them exchanged glances.

"So why are they here?"

Wade glanced at Jeb, who stood by the door. He knew from walking in there were three men outside, ready to escort them onstage when they were called to do so. "Because snagging me to leverage her is a real threat."

There weren't many times he found his band speechless.

Now was one of them.

"Her to get to you I understand . . . but you to get to her?"

"She's that special?" Gus was the only married man in the band. He and his wife of five years had two kids and one of the strongest relationships Wade had ever seen.

"She is. As in, I think she's it." Actually, he knew she was it. It was just going to take a little more time to convince her of where she needed to be.

Gus offered a knowing smile and clasped Wade's hand in a shake that formed a bond. "Congrats, man. I'm happy for you."

"Guess this means we're not going for drinks after the show," Luke, the youngest member of the band, said.

"I'm sure you and Sebastian will find plenty of female companionship to fuel your evening without me."

Luke removed his hat in an overly dramatic fashion and pressed it to his chest. "We'll do our best, won't we, Seb?"

"A sacrifice I'm willing to make," Sebastian replied, patting his chest.

A knock on the greenroom door directed their attention. "Five minutes."

Wade turned to the mirror. "That's our cue, boys. Let's see if these city folks know a little country music."

⁓☺

"You have it bad!"

Trina turned down the stereo that filled the room with Wade's voice and focused her attention on Avery as she walked into the room. She used one crutch and the walking cast the doctor had put her in before they left New York.

Cooper attempted to be a shadow but somehow seemed to fail as he walked by the room.

"I do," Trina told her friend while she sipped on her glass of wine.

"Do you have more of that?" Avery pointed to her drink.

"Is it okay with the medication you're taking?"

"So long as you don't plan on taking advantage of me, I'm sure one glass isn't going to hurt."

Sadly, Trina knew firsthand how true that statement was.

"Fine."

She crossed to the bar to pour her friend a glass.

"The quiet is going to kill me," Avery said after her first sip. "I don't know how you do it out here all alone."

Trina glanced toward the opening of the great room. "I'm never really alone."

"You know what I mean."

"What about you? How will it be back in LA?"

Avery turned her head. "I'll be fine."

"Avery?"

"What?" Avery might be able to fool many people, but she didn't fake well with Trina.

"I know you."

"I'll be fine. I won't let Scarface own me."

"It's not that simple."

"Says who? I'm only sorry I didn't get a punch at the man who altered my appearance for the rest of my life. If it would make a difference, I'd dig him up and kick him in the face to show him how it felt."

The image had Trina swallowing hard.

Trina snapped out of her grave-digging trance almost as fast as she popped into it. "So Wade . . ."

She didn't want to change the subject but didn't quite know what to say following Avery's dip into the macabre. "I'm bummed I'm not there."

Avery shrugged. "It's good to have time apart."

"I know that."

"But you miss him."

"I've leaned on him a lot since we met. It wasn't that I looked for him to answer my questions so much as support me in asking them."

"I get that."

"I realize that Fedor and I . . . that we weren't . . ." Trina glanced toward the open room, to whoever might be listening. "But we did talk. It was nice to bounce ideas off someone you shared something with."

Avery sighed. "Bernie and I had that, too."

Trina lowered her voice. "With Wade, it's that friendship and a lover in the same person. I can't help but think that's rare." She paused, sipped her wine. "I'm falling in love, Avery."

Her friend moaned. "I know." Over her bandaged nose, Avery glared. "I really want to hate your guy . . . you know that, right?"

Trina laughed and hung her head. "How is that working for you?"

"It isn't!"

Trina laughed louder.

⌒

Sometimes, when you wanted things done right, you needed to do them yourself.

Ruslan pulled the cuff of his jacket and squared his shoulders.

"Find her, bring her to me."

Zakhar disappeared into the thick crowd of rowdy, drunk urban cowboys toward the front of the stage.

"Hello, Las Vegas!" Mr. Famous himself tilted his hat to the crowd.

A chaotic cheer went up.

"How's everybody doin' tonight?"

Ruslan weaved his way through the crowd.

"Hope you don't mind if I take a couple of pictures. I have someone back home who really wanted to come." Wade turned his back to his audience, lifted his phone in the air. "Say *country!*"

He turned back around, waved his phone in the air. "Not sure how I'm gonna get this to all of you. Guess I'll upload it on Instagram." He fiddled with his phone before setting it aside on the stage. "Let's get this party started."

The band struck a note, and the noise in the arena made it impossible to think.

∽

Trina opened the image on her phone and enjoyed the giddy buzz inside her body. Wade was onstage, an arena full of fans with bright lights and cell phones was a sea behind him. He captioned it, Wishin' you were here!

The fact that he was onstage right then, doing his thing, and taking even a second out of that to text her a picture gave her hope that they could work.

She snapped a selfie in her reply. Wish I was, too.

She hit send, knowing he probably wouldn't respond until after the show.

She set her phone aside and reached to refill her glass.

"Someone is all smiles over there." Avery looked up from her phone and the game she was playing on it.

Trina showed her the picture. "I can't wait to watch him in person."

"I'm sure we can pull up some YouTube videos to tide you over."

Trina set the bottle down, took a sip. "I'll wait."

Avery didn't look convinced.

Her phone pinged with an incoming message.

Trina's heart fluttered. He wasn't really texting her, was he?

She smiled, prematurely, before the image came into focus.

Then she dropped her glass of wine and yelled, "Cooper?"

Avery jumped. "Jesus, Trina."

Cooper ran into the room, gun in hand.

Trina's hand shook as she showed him her phone. "Ruslan is there."

Cooper turned a full circle.

Trina pointed on her phone. "At the concert. This is him."

Avery pushed to her feet and limped over to see.

"Who sent you this text?"

"I don't recognize the number."

Cooper put his gun away and picked up his phone as the one in Trina's hand rang.

It was Lori.

"Reed just got a text."

"So did I."

"Ruslan is in Vegas."

Trina tried to calm her breathing down. "I know. What do we do?"

"Reed will be on a plane and in Vegas before the show lets out."

The phone beeped in her hand, and Trina pulled it away from her ear to see who was trying to break through. "It's from that number again. A video call."

Trina didn't hesitate as she disconnected with Lori and picked up from the anonymous caller. She half expected to see her ex-father-in-law on the other side of the line.

She didn't.

Sasha's image flickered into place. "Are you both there?"

"I am." Trina heard Reed's voice but didn't see his face.

"I am," Trina said.

The noise in the background where Sasha was calling blared into the phone.

"First thing. Calm the hell down. I have him in my sight. Second . . . get off your fucking phones. I can't jam all your shit at once. Reed, you're secure, Trina's phone isn't on the map yet. I take it someone yakked on a text about the information at the bank."

"Lori took pictures."

"Which means Ruslan knows what you have on him." Sasha had a half smile on her face. "And he's nervous."

"What is he doing there, Sasha?" Reed asked.

"Right now he is watching the cowboy's show from the back east end of the arena."

"He isn't there for a social visit."

"No, he's grasping at a lifeline. How soon will you be here, Reed?"

"I'm getting in my car now, forty minutes in the air once I'm on a plane. I'm an hour and a half out, sooner if I can push the pilot."

"Bring reinforcements. He's reaching the end of his freedom, and he won't go out alone if he can take someone with him. He has tabs on all of you. Radar on the locations of your phones, texts, and e-mails. Lori, Avery, Shannon, Wade . . . everyone. The only secure contacts are these three lines. Do I make myself clear?"

Trina couldn't stop shaking.

"Yes."

"He has five men. Two flanking him, two on the side of his main man."

"We need to warn Wade," Reed said.

"I'll take care of that. Telephone conversations only. No texting, no e-mails. Now get on the plane, Reed. You owe me. This is going down tonight. It ends, tonight!"

Just when Trina was about to hang up, Sasha spoke to her in Russian. "I have waited a lifetime for this day, don't panic and fuck everything up."

"Don't let anything happen to him," Trina pleaded.

Sasha hung up without comment.

Chapter Thirty

He loved his job. The screaming women calling his name and telling him they wanted to have his babies, the men waving their hats in the air, his audience never got old. From ballads to songs meant to swing your honey around the dance floor, Wade sang and danced around on the stage. Much as he tried to pick out a face here or there toward the back of the crowd, he couldn't make out much past the first ten or twenty rows. Those fans screaming and taking videos of him in the first few were given plenty of winks and smiles.

Before he finished his fourth song, Wade tracked a familiar face in the second row.

What was Jordyn doing there?

The woman didn't know when to quit.

He didn't think anything outside of putting a ring on Trina's finger would stop her from trying. Even then, he could see Jordyn flirting with a push-up bra and a smile.

Wade shook his head when she made eye contact, and then directed his attention beyond the second row.

The band worked their way into the fifth song, and Wade lost himself in the music. Forty minutes into his set, Sebastian began his drum solo, giving the three of them a couple of minutes offstage.

"The crowd's on fire," Luke said when one of the stagehands gave him a cold water.

Wade found Jeb within spitting distance. "How are we doin'?"

Jeb gave him a thumbs-up.

"I saw Jordyn down there. You know about her being here?"

Jeb shook his head. "I can keep her away if you want."

"No. I'll take care of it after the show."

"You got it, Boss."

Wade rolled his eyes while someone handed him a fresh shirt. He stripped down to his jeans and shoved his arms in right as Sebastian was finishing up. He managed one button before taking the stage again.

The ladies roared.

You can look, he mused. *But I have someone special that gets to touch.*

They played into the second half of the show.

When Wade scanned the first couple of rows, Jordyn wasn't there.

Maybe she got the hint.

Or maybe she was waiting in the wings to corner him.

Unable to help himself, Wade sang his way to the left side of the stage and glanced toward Jeb. A woman was walking away, but Wade couldn't tell who she was.

He pushed Jordyn out of his mind and sang to Trina, even though she wasn't there.

That's when he noticed his mother.

She filled the spot where Jordyn had been, her eyes wide and her smile just as brilliant as ever.

He mumbled the words of his own song and faked his way through.

He had to concentrate or he'd end up singing his frustration with her presence.

He made a motion with his hand, as if to tell his mother to stay right where she was so he could keep an eye on her.

She smiled, like she did when he was in the fourth-grade talent show, and Wade forced himself to relax.

He made it through the song and turned to Gus. "Buy me a few minutes."

There weren't many times he couldn't make it through a set without needing to pee, so Gus looked confused. Then he smiled and started a slow intro to the next song.

Wade rushed offstage to find Jeb.

By the time he got back out, his mother had already disappeared from the audience, and Wade relaxed.

⌒ᔅ

Ruslan lifted his phone after it buzzed in his breast pocket.

Everything is set. Waiting for your instructions.

Much as he didn't like being this close to the action, he wasn't about to leave this up to just anyone to handle.

With a final glance toward the stage, Ruslan turned on a heel and strolled away. Two hired hands flanked his sides.

He slowly made his way out of the arena and onto the casino floor.

Eyes followed him, he could feel it.

He paused at a craps table, made eye contact with a busty blonde, then turned and walked away. The hotel elevator took him up to his room on the twenty-eighth floor. Double doors opened to an empty suite.

His guards flanked the doors, once they were shut, and folded their hands.

Ignoring the "No Smoking" sign on the bar, Ruslan lit up a cigar while he poured himself a drink.

He looked at his watch.

Wade's show should be ending any minute.

Ruslan put his phone to his ear.

It rang once.

"Put me on speaker."

His voice was encrypted.

He waited until he heard a female voice.

"You're going to look into the camera and say exactly what I tell you to say." He pulled two silver balls from his pocket and shuffled them between his fingertips.

"Who the hell are you?" The woman screamed the question.

"Remind her of her manners."

Ruslan waited, heard the sound of flesh hitting flesh.

She cried out.

"Now . . . let's do this again. You're going to look into the camera and say exactly what I tell you to say."

"Okay, okay. Don't hurt me. I have money. Please don't hurt me."

Ruslan's hands itched to be the ones inflicting pain.

⁓

Wade said a final good night to the crowd while he and the band took a bow and waltzed off the stage.

The roadies swept in after them, collecting anything they left behind, while the lights in the arena lit up, signifying that there weren't going to be any more encores.

Jeb was at his side as one of the roadies shoved Wade's cell phone into his hands.

"Where is my mother?" Wade felt Jeb's energy before the man opened his mouth.

"We gotta go."

Two more bodyguards flanked Wade's front and back, their eyes in constant motion.

"What happened?"

"Wade?" Gus called out as he stepped close.

One of the bodyguards cut him off.

Jeb pulled on Wade's arm.

"Where is Vicki?"

Jordyn ran up behind the stagehands. "You were on fire tonight."

Wade didn't look at her twice. "Jeb?"

He paused. "We can't find her."

Wade's blood chilled. "Where is my mother?"

"Wade?" Jordyn pushed between him and Jeb.

"Did you bring her here?"

"Who?"

"Vicki? My mom?"

Jordyn placed a pout on her lip. The one that she'd used to get her way when they were dating. Wade saw through it then and hated it now. "I want a second chance. Your mother loves me. Doesn't that count for something?"

Wade pushed Jordyn aside. "Where is she, Jeb?"

The background music in the stadium filled the PA.

Wade started for the stage again as his bandmates gathered around.

"What's going on?" Gus asked.

"My mom is here."

Gus smiled. "Where? I could use a dance partner tonight."

Wade turned to Jeb.

"We can't find her."

Panic, like nothing Wade had known before, filled every cell in his body.

"We need you out of here."

"Not without my mom."

Jeb took hold of Wade's arm and didn't let go. "Ruslan is in the building. I have the house security at every exit."

"What's going on, honey?" Jordyn's words made him want to throttle her.

Wade turned, put two fingers in front of Jordyn's nose. "Did my mother tell you it was a risk for her to come?"

"She said there was some drama with your new friend . . ."

"Trina is more than a friend. That drama—"

"Wade? We have to go!" Jeb pulled on his arm and didn't let him finish his sentence.

"We're over," he called behind his back. He forced his feet in the direction Jeb was pulling. "Make sure she gets home."

"I already have that handled."

In less than two minutes, Wade was tucked into the back of an SUV and driving away from the venue.

"I need to be back there, looking for her."

Jeb had his phone in his hand, the receiver to his ear. "How far could you look? The front row?"

The driver took the corner too fast while Wade's phone buzzed.

He pulled it from his pocket, saw his mother's number pop up on the screen with a photo text.

He clicked on the image and froze. "Good God."

"Wade?"

"Sweet Jesus, Jeb, look at this."

His mother was tied to a chair, her lips swollen.

"You can't have my son. Kill me. I don't care." The image switched to what looked like a live feed outside of a ranch house that looked familiar. The scene flashed to Trina helping Avery inside the doors of her house. His heart plunged. The next video image was of Trina's father, and a woman who Wade had to assume was Trina's mother, as they sat half-asleep on a sofa, watching a television. The image then switched to a high-rise building he'd never seen before, then to Aunt Mavis's living room. "My bombs will kill everyone you love." Someone offscreen lifted a gun and placed it on his mother's temple.

"No. No. No!" Wade screamed into the phone.

Vicki closed her eyes, pulling away from the barrel of the gun as far as she could.

The screen went dark.

"What the hell?"

Jeb's face was just as horrified as Wade's.

Wade's phone buzzed.

Turn the car around.

Wade pushed on the front seat. "Turn the car around."

"Hold up, Wade. We don't know what we're dealing with here."

"Yes we do, we're dealing with a sociopath. Call Reed, turn the car around, show them we're following instructions."

"The phone isn't secure. If I call Reed, Ruslan will know."

Wade looked at the driver. "Is his phone secure?"

Considering Wade had never seen the driver before in his life, he assumed the man wasn't connected to any of them outside of a car service.

"Give me your phone. Turn the car around, find traffic." Which, on the Vegas Strip on a Friday night, wasn't a problem.

The driver handed Wade his phone.

"Reed and Trina have the only secure lines."

Since Wade had memorized Trina's new number instead of putting it in his directory, he dialed it first.

"Hello?" She sounded distraught.

"Oh, baby, are you okay?"

"Wade?" She started to cry.

"Shh, I'm okay. Listen carefully. Get out of the house, but don't leave through the front gate. Call your parents, my aunt. There was a condo . . . high-rise, I don't know who that is."

"What are you talking about?"

"He has bombs. Get everyone out quietly. There are cameras everywhere."

Wade's personal cell phone buzzed.

Fremont Street

Wade showed the text to Jeb, who told the driver where to go.

"What does he want?"

"I don't know, but I'll find out. He has my mother, Trina. At gunpoint."

"No."

"I'm headed toward Fremont Street."

"He's desperate."

"I know."

"I'm so sorry."

"Stop it. Get out of the house and tell Reed where we are."

"Please be careful."

Wade hung up. "Now what?" he asked.

"Even if Trina manages to get everyone else out, he still has Vicki," Jeb said. "He needs her for leverage."

"Which means he won't kill her."

"I hope you're right."

༄

Trina used a conference call function and dialed Reed's and Sasha's numbers.

Sasha answered first. "This had better be important."

"Talk to me" was Reed's answer.

Trina ran through everything Wade had told her while Cooper maneuvered Avery through the house and out the back door. Cooper had spoken directly to the cameras Trina knew were being monitored by Reed's team, and with any luck, they were evacuating the locations as rapidly as Trina was preparing to leave her Texas home.

"Fremont Street?" Sasha clarified.

"That's what he said."

"How far are you out, Reed?"

"Getting off the plane now."

"I have my eye on Ruslan. You find Wade and he'll lead you to the girl."

"You know where Ruslan is?" Reed asked.

"He's sitting in a hotel room, far away from anyone with a hostage. He's a murderer, but he isn't stupid. I have him, you take care of Mr. Country and his mother."

"I've got to go. Wade said he had a bomb here, and I can't have one more death on my conscience," Trina said.

"Go, Trina, get out of there. Leave the cars behind. Ruslan likes planting bombs in cars."

"How do you know all this?" Trina asked Sasha.

Sasha didn't answer. "Reed. I need an all clear when you have the hostage."

"You got it."

The line went dead.

Trina glanced at the faces looking at her. Cooper held Avery under her shoulder. Trina's housekeeper, Stella, stood clenching her bathrobe. "We head to the barn, quietly. Do you know how to ride a horse?" she asked Cooper.

"How hard can it be?"

"He can ride with me," Avery said.

Trina crossed to the fireplace and removed the shotgun that hung on a rack over the hearth. She pulled back the stock to find it loaded with two rounds. "If this is some ploy to get us out of the house, it worked, but we won't do it unarmed. Avery, bridle two of my mares. I'll wake the Folsoms and get them out." The Folsoms were a husband and wife team that handled the livestock.

"Not without me," Cooper said.

"And leave Avery and Stella alone? No, you stay with them. I will wake the Folsoms. We don't have time to argue."

"Damn it."

"Let's go." Trina opened the door and felt a rush of unexpectedly cold Texas air.

∽

With a laptop open, Ruslan watched the blips on his monitor for sudden movements.

Texas was sleeping. No one in. No one out.

Wade's aunt snored like a truck driver.

Trina's parents had gone to bed without realizing that their room over the garage would be blown to pieces if he made the call.

But the target Ruslan wanted to pull more than any was the bitch lawyer's building in Los Angeles. He couldn't get close enough to place the explosives in her room, but they were close enough to keep her from sleeping soundly for the rest of her life.

Blips on the radar told him no alarms had been sounded.

Wade's locator placed him two miles outside of Fremont.

There were men there to take him once he stepped out of the car. He was the hostage that would get Trina to do whatever Ruslan wanted.

∽

The last two miles to Fremont Street were excruciating.

Jeb handed the driver's phone over to Wade. "Reed."

"Hey."

"How ya doing?"

Wade wiped his sweaty palms on his jeans. "Not bad for a man about to walk into a trap."

"I just landed on the helipad on the top of the Golden Nugget. There are four of us. We are dressed like tourists and armed like ISIS. When we break silence, you will know it. Take cover and get out of the way."

"And in the meantime?"

"You have to trust that we are watching you. I have your phone on radar."

"What if they take that?"

"Are you wearing your boots?"

Wade looked at his feet. "Yeah."

"Right buckle."

Sure enough, there was a decorative stone that wasn't on the left boot. "Stalk me anytime, man."

"I only bug people I like. Follow their directions. And, Wade . . ."

"Yeah?"

"They need your mother alive to get to you. When they get to you, they get to Trina."

"Is Trina safe?"

"Yup. Okay, we're on the ground floor, spreading out."

"I owe you a beer, Reed. Keep us both alive so I can buy it for you."

"You're on."

Wade hung up as the car pulled to a stop off Fremont Street. The famous Fremont Experience was midway through the light show in a canopy over one of the oldest streets in Vegas. The crowds were busy craning their necks to watch the show. Some were lying on their backs, heads resting on towels or blankets to keep the grime off their clothing. None of them seemed to notice a dark sedan pull up and idle.

Wade's phone buzzed.

Step out of the car, alone. Leave the phone. Lose the hat. Turn in a circle, hands where we can see them. Put on your bodyguard's coat and walk towards the Plaza Hotel.

"I'll follow."

"No, you won't."

Jeb pressed his lips together.

"You know they will spot you. Reed has a better chance of going undetected. Ruslan still thinks he's in LA."

"You pay me to protect you."

Wade grabbed the door handle before he lost his nerve. "Fine. You're fired." Wade pushed out, dragging Jeb's coat behind him. He had some hope he wouldn't instantly be shot when he didn't see a red dot on his chest as he turned around.

He shrugged into Jeb's oversize coat, turned up the collar, and started walking down the street. He weaved through the crowd, avoiding eye contact in hopes that no one would recognize him. People passed by, most holding drinks and looking at the lights flashing above their heads. The music from the show deafened his ears more than the speakers he had onstage. Or maybe he was hyperaware of every sound and every sudden movement.

He felt the weight of eyes and started to look around. If he could just see Reed, he'd feel so much better.

No, instead he noticed a man wearing a black leather jacket watching him from across the street. He didn't look away when Wade met his eyes.

The stranger nodded to the right.

Wade looked around before he complied.

His heart pounded loud enough to dwarf the music.

There wasn't a deserted alley off Fremont, but the side street he walked down was close. He followed Leather Jacket Man as he turned in to the back door of a Korean barbeque kitchen. He stepped around the tables filled with pots and pans and odiferous food without so much as one employee looking up to see who walked by. If there was one time in Wade's life he wanted to be noticed, it was when he was walking toward what could be a life ending experience. Apparently, that wish wasn't going to come true.

Leather Jacket Man up close looked like a cross between a crack addict and a meth head. Twitchy, without a lot of teeth. Wade couldn't help but think he was someone Ruslan used to lure Wade to their current location but would probably have him tossed off a bridge before the night was over. Wade had a strange compulsion to warn the man.

He decided not to push his luck.

Leather Jacket Man stood in front of a tiny elevator with the door open. He waved Wade inside, pressed a button, and stepped out before the doors closed.

Leather Jacket Man wiggled his fingers in a comical goodbye and sealed Wade inside. "Top floor." Which was only six stories. It was old Vegas, and outside of the hotels, many of the buildings were old construction with low ceilings and tiny elevators.

When those tiny elevator doors opened, Wade took a cautious step outside.

Someone grabbed him from the side, threw him against the wall, and started patting him down.

Wade's instinct was to push back.

He squelched it.

The man checking every pocket and touching every part of him was nothing like Leather Jacket Man. This guy was a house. Bald head, dark skin. Slavic? Hispanic? Wade wasn't sure. Or maybe he was American and his parents had been in the circus.

Either way, this man wasn't twitchy or timid. "Where's my mother?"

Baldy pushed Wade toward a lone chair in the virtually empty room and turned on an old television set.

Vicki sat in a chair, in a room that looked a lot like the one Wade was in now. She pulled at the restraints holding her. Her mouth was stuffed with some kind of towel, and duct tape wrapped around her head.

A voice through the speaker of the TV sounded like Donald Duck after he inhaled helium. "Sit down, Mr. Thomas."

The last thing Wade wanted to do was sit.

Then two more of Baldy's friends stepped into the room.

Wade lifted his hands and sat. "Okay. Sitting."

"Let's begin."

"Let her go."

"I'm sorry, Mr. Thomas. Do you think you're in charge?" The voice was almost impossible to take seriously.

"If you want my help, you'll let her go."

Apparently that was the wrong thing to say.

His mother stopped struggling and stared off camera. Without warning, someone the size of Baldy walked over to Vicki, grabbed her middle finger on her left hand, and dislocated it.

Wade yelled "Stop!" while his mother screamed through her gag.

"God damn you!" Wade kicked the chair across the room.

Baldy moved in with one of his friends and held him while the third man reminded Wade why he avoided bar fights. Two hits to the gut without the ability to guard himself, and he felt the need to throw up.

Baldy shoved him into a chair.

"Let's try this again . . ."

Chapter Thirty-One

It wasn't a trap.

Trina and her band of travelers arrived at her closest neighbor's house, half an hour away from hers. It was cold, and dark, and she was a little surprised they didn't get shot at. Chances were if they had arrived in a car or on foot, they would have seen someone with a gun at the door. But six people and three horses, some in their pajamas . . . they looked like a homeless troupe instead of bandits.

Once they were safely inside the neighbor's home, Cooper called in to his headquarters.

When he got off the phone, Trina pounced on him for information. "Well?"

"Reed has eyes on Wade, they are scrambling to find Vicki. They have her located in the same building, they're going floor by floor to find her."

"And Ruslan?"

"Radio silence from Sasha. We have to assume she's waiting for the all clear."

"What about my parents, Wade's aunt?"

"Everyone is accounted for. Lori and Avery's building has a mysterious fire and has been evacuated. A bomb threat will follow to clear the building before anyone can go back in."

"Shannon?"

"Safe."

Trina stared at Avery. "Now what?"

"We wait."

"I knew you were going to say that."

◦⌇◦

"Why don't you do away with the Disney voices and make your demands like a man, Petrov?"

Wade's comment earned him another punch.

"I want what is in that safe, and I want the letters."

"The safe in Arizona?" Wade looked around the room, purposely stalling. *Where the hell is Reed?* "*When we break silence, you'll know.*"

Well, break the fucking silence already.

"What about the letters?"

"Trina doesn't have the letters."

"You're lying."

He looked at the camera. "I was told she didn't have them."

"Katrina lies."

Keep him talking. Buy time. "Says Donald Duck."

Wade saw the punch coming, tightened his abs.

He coughed several times, felt bile rise in his throat. "Fine, whatever. Someone have a phone? Let's call her right now. Of course, she's bound to call the police once she realizes what's going on." Wade calling her would give them the trace they needed to find out where she was, which wasn't a risk Wade was willing to take.

"You'll have to convince her not to if you want to live to see another concert. If you want to see your mother alive again."

C'mon, Reed.

"You could have a career in music, Petrov. I'll be Alvin, and you be the chipmunks."

Wade's head flew back with the punch. "Not the face."

"Clearly you're not taking me seriously, Mr. Thomas. Let's see how well your mother likes looking in the mirror after I remove her ear."

Vicki started to shake her head, and the next thing Wade saw was the floor as the camera fell and went blank.

At the same time, Reed's team broke the silence.

Wade used the distraction, buckled his knees, and dove for the floor. Between attempting to hold Wade up and pulling their guns out, the men holding Wade let go.

The window on the east side of the room crashed open and someone kicked in the door.

Wade covered his head and ducked around a half wall and heard a few soft popping sounds and the heavy thud and grumbling of men.

The room grew silent outside of Donald Duck's voice. "Zakhar?"

Wade looked up to see two men wearing street clothes and face masks that made it difficult to see the color of their eyes. One of them had to be Reed, but Wade couldn't make out which one he was.

They hadn't shot and killed the men in the room, but they would be wiping their asses with their left hands for some time to come.

The team worked quickly and quietly, wrapping bloody hands, feet, and mouths together.

"Which one of you—"

"Uh-uh." One of the masked men put a finger to his lips, tossed Wade the duct tape.

"Zakhar?"

Wade ignored Donald Duck.

That is, until a woman's voice came through the speakers.

"Hello, Father."

Wade froze. So did the other men in the room.

Donald's voice was replaced by something much more serious. Ruslan's.

"Natasha?"

One of the team turned to Wade, their voice altered, but not in a duck kind of way. "You have no idea who we are."

The masked man Wade assumed was Reed turned to leave.

"Where is my mother?"

The man pointed out the door. "One floor down."

As fast as the masked men arrived, they left.

Wade ran out into the hall.

∽

He was staring at the living dead.

A zombie, and vampire . . . Natasha was at the bottom of a cliff with a broken neck. Only, the woman staring at him now was her, reincarnated and calling him *Father*.

"You seemed surprised to see me." She walked around the chair in the sitting room, her long, lean legs enveloped in black spandex.

"Natasha is dead."

"You would know that, since you killed her."

"I don't know what you're talking about."

This woman's eyes narrowed. "Don't insult me."

A memory burned bright in his head. "You're the daughter."

She held a hand to her chest. "I'm touched. You remembered."

Ruslan looked beyond her, toward the door, and called out to his men in Russian.

The woman laughed, responded in Russian. "They have drugs so powerful in Africa that one drop into the bloodstream and phew! Down you go. I have waited my whole life for this moment, do you think I'd let two thugs at the door stop me?"

"What do you want?" Ruslan asked in English.

"You dead would be ideal, but I'll settle for life in prison without a chance for parole."

He kept his hands from reaching for the gun he had at his hip. "How do you plan on managing that?"

"I waited until you screwed up. You've been doing that quite a lot since you killed my brother."

∾

"Mama?"

Wade lifted his mother off the floor and into his arms. The pain in his side told him not to walk very far.

"I should have stayed home," she said as she dropped her head on his shoulder.

"Are you okay?"

She looked up at him, her eyes swollen with tears. "I didn't want them to hurt you."

He took care in setting her back in the chair, although seeing her there made him want to run out of the room.

Sirens grew closer.

"Wade? Vicki?" Jeb's loud, booming voice, along with the sound of running footsteps, came from the hall.

"In here."

Jeb paused at the door long enough to take in the situation. He kicked the side of a wounded man lying on the floor, his body bound in a way to keep him from moving until he had assistance.

"Help is on the way."

Wade looked around the room. "Help has already been."

Vicki lifted her eyes to Wade. "Do they have Trina?"

The mere mention of her name brought pain to his chest. "I don't—"

"Trina is fine," Jeb announced.

"They showed me a video of my sister's house. Did they get to her?"

"They're fine, Miss Vicki. Bomb squads are already there, and Mavis is far away."

They all paused when they heard a woman and a man arguing through the communication system Ruslan had put in the room.

The scene from miles away unfolded for them to hear.

∽

"Fedor committed suicide."

Sasha watched the irises in Ruslan's eyes contract as he continued his lies. "Fedor ate a bullet, but he didn't put the gun into his mouth willingly. You were there, snuck up on your son to try one final time to get him to come over to your side. You even convinced the housekeeper to let you in."

Ruslan's jaw twitched, his fingers rubbed together.

"The police know all about Cindy. How long had she been on your payroll?"

He didn't answer.

"What happened, Father? Did your weak son protest a little too loudly? Did he manage to get a punch or two in?" She moved slowly to the front of him, buying a little time as she brought his crimes to the surface. There was no way Reed had mistaken her *all clear*. It was only a matter of time before he arrived with backup.

"Or did he slice you open? The knife he used to carve his trinkets never was found. An observation that will come out now that this death has been labeled suspicious and homicide is involved. Your blood had to have been shed, or why would you have brought in a team to clean up your crime?"

A bead of sweat pooled on Ruslan's forehead.

His hand twitched.

"Fedor cut you, and you repaid the favor by blowing him against the wall. Didn't that hurt? Just a little?"

"I lost my son long before he died."

Get him talking. A confession, even one that would likely be thrown out, was better than no confession at all.

"With Fedor dead and Alice having tea with the grim reaper, you were weeks away from throwing her entire estate to the courts to get your share."

"You can't prove that."

"Cindy was your informant on the inside. The housekeeper always knows what's going on. You knew about the separate bedrooms and the lack of noise coming from the honeymoon suite. You made sure the housekeeper knew how she would die if she said anything. You paid her off. Since no one was around, poking questions, she kept quiet. She was a loose end you had to tie up. But a bad brake job? Really, Father? I knew then you were close to the breaking point . . . you don't make those kinds of mistakes."

"I had nothing to do with her accident."

"No, but Zakhar did. I doubt your man's loyalty will go so far as him allowing you to stay free while he rots in jail. Much like you tracking all the players, I have been watching you."

Ruslan ran a palm on his pants, her words penetrating his brain.

Her pulse ticked a steady beat in her neck. Every muscle in her body was ready for him to pounce. He was big, but she was faster.

"You intercepted Avery's call. You learned about the blood left in the room and hired a drugged-out murderer who couldn't follow instructions and a cleaning crew that wouldn't know the term *stealth* if they looked it up in a dictionary. You wanted Avery out of the picture since she saw what you left behind. But your bankroll has been dwindling, can't quite afford the help you once had."

"You can't prove anything."

"Did you miss the part about me tracking you? Alice hired me to keep her son and daughter-in-law alive." The desire to get in the man's face and smash an elbow into his nose was so strong Sasha could taste it. "Once you killed Fedor, that only left Trina. With the support of her new family of friends, that gave me time to watch you . . . watch and wait for you to fuck up. With everything I've found, and the evidence left behind by your unassuming ex-wife, you're going to be mopping the floor in prison with your hundred-year-old ass."

Ruslan kicked the coffee table over as he stood and reached for his gun.

Finally!

One round kick and his gun was sliding across the hotel floor. Her second kick to his chest was pure satisfaction.

She moved in, fast. Managed two blows to his face before he blocked her elbow by shoving his shoulder into her torso.

Sasha used his move to capture his head and force it to her knee, repeatedly. "That's for Avery!"

When she felt his body go lax, she pushed him away and sent a kick to his groin. "That's for Mom."

Ruslan spat blood to the floor and charged.

Sasha fell back, the table breaking their fall. And Ruslan started punching.

The pain of his meaty fists fueled her anger. She bucked with her hips and rolled to the side. Her knee met his groin again.

"You're a filthy whore, just like your mother."

He sent a fist to her stomach.

"You take a punch better than your mother. Weak woman didn't even put up a fight when her neck snapped." He threw her off and scrambled to his feet.

Sasha rolled onto the balls of her feet and sent a fist to his face.

He moved out of reach. "Your brother shared your loyalty to the *pizdas* who bore you." Ruslan held up his arm, showing a scar that spread from his wrist to midforearm. "No one cuts me and lives."

Sasha managed a fist to his face and went in for more.

He ducked and came up fast with both hands to her neck.

Air immediately stopped entering her lungs.

She twisted, attempted to make space.

He held on tighter.

Don't panic.

Her legs were in motion, her blows reaching him, but he didn't let go.

The room started to dim.

"My only regret is not taking Alice out when I had the chance."

Her struggles started to fade . . . a little more pressure and her windpipe would shatter.

This wasn't going to happen. All this work, and she was going out because of his hold on her neck.

Her lungs burned and her body lost its fight.

The room exploded in sound and her frame fell to the floor.

Sasha gasped in several pained breaths as her eyes fell on the man who shared her DNA. He was lying against the wall, his shirt quickly soaking in his blood.

A uniformed security guard stood over her.

She met Ruslan's eyes as he took his last breath.

Sasha hung her head between her stretched-out arms and attempted to stand.

Reed swept in behind her and helped her up.

"Took you long enough," she choked out.

He looked at her neck, and her face. "We need a medic!"

Chapter Thirty-Two

Trina stood on the tarmac as the private jet rolled to a stop and the small gangway lowered.

The Texas sun blazed down as the wind whipped her hair around her face. Dark sunglasses covered her tired eyes, hiding the circles that makeup couldn't manage.

The media was out of reach, but that didn't mean their lenses wouldn't capture this moment.

Jeb walked down the stairs first and stood at the bottom as Wade filled the doorway.

Trina held her breath and waited for him to see her. When he did, he skipped a step and opened his arms.

She ran into them.

Her lips found his, his hat fell off.

He was alive, and whole . . .

She pulled away. "I thought I was going to lose you."

"Shh, not done kissing you yet."

Okay, she could work with that.

When she squeezed his waist, he winced. "Easy, darlin'."

Her hands rubbed over his rib cage, felt a bandage in place. She started to pull at his clothing. "They said you were fine."

Wade brushed her hands away. "Couple tiny fractures."

"You're broken?" No one told her that.

"Just a rib or two. Simmer down. I'm fine."

"Wade Michael Thomas, you told me you were fine."

He chuckled as he reached down to slowly pick up his hat. "Oh, the middle name. I find that strangely sexy, coming from you."

"Let's get you home."

"Are we bomb free?" he asked as she limped him to the waiting car.

"Yes, they found one at my gate and one in your garage."

"I heard." Wade climbed in first and Trina followed.

The car drove them from the small airport directly to Wade's ranch, where Trina planned on staying until he kicked her out.

"How is your mom?"

"She's a pretty strong woman."

"If it wasn't for me—"

"Don't." Wade placed a finger over her lips. "My mother had no business in Vegas. If it wasn't her, Ruslan would have taken someone else. Jordyn, one of the guys in the band. The end result would have been the same."

"But your mom. She's never going to accept me now."

"She isn't going to be given a choice."

Trina squeezed in close, felt the weight of Wade's arm over her shoulders.

"How is Sasha?"

Wade rested his head against the back of the seat. "Couldn't really tell ya. According to Reed, who technically didn't show up until the police were standing over Ruslan's body, Sasha answered the questions the police asked, and then AWOLed from the ER before her X-rays were read."

"That's crazy, he almost killed her."

"She had every reason to kill him." Wade had heard the entire conversation, right up until the gunshot that ended everything. The microphone Ruslan had used was left on and forgotten, which gave the police everything they needed to pin murder, kidnapping, and black-mail charges on a dead man.

"I wonder if I'll ever see her again. I have so many questions of my own."

"Something tells me you will."

"Is this all really over?"

Wade ran a hand over her hair as she rested it on his shoulder. "Baby, I hope so. I can't keep up with your level of partying," he teased.

In the front seat, Jeb laughed once. "Amen to that."

Trina leaned forward and placed a hand on Jeb's shoulder. "I didn't even ask how you were doing."

"I'm fine. Just fine. In need of a job, if you have any openings. Seems my boss fired me a couple of days ago."

"What?"

"He's lookin' for sympathy. If he wasn't employed, he'd be gone."

Jeb twisted in his seat, the smile from his face gone. "Take that back, Cowboy, or I'll break your other ribs."

Trina actually thought Jeb was serious.

Wade hesitated.

The car was silent for several seconds before Wade cracked a slight smile and nodded once. "All right, then."

The man code of unspoken agreements had unfolded right in front of her. It was handshakes and *I got your back* all wrapped up in a single look.

"But since you want to rehire me, I think I'll be asking for a raise. Hazard pay."

Wade laughed, held his side. "Stop. It hurts."

They pulled up to Wade's ranch to the fanfare of a homecoming. Trina didn't recognize all the faces, but she did single Vicki out of the mix before the car was put in park.

Her eyes skimmed over Trina before falling on her son.

Wade pushed through the crowd and hugged his mother. "How are you feeling?"

"I've been thrown from horses. I'm fine."

Wade kissed her forehead and stood back.

"I'm so sorry," Trina told her.

Vicki blinked, looked at her son. "So am I."

"I know what you're thinking, Ms. Thomas." Trina used her last name to create distance. "If Wade hadn't met me, none of this would have ever happened. And you'd be right about that. If something had happened to you or him, I would have never forgiven myself. But apparently someone, somewhere, has other plans for us. I'm sorry you don't like me, I truly am. But I'm not going anywhere. Not unless Wade wants me gone. If men with guns and big fists can't drive us apart, I don't think you're going to manage. So I suggest we find some common ground, like the fact that we both love your son, and figure out a way to get along."

Vicki looked around at the faces that were trying not to listen.

Wade shuffled his feet. "Trina just tossed you an olive branch, Mama. I really think you should pick it up."

Vicki's eyes lost their hard edge and started to mist. "He's my only son. He's all I got."

"He's a pretty tough guy. I don't think he's going anywhere."

"*He* is standing right here, and wouldn't mind a cold beer and a couch."

His words snapped Vicki out of her *I'm going to put my energy into hating Trina* trance.

They bumped around each other in an effort to help Wade get comfortable.

Vicki brought him a beer and held up her bandaged hand. "You're going to have to wait on that pie until this hand is better."

"I think I'll be waiting longer than that."

Vicki smiled.

"I can bake a pie," Trina offered.

Vicki and Wade both turned to stare.

"What? I can cook. I just don't do it very often."

Vicki shook her head. "It's all over now."

Wade chuckled as his mother left the room.

Trina helped him remove his boots.

He slapped her ass when she straddled his leg to find the leverage she needed to wiggle a boot free.

"Hey!" She tossed one boot aside and moved to work on the other.

"I do like this view."

She left his other boot on the floor, and then turned to straddle his hips.

He pushed her hair over her shoulders before resting his hands on her waist.

"God, you're beautiful."

She blushed. "Wade."

"You're a flower unfolding in spring, the last rays of a sunset before the light is gone, stars in a clear Texas sky, you're breathtaking."

Trina looked up and tilted her head. "Go on . . ."

Wade chuckled. "I heard what you said back there."

"When I said what?"

He squeezed her hips. "That you loved me."

"Oh, that . . . well . . ."

"There are a lot of women that tell me they love me."

Trina pushed her thoughts about all those women aside and looked Wade in the eye. "But I'm the one that means it."

He ran his hands up her sides and pulled her down to his lips. He was slow and easy, and he filled every ounce of her.

"I'm a traditional man," he whispered between his kisses. "I wanted that fancy dinner and walk in the moonlight when I told you I loved you."

She smiled and looked him in the eye. "You don't always get what you want. Besides, I don't need fancy anything. I just need you. I was a walking shell when we met, half empty in every way. Now I'm so full I'm spilling over."

"Oh, darlin', you sure you've never written a sweet song before?"

She giggled. "If you think my words are sweet . . ." She wiggled her hips over his lap, and the edge of his jeans tightened. "Just wait until those ribs of yours are well enough for me to show you how full I am."

He cupped her butt and crushed her closer. "Honey, the doctor said my ribs were broken, the rest of me is workin' just fine."

Her eyes widened.

They both looked toward the stairs that led to the bedrooms.

Trina hopped off his lap and reached out her hand.

"Show me."

The letters arrived a week later, certified, with no return address.

Half the letters were opened.

Wade sat beside Trina as she read each one.

> Dearest Trina,
>
> By now you and my son have undoubtedly searched for any possible reason for my changes in my will. But they are painfully simple. Leaving my estate to you will keep my son, and possibly even my sisters, alive.

If left to Fedor, Ruslan will undoubtedly have him killed. I cannot bear the thought of my impending death risking his life. Ruslan has killed, and will do so again. Enclosed evidence, twenty-six years old, of the murder of his mistress.

The guilt I have harbored all these years is only abated by the fact that Natasha's death would never put Ruslan in prison for his entire life. The evidence I obtained was from an investigator I hired to track Ruslan at the time of our marriage. My thoughts were to find proof of his crimes and use the evidence to escape my tortured marriage. I never thought I'd be witness to a murder of an innocent woman.

I'm sorry, Fedor. I'm sorry to burden you with any of this after my death. But I didn't see another way. I know about you and your wife. I also see how you look at her. I hope that you will both use the year I've given to adjust to this change and find a way to stay together. But even if you don't, the money has to stay with Katrina. Or he will kill you to get to it.

Hold on to the evidence and wait until he makes a mistake.

He will.

I just pray it isn't lethal for any of you.

Alice

The second letter proved even more enlightening.

Dearest Fedor,

These letters are coming to you from your half sister. I have no doubt she is reading these before they come to you. I have absolute faith that she has investigated Natasha's death and has learned who her father is.

I could not prevent her mother's death any more than I could stop cancer from killing me. I have done everything I could to give Sasha a life and the skills she would need to survive if the day ever came that Ruslan learned she was alive. I used charities to disguise the path of money given for her education and home during her young years, and then hired her to watch over you and Trina from the moment you married.

I hope my deception is met with understanding. Your father's reach is so vast that had he known she was alive, or worse, that I was her secret benefactor, he would have had her killed.

Now she has the skills to learn of her heritage and stay alive. I pray, out of some loyalty to me, that she honors my wishes and delivers these letters to you.

Family is all you have when you leave this world.

I hope you all find it in your hearts to accept each other.

While your bond is through a monster, that doesn't make either one of you evil.

I love you, Fedor. And I have grown to love your sister as if she were my own.

My last letter will come after the anniversary of my passing.

The delay is my way of giving your father time to make some kind of mistake that Sasha can use against him. I have left your sister a tidy sum to help in her efforts, and hope that if she needs more you and Trina will provide it for her.

But I doubt that will be needed.

It seems Trina has a very powerful group of friends that, once they learn of these letters, will see to it she is safe.

Be kind to one another.

With all my love,

Mama

The last two letters weren't opened. They came directly from the law offices of Dwight Crockett.

Dearest Katrina,

I know you care for my son. Although I had hoped it would be deeper than what I know to be true. I can't, and won't, ask you to return the estate to him. To do so while Ruslan is still alive simply puts a target on his back. Ruslan can't get to you. I've seen to it with my choices.

I have seen your heart and know you will do the right thing if the day ever came. I have been honored to call you my daughter-in-law, if only for a short time. I'm humbled that my son loved me so much he would take such extreme measures to see me smile in my last days.

Be kind to each other.

All my heart,

Alice

My loving son,

It pains me to say goodbye but know I am no longer suffering, and I am watching over you. If there is a way to reach out and prove I'm there, rest assured I will.

Your aunts will always see to your needs, you know that. Money has never ruled your life, and I'm certain you won't let it now.

I love you.

Mama

Trina finished reading the letters and waited for Wade to catch up.

It took well over an hour before they could talk about them. Even then, it wasn't to go over any single piece of information, but to discuss the collective whole.

"So what now?"

Trina sat up on Wade's balcony, overlooking the vast span of his property. The world worked below while she stretched out on a lounge chair, contemplating life.

"I've already tried to give back everything to Diane and Andrea. They refused. Said they wanted family more than the money. They thought, with everything that had happened, I'd find plenty of ways to spend my share of the company that would prove worthwhile. They said if it wasn't for me, Ruslan would have never come to justice and would always be a threat for them and their own families."

"How do you feel about that?"

"I'm not sure."

"You have a whole lifetime to figure it out."

"First thing I need to do is sell a few houses."

"New York?"

"That's the first to go. Avery wants to fly back next month and continue where she stopped."

"You're kidding."

Trina didn't like the feeling in her gut about the whole situation. "She's battling some personal demons. I'm going to go with her."

"You sure about that?"

"It doesn't have the hold on me that it once did. But if you wanted to come along . . ."

"Is there a question?"

"Of course there's a question. I'm not assuming anything. Well, other than spending all my time here at your place. Stella and the Folsoms think I've abandoned my place."

"You should sell."

She tilted her head to the side. "I'm not selling."

"Fine, keep it. But we won't be there very often."

"Is that right?"

"Yeah, if we have a fight, I'll sleep on the couch like any normal man, not let you leave to your own house three hours away."

"You and I don't fight."

"I'm sure we will. Every couple argues."

"We're not like every other couple."

He leaned back, tilted his hat until it shaded his eyes. "Are we going to fight over not arguing?"

"That's an oxymoron."

"You can disagree with yourself. I'm thinkin' of takin' a nap. You're wearing me out all night long with your overactive sex drive," he said as he smiled under the brim of his hat.

"I'm wearing you out?" She kicked his boots off the railing, and he jumped up and pulled her out of her chair.

"Someone is feeling much better these days."

"Someone is. Now grab your purse, we need to go shoppin'."

"Shopping?" She glanced at the bed in the room just beyond the porch, hoping to exercise her sex drive.

"Yup. We need some boots, and a hat. Two hats, one for here and another one all blinged out so I can take you dancin' tonight."

"You're finally gonna dress me for the part?"

He lifted her hands and kissed the backs of both of them. He paused over her ring finger and gave it a hard stare. "Darlin', when I get done dressing you, there won't be a soul on this earth that doesn't know you belong to me."

Epilogue

"You know, as First Wives Club meetings go, this one has to be the best." Avery lifted her glass of champagne for a toast. "To Lori, with her newly engaged badass self."

Lori beamed while looking at the ring Reed had finally put on her finger a month before. Wedding plans were in the works, which gave the four of them plenty of time together while they hammered out all the details.

Trina sipped the sparkling wine in celebration before scooting out of the way of one of the stagehands.

The four of them sat in the wings of the concert hall, waiting until the very last second to walk down to their front row center seats.

Since she'd met Wade, this was the first concert she'd attended. Everything inside of her buzzed with excitement. The guys in the band had welcomed her into their fold with warm hearts and big hugs. They liked how she made Wade smile, and the music he was working on was a windfall for all of them. At least that's what the band had told her.

The roadies were finishing changing the set from the warm-up band as Wade and his guys walked through the backstage crowd.

Wade let out a whistling catcall and snagged Trina around the waist. "I'm taking this one, boys," he teased his guys.

"It's the hat, isn't it?" Pure cowgirl and picked out by her own country stylist. Even Wade's mother liked it, and that woman never approved of anything dealing with Trina.

"You can have her. I personally prefer blondes." Luke winked at Avery.

Avery waved him off with a turn of her head. "Oh, hell no. I'm out. See ya down there," she called as she walked away.

"Dude, she just dissed you hard," Sebastian teased Luke.

"Don't take it personally, Avery doesn't like musicians."

"Except me, she loves me." Wade patted his own chest.

"Don't flatter yourself. She tolerates you."

Wade swept Trina up for a kiss. "What about you?"

"Oh, I love you, but I only tolerate so much." She slapped his butt.

"Break a leg . . . or whatever one says before a concert," Shannon said before following Avery's lead.

Wade winked.

Lori patted Wade's shoulder. "Reed said he'd see you from the floor and after the show."

Wade kissed her cheek. "Enjoy."

Lori walked off.

He ducked his head close to Trina's. "I'm a little nervous," he admitted.

"Because of me?"

"What if you don't like it?"

Trina busted out laughing. "Not possible. Besides, I've been listening to you sing to me for months."

"Still."

"You know what they say. For stage fright, just picture the audience naked."

His eyes traveled up and down her denim miniskirted frame. "That is not helping."

She lifted on her tiptoes, as much as she could in a pair of boots, anyway, and kissed him. "I could say that if it bothers you, I'll stay away from your concerts. But that would be a total lie. So deal with it." She kissed him again. "I love you. Sing your heart out."

"Ready, Wade?" one of the stage managers interrupted them.

Trina slipped out of his arms and blew him a kiss before she jogged out of the wings and down the back staircase to the concert floor. She smiled at the security guard stationed there and slipped through plenty of strangers before meeting her group.

Trina turned a full circle and took in the sheer mass of people. "Phenomenal, isn't it?"

"All here to see your guy," Avery said.

Reed walked up, double fisted with a beer in each hand. "Hey, ladies."

A round of hellos went up as the lights in the concert hall went down.

The crowd started to rumble, and when the strings of an electric guitar hit a chord, everyone went wild.

Through the fancy lights and the smoke, Wade walked onstage and hit the first riff of his opening song.

And Trina fell in love all over again.

God, he was good. He sang of good times with old friends, and everyone around her sang right along with him.

Wade found her spot and smiled at her as he performed. She wasn't sure if he was picturing her naked, but he didn't seem all that nervous once the song ended.

"Hello, Nashville!"

The crowd went wild.

"How y'all doin' tonight?"

The audience responded.

"It's been three months since I've been onstage, I was goin' through withdrawals. Thanks for joining me on this last-minute gig."

"Anytime!" a man standing behind Trina yelled.

"Tonight's a mighty special night for me. You see, I have someone special in the audience, watching me for the first time."

Avery bumped Trina's side.

Trina squeezed her eyes shut. When she opened them, Wade was smiling down at her. "In fact, I wonder if y'all wouldn't mind if I brought her up onstage for just a couple minutes so I can introduce you to her."

Trina started shaking her head. "Oh, God. He is not . . ."

Next thing she knew, Jeb was standing in front of her with a step stool she could use.

Wade reached out his hand. "C'mon, darlin'."

"I'm going to kill him."

Trina's entire body shook as she let Jeb help her to the first step, and Wade pulled her up the rest of the way.

She couldn't look up for fear of passing out.

"Trina, honey . . ." Wade lifted his hand to the audience. "This is everyone . . . everyone, this is the love of my life, Trina."

A rise and fall of her name rose in the room.

That was when she realized just how many eyes were on them.

She swallowed, hard. "Hi."

Wade leaned in and talked low into his microphone. "Just picture them all naked. Totally works."

Everyone laughed.

Her knees felt weak. "It's okay, darlin'." Wade waved toward the wings. "Let me get you a chair."

Next thing she knew, there was a chair under her, and someone pushed her to sit. All she really wanted to do was get off the stage. While she was politely smiling, she was thinking of all the ways she'd get back at him for this little stunt. She glanced at her friends on the floor, who stood there with cell phones pointing in her direction.

"Wade," she said through clenched teeth.

He lifted a hand in the air. "Just a minute. I have something I need to do here . . . boys?"

The sound of the bass and lead guitar hit a pleasant note. At first Trina thought Wade was going to sing to her onstage.

Then he dropped to one knee.

All of the nerves and anxiety about a zillion eyeballs on her disappeared.

Wade pulled out a box from his back pocket.

Trina stopped breathing.

The arena was a mix of silent rustling and muttering between people. But Trina didn't hear any of it. She only saw Wade and the mist in his eyes.

"Darlin', I started falling in love with you that first night, when you leaned over and said, *Wade Thomas who?* I've been fallin' hard ever since. I had no idea what I was missing in my life until you walked in it. You know how much I love you."

Trina started to cry. *I love you*, she mouthed.

Wade opened the box. "I would be deeply honored if you would wear my ring and let me call you Mrs. Wade Thomas. Trina, my love. Will you marry me?"

She was nodding before he finished the question. She threw herself into his arms and met his kiss.

Someone cut his mic. "I love you," he said just for her.

He kissed her again, stood back, and slipped a ring on her finger. It was big, and blingy, and if size was an indicator of love, there was no doubt of Wade's for her. "I love you," she said out loud.

Wade lifted her off her feet and spun her around.

The audience went crazy.

His microphone was turned back on as he handed her off to Jeb.

"Now get off my stage, woman. I have to pay for that ring," he teased.

Again, the crowd laughed.

Trina was surrounded by her friends, and Jeb had acquired two more bulky guards to stand by.

Wade stood there for a second before turning to his band. "Hot damn, I'm the luckiest man in the world."

And then he sang.

And it was Trina who felt like the luckiest person alive.

She lifted her phone to take a picture of her fiancé and saw a text image.

When she opened it, it was a picture taken only seconds before, from several rows back.

It was from Sasha.

Congratulations.

Instead of turning around to find her, Trina sent her reply. Thank you.

She had more than one guardian angel looking over her shoulder. Two had halos and one wore spandex.

Acknowledgments

It's that time again, time for me to pause and think of all the people who helped me reach the words *The End* in this book.

As always, Jane Dystel, you never struggle for the right words needed for encouragement. Thank you and your entire team for helping me reach my dreams.

Thanks to everyone at Montlake for seeing the big picture and giving me the creative elbow room I need to write the best book in me each and every time.

Thank you, Maria, for taking me on and making the transition of staffing changes seamless.

Kelli, my steadfast editor . . . you know how much I love you. Thank you for helping me make my books rock.

Now back to Ellen Steinberg . . .

I'm writing this dedication and acknowledgment as I sit in my new home overlooking the Pacific Ocean off the coast of San Diego. I was looking for a real estate agent and somehow gained a friend. Thank you for your patience in finding the perfect home for me to write the next few chapters of my life. I look forward to sharing lots of sunsets and bottles of bubbly on my deck. Thanks for all the coaching in those pesky Russian words that shouldn't be repeated in polite company.

You're an unexpected blessing in my life, Ellen.

Here's to many years of friendship.

Cheers,

Catherine

About the Author

New York Times, *Wall Street Journal*, and *USA Today* bestselling author Catherine Bybee has written twenty-eight books that have collectively sold more than 4.5 million copies and have been translated into more than a dozen languages. Raised in Washington State, Bybee moved to Southern California in the hope of becoming a movie star. After growing bored with waiting tables, she returned to school and became a registered nurse, spending most of her career in urban emergency rooms. She now writes full-time and has penned the Not Quite series, the Weekday Brides series, the Most Likely To series, and the First Wives series.